Valentina's Rules

Spanking was one of the things on Valentina's list of 'don'ts' – her rules about the sexual things a girl shouldn't do because they were disrespectful. They included anal sex, striptease, doggy position, bondage and spanking – along with a lot of other things I couldn't remember. Some of them I'd never understood, like striptease, which is just fun, and going in doggy, which I adore. I knew she was on to something, though, because men always seemed to worship her, while most of my boyfriends had been about as disrespectful as it was possible to be. John McLaren having me in the changing rooms at a squash court and telling me he had a dinner date with another girl while I was actually sucking his cock clean came to mind. Valentina would have probably bitten it off, but then, that sort of thing would never have happened to her in the first place.

Other Books by the author:

Noble Vices

Valentina's Rules
Monica Belle

BLACK LACE

Black Lace books contain sexual fantasies.
In real life, always practise safe sex.

This edition published in 2003 by
Black Lace
Thames Wharf Studios
Rainville Road
London W6 9HA

Design by Smith & Gilmour, London 3|09049514 8
Printed and bound by Mackays of Chatham PLC

ISBN 0 352 33788 5

1

I don't usually pick men up at golf clubs.

No, that sounds awful. I don't usually pick men up at all. Usually, I go on a double date to make a friend feel safe and end up being talked at by her gorgeous date's less than gorgeous mate. As often as not the friend is Val: Valerie Lacy at school, the daughter of a train driver and a serial smoker; now Valentina de Lacy, who never admits to parents if she can possibly help it. She was the reason I was at the golf club. I could remember the conversation:

'You must come, Chrissy. It will be unbearable without you, and nothing but dreary old buffers.'

She'd gone on for some time until I'd finally given in and said I'd come. Only now I was there, she wasn't. But Michael Callington was.

He was the reason she was supposed to be there. And it had nothing to do with golf. She was the social secretary for her company and she wanted to book him for some upmarket, corporate wine-tasting event that the Callingtons were noted for giving. He had suggested the golf club as a convenient place to meet. She had accepted, bullied me into coming to give her moral support, and then left a note with reception apologising for not being there.

I wasn't sure what she had expected him to be like, but it must have been very different from the reality or she would have made an appearance. I suppose it was because he was a wine merchant. Wine merchants are supposed to be crusty old men with red noses or bristly moustaches, sometimes both. Michael Callington had neither, and he wasn't old.

He was maybe twenty-eight, maybe a little more. He was also tall, with striking pale-grey eyes and a languid poise that exuded strength and confidence. Confidence is something I am sorely lacking in, and I adore it in men. I don't mean the sort of brash, boastful confidence of men who're not really sure of themselves underneath, but the calm, easy confidence of a man absolutely certain of himself and happy in his skin. That was Michael.

Normally I would hardly have dared talk to a man like that. This was not normal. He was so attractive he was making me melt, and I had the excuse to introduce myself. So I did it. I did it pink-faced and full of apologies for not being Valentina, but I did it.

By the way, I really was sorry that I wasn't Valentina, and it had nothing to do with her broken appointment. I always try to tell myself I wouldn't rather be Valentina, but I'm never very convincing. You see, I'm five foot one; she's five foot nine. She looks as if she belongs on a catwalk; I look as if I belong in a cake shop. She's slim, leggy and blonde, with a tight bottom, a slender waist and breasts you couldn't buy for anything. I'm ... well, voluptuous is probably the kindest word, with a big round bottom and breasts one unkind boy at school once described as 'over-inflated footballs'. If I do have a small waist it just makes the rest look bigger. A snub nose, freckles and curly brown hair don't help either. OK, sometimes I do wish I was Valentina, but who wouldn't?

It's not just that either. She always knows what to

do, what to say, what to wear, everything. She reads all the right magazines, and sometimes I think she ought to edit one. Any subject, and Valentina knows what to think, what's in and what's out, what's going to make everyone admire her and what's going to make everyone laugh ... at me. She has life worked out, with a rule for every occasion. I just muddle along.

So I tried to make small talk with Michael, expecting him to be polite but cold. Instead, to my great delight, he was warm and welcoming. I put his friendliness down to drink, but kept chatting. One of Valentina's many rules for dealing with men is always to pretend to be interested in the same things they are. He was a wine merchant and he played golf – that was all I knew. The sum total of my knowledge on both subjects could be written on the back of a postage stamp, but I do at least drink wine, so I tried that. Ten minutes later I'd been invited to a tasting his company was giving in Central London.

Telling myself it only meant he wanted to sell me some wine, I tried golf. Unfortunately the first question I asked turned out to be so silly it made him laugh. It also made him offer to take me out on to the course and show me how to do it. I accepted.

So there I was, along with Michael Callington, in what in most contexts would have been a highly compromising position. To teach me how to use a club, he stood behind me and placed his hands over mine on the shaft. With him being a foot taller than me, this was easy. It was also very intimate, with my bottom stuck out into his lap so that I could feel the bulge of what was in his trousers against the top of my bottom crease. Not only that, but every time he moved to swing the club, it made him rub against me.

I may lack confidence, but I'm not completely naive. Nor was he. We both knew what was happening, and before long we were doing it on purpose and making a joke of it, with me wiggling my bottom as I got ready to hit the ball, and his grip growing ever tighter. I'd got him hard and my panties were damp. It was instinctive and inevitable. When he offered to show me how to drive and sent the ball deep into a clump of birch and gorse, I had no idea what we were going to get up to – me and this well-respected wine merchant. Into the bushes we went. No sooner were we safely out of sight than he had taken me in his arms.

Another of Valentina's rules for dealing with men – never give too much too soon. I could never keep to it. The idea that sex is something women should ration I could never understand. I like it too much, and once I'm going I can't hold back. She'd have left him with a teasing word that held the promise of more whereas I pulled down his zip and took his cock in my mouth. He was big and silky smooth, and absolutely rock hard. I think he was a bit surprised, but if there is one thing I do know about men, any man, it is that once his cock is in a girl's mouth, he won't stop.

Michael didn't, but began to stroke my hair as I sucked on him, first as if he was petting me, soothing me maybe, then lower, his fingers finding the nape of my neck to tickle in among the short hairs. That was just too much. One tug – my jumper and bra were up, my boobs in my hands. Two tugs – my jeans were open. Three tugs – I was bare from my neck to my knees with my bottom stuck out behind, praying he had enough sense to take control.

He did, without a word. He withdrew from my mouth. Down I went, on to all fours, sticking my bottom up as he got behind me. In went his cock, sliding greasily into my soaking pussy so easily that he was in me up to his balls before I really knew it. His hands came round to take my breasts and he was fucking me.

I love to be taken kneeling, showing everything, with a cock going into me really deeply. Michael was good too, stroking my nipples as he fucked me, and so fast. He was pumping away until all I could do was pant out my ecstasy into the curtain of hair hanging down around my head and pray he wouldn't come before I was ready.

He didn't, but what he did do was something no man had done to me before. Once he'd given me a thoroughly good pumping, he pulled out. For one awful moment I thought he was going to bugger me, and then the head of his cock was against my clit and he was rubbing. I just melted completely. My mouth came open, my face went into the grass and my bottom went higher still.

It was so rude, with my bottom cheeks spread wide to him as he masturbated me with his lovely cock, but it was perfect, exactly what I needed. All I could do was clutch at the grass and pant out my feelings, but I didn't need to do anything else. He was completely in control, teasing me towards orgasm as I wriggled and squirmed on his erection, with my boobs rubbing on the ground and the head of his cock bumping on my clit, bumping and bumping and bumping . . .

I just came, an orgasm in a thousand, with my entire body focused between my legs and what he was doing to me. Pulse after pulse of pleasure went through me, and I must have looked unspeakably rude from the rear, in fact, unspeakably rude full stop. I was kneeling on the ground with everything showing and my mouth full of grass because I was trying to stop myself screaming out loud.

He slid his cock back into me as my orgasm started to fade, and began to ride me once more, harder and faster than before. His hands found my boobs again and he was squeezing them tight and rubbing my nipples, and kissing my neck, and pumping against my bottom to bring my orgasm right back up again.

I couldn't take it though. His whole weight was on my back, just about, and I collapsed, face down in the mulch, just as he came. His cock pulled out, jammed between my bottom cheeks and there was something hot and wet in my crease and on my back. I let him do it, something no boyfriend would ever get if he asked, finishing himself off by rubbing his cock in my bottom crease. All the while he was mumbling compliments about how pretty I was, although I wasn't at all sure if he meant my face or my bottom.

So that was my brief and passionate first encounter with Michael Callington. He was completely cool about it, apologising for making such a mess and offering to clean me up with his handkerchief. I declined, not entirely sure about having my bottom wiped by a man I'd just met, whatever we'd done.

We abandoned the ball and any pretence of him teaching me golf, and went back to the club house for a more thorough clean-up and a drink. I was pretty embarrassed, really, by my own passion, but when I'd cleaned up and found him seated at a club-house table it was to find him as calm as ever, waiting for me with a half-bottle of white wine in an ice bucket.

The next hour was spent chatting as if we'd been friends for years rather than having just shared a knee-trembler in the bushes. He introduced me to his father, Major Malcolm Callington, an older version of the son, whose eyes made his appreciation of my figure embarrassingly obvious. He was the soul of politeness though, and made a point of insisting I come along to the tasting Michael had mentioned.

That was that. He had to get back to work and his father had a round booked. So I left too, cadging a lift in his great black Rover as far as Highbury Corner and walking the rest of the way to my flat. He kissed me goodbye with real warmth, and reminded me about the tasting once more. As I walked I was floating. I was sure I was on to a good thing. Looking back, it was a little embarrassing, but the sex had been good, no doubt about it. Impatient and spontaneous and very horny. Not only that, but I could be very sure that if Valentina had been there it wouldn't have happened. Instead he would barely have noticed me, and been enthralled with her instead. They always are.

As it was, we'd done it, and he was keen to see me again. He'd been pretty complimentary too. OK, mainly in a rude sort of way, but then that's men for you. I like rude men, anyway, at least in the sense of men who are confident in their sexuality. I like men who are confident full stop. There's nothing worse than a man who gets embarrassed about it or is ashamed of himself afterwards.

I was vaguely expecting a message from Valentina apologising for not turning up. Of course there wasn't one, but I rang her anyway, to be told that she'd been invited to sit in on a meeting chaired by the president of her firm, which was so important she had forgotten all about me. I did get to tell her about Michael though, all but the very rudest details. After all, it was the first time in all the years I'd known her that I'd come off best.

I had to see the guy little Chrissy Green had bonked. He couldn't possibly be as cute as she said. At least, not by any *real* standards of being cute. Cute is relative. There is Chrissy Green cute and then there is Valentina cute.

I mean, she said he was tall. Next to Chrissy, anyone is tall. She said he was good-looking. Compared to some of the men she's been out with, I was sure he was. She said he was confident and passionate and skilled and considerate. Well, this was Christina Green, expert in clumsy fumbles in the backs of second-hand cars with second-hand boyfriends. I needed to meet him anyway, as he'd been recommended to the chairman as running the best corporate wine tastings available, and so he was a must for the company social club. So I rescheduled the meeting.

What I expected was some pompous public-school boy, probably shorter than me, probably a bit over-weight and probably following me around like a puppy within a minute of meeting. What I got was Michael Callington. He was over six feet tall and absolutely drop dead gorgeous. He was also no puppy; anything but. He even had the nerve to comment on my breaking the previous meeting at short notice. If it hadn't been for the chairman's recommendation I'd have told him to get stuffed, but of course I couldn't.

Aside from that he was perfectly polite, but didn't show the slightest interest in me. That was too much. Sure, Chrissy had probably been slobbering all over him, but he'd gone for it. She'd never have dared lie, so I knew it was true, but if she hadn't told me what they'd done I would have thought he was gay.

All I wanted was a little interest from him and I'd have left him to her. As it was, it took an entire bottle of champagne and several heavy hints to get him to invite me to his flat after work, ostensibly to taste some of the wines he would be showing for the company.

I knew exactly what I was going to do. After leaving the office I would let my hair down and adjust my blouse to leave just a little bit of cleavage showing. Once there I would flirt a little, show off a little, until he finally got the hint and made an advance. I'd turn him down, expressing astonishment that he could have so clumsily misread the signals. Then I could report to Chrissy that he'd tried it on but I had refused to have anything to do with him. I would even imply that I'd made the choice both out of loyalty to her and because he wasn't really good enough for me.

Unfortunately it didn't work out that way. His flat was a big airy warehouse conversion overlooking the Thames. Everything about him suggested that he and his family had serious money. There were various bits of yachting stuff around, and when he noticed my interest he showed me out on to the balcony of his bedroom. There, seven storeys down, was a yacht a good twenty metres long – not cheap. That also meant he had mooring rights in the creek by the side of the flats – not cheap either. Finally there was the photo of some old boy standing with him outside a country house – not cheap at all. Wealth wasn't the only thing he had either. There was an oar with a pale blue blade up on one wall, which made him a Cambridge rowing blue. Various team photographs recorded other sporting triumphs, mostly to do with rowing or sailing. So he was not just gorgeous, but wealthy and a sportsman.

He couldn't possibly be interested in Chrissy Green! She just wasn't in his class. It is pathetic the way she throws herself at men, and I could just imagine what had happened, with her all over him and him shagging her more out of pity than sexual desire. Inevitably she was going to think it would mark the start of some great romance and, just as inevitably, it wouldn't. It was actually kind of me to put a stop to it sooner rather than later, so that she didn't get badly hurt.

I'd given up all intention of turning him down, but it wasn't going to happen that evening. That's the thing about men. Give in too easily and they lose interest. Hold back and they want more. It doesn't matter how attractive they are. Deep down they're all the same, and Michael Callington would be no different.

So I played it cool, nothing obvious, but a little hint now and then to suggest that I might be available, and to keep his juices flowing. He gave no sign of even noticing, but I knew he had, if only because he'd responded to Chrissy.

He'd lined up six bottles and was explaining why he'd chosen each as I pretended to listen, all the while admiring the way his muscles moved under the loose white shirt he had on. There was all sorts of pretentious technical stuff, but I didn't really catch it, except to note that he was going a long way round to explain to me that the glass of Chablis he'd given me was dry and light.

I drank the Chablis, and the Australian Chardonnay that came after it, and the light red that came after that, which I'd never heard of. I was sure he was trying to get me drunk, and played along with it, even undoing another button on my blouse as I finished the third glass. He poured a fourth, a strong Australian red, his hand as steady as ever. His hands were beautiful, elegant but strong, and it was all too easy to imagine them on my body, which was where I was sure he wanted them.

By then I'd realised what he was doing, playing me at my own game. It was easy, you see, with a little slut like Chrissy, who'll go with anyone half-decent who makes a pass. He wouldn't have cared that much anyway, happy if she did, not really bothered if she didn't. With me it was different. He didn't want to take any risks.

I went to a sofa and stretched myself out, giving him every opportunity to admire my legs and to look down my blouse. He came close, to sit on the arm, still talking, still cool and professionally detached. I leaned my head back, looking up into his beautiful pale eyes. Still there was no reaction, and as I finished my glass, he took it and went to fill it again.

Four large glasses of wine isn't *that* much, but I hadn't eaten. I knew I was in danger of getting drunk, but if I was, then so was he. The fifth wine was something sweet and rich and strong, not my taste at all, but I drank it anyway. So did Michael, talking in between sips. I never heard a word, but just watched his face and body.

I swear I don't remember putting my hand on his leg, but I do remember him taking it off again, gently but firmly. That was it, too much. If he could fuck Chrissy Green with her great wobbly bottom and her ridiculously big breasts and her little stuck-up nose and her 'butter-wouldn't-melt-in-my mouth' attitude, then he could fuck me. I stood to put my arms around him.

He tried to pull away, but not hard enough. I kissed his neck, nibbled on his ear, then pressed my mouth to his. For an instant he resisted, then gave in, his mouth opening under mine, and I had won.

His arms came up around my back, his big, strong hands pulling me in, his finger slipping up to the nape of my neck. I should have pulled away, slapped him even. Part of me wanted to. It was a very small part. I was going to have him.

A hand went lower, cupping my bottom through my skirt. I let him have his feel, to find out how much nicer my cheeks were than Chrissy Green's; how much smaller, how much firmer. Already I was easing him down on to the sofa, intent on climbing on top, intent on having him lick me before I mounted him and thoroughly enjoyed his, lean, hard body.

He let it happen, only to turn me at the last moment with one easy motion, and down I went, on my back. His hand was still under me, inching my skirt up, the other holding me to him tight, too tight to get away. Again I should have struggled, taken control, but he was too strong and I was too drunk and too urgent.

So up came the skirt, bunched around my waist, with my legs up high and wide, in a thoroughly undignified position I could do nothing about. I didn't even want to very much because I could feel the bulge of his cock through the front of my panties and it was very promising. He had also begun to kiss me again, only now with real passion.

His hand went down to fumble with his fly and I realised that he was just going to fuck me, then and there. Again I tried to make myself resist, to tell him to slow down, to undress for me, to lick me, play around for a bit first. Again I just couldn't, being too drunk and too aroused to even push him away for a minute. Instead, his cock came out, my thong was pulled aside and he was in me, filling my sex to leave me open and urgent beneath him as we began to fuck.

From the moment he responded to my kiss he had been the one making the decisions, and he continued to do so. He held me tight as we fucked, with enough of his weight on me to keep me firmly in my place. All I could do was lie there with my legs open and let him do it, pumping away so fast and with so much energy that I was soon completely breathless and couldn't have got up if I'd wanted to.

He'd been so quick, so urgent, that I thought he would come more or less immediately, and probably up me. If he had I'd have ended up masturbating in front of him. I didn't need to. After we'd been fucking long enough and fast enough to send me dizzy with pleasure he took out his cock and began to rub it on my clit. It was so good, so good that every last tiny scrap of my reserve just disappeared. I was squirming myself against him wantonly, frantic to get better contact between his cock and my clitoris. He just went on rubbing, still holding me, still kissing, as he brought me up to an orgasm over which I had no control whatsoever.

It was the best, pure, perfect rapture, my body responding to him by instinct, to send me into a wriggling frenzy, a totally uninhibited writhing and bucking underneath him. I don't know how he judged it, but no sooner had my orgasm begun to fade than he had pulled away, to take me firmly by the head. A tiny, lone voice in the back of my head was screaming out that I don't suck after fucking but it was too late. His cock was in my mouth and I was doing exactly that, sucking

13

the taste of my own sex, then of male come as he did it full in my mouth. He kept my head firmly in place until I'd swallowed the lot, but he didn't have to. I'd have done it anyway.

I did manage to call him a bastard afterwards, but I didn't really mean it. He just grinned. It was the same in the bathroom. I did feel a little put upon, because when I have sex I like to be in control. I kept trying to tell myself he had been too rough, too quick, too domineering. Unfortunately he hadn't. He'd been just right.

As I sat down to the glass of port he'd poured me, I was wondering how I was going to tell Chrissy that Michael and I were now lovers.

2

Michael didn't phone all week. Not that I really expected him to, but I felt he might have done. All I really wanted was a 'Hi, Chrissy, see you at the wine tasting', or maybe 'It was great to meet you, Chrissy, maybe we could get together again some time'.

I wasn't expecting it because he didn't seem the sort to get flustered over women. Far from it. He was the sort women got flustered over. He seemed to take life in his stride, strong, calm and easygoing. There would be no emotional crises for him, no getting worried over the sort of things I can spend hours agonising over. What with his wine business, his sport, his friends and so on, it was easy to imagine that it might never even cross his mind to phone me.

The trouble was, I didn't know where we stood, and I wanted to. He might be happy to just let things develop in their own time. I wasn't. I didn't have his confidence. I wanted reassurance. The more time passed without that all-important phone call, the less certain I became. I wanted there to be something special between us, but I didn't want to assume there was and end up looking pushy, or a complete idiot. Worst of all, I didn't want to end up looking bad in any way in front of Val – sorry, Valentina – who was bound to be there.

I didn't know anything about the event, either. It was at somewhere called the Home and Colonial, which was apparently an ancient club in St James's, and sounded stuffy and formal. I had no doubt at all that I would be expected to dress and behave a certain way. I also had no idea what I should do at a professional wine tasting. Ringing Michael was out of the question, as I'd have looked both pushy and foolish. So I rang the only other person I knew who would have all the answers: Valentina.

She was highly amused by the state I'd worked myself into and, sure enough, she was going to the tasting as well. Rather than answer my questions on the phone, she suggested going shopping, so that she could be sure I bought the right things. She would fill me in on etiquette between shops. I knew it meant I would be paying, but she was doing me a favour. Also, for all that she seems to be on the fast track to the top of the legal profession, she doesn't actually have all that much left to spend after her expenses.

One thing I can always guarantee about Valentina is that she will tell me the truth. Most of my girlfriends tell me I shouldn't worry about the size of my bottom, and I look fine and don't need to worry about drawing attention to it. Not Valentina. Her of the perfect flat, firm and exquisitely feminine bottom. She says mine is big and wobbly. Not wishing to end up looking a complete bloater, I needed the truth.

It was what I got, in abundance. We met at Knights-bridge tube station and spent a busy afternoon wandering around the stores looking for ideal outfits. As usual, all the designer labels seemed to have been tailored for her, while none came close to fitting me. After two hours she had seen so many things she simply had to have that my generosity was beginning to wear thin. As always she knew exactly when to stop and turned her attention to me.

She had gone for a choice of two very elegant dresses, both well-known labels and both just revealing enough to be acceptable at the tasting. I wanted something similar, as I felt that anywhere so old-fashioned, a dress was sure to be appropriate. She dismissed the idea, pointing out that we weren't in the eighteenth century, or even the nineteenth, and that we hadn't seen a dress that would fit me properly anyway. Her view was that a trouser suit in a dark colour and a light cloth would suit me best.

There was nothing in the area that she felt suitable, but we finally got lucky in the Fulham road with a black outfit for just forty-five pounds, which was certainly good value. Valentina said she was too exhausted to shop for accessories for me, and my feet hurt too much to disagree. I was also badly in need of a drink, so we found a cafe in a side street and I got my lecture on etiquette over a bottle of chilled white wine.

Without her help, I would have made a complete fool of myself. For a start, I'd expected to have to spit out what we tasted, and would probably have done it in the waste-paper basket or something equally crass. I'd also expected it all to be laid on for us, with one wine followed by another, and Michael or one of his colleagues telling us about each. Instead, I learned that there would be a long line of bottles on tables, from which we could help ourselves. Also, it was considered impolite to take more than one third of a glass or to sample the same wine twice. There was even a correct order in which to taste them. Without Valentina to help, I knew I'd have got every single step wrong, and by the time she eventually left to get ready for some date or other, I was feeling immensely grateful to her.

I was also a little drunk, having got through more

than my fair share of the bottle, and more than a little horny. She had met Michael in the week to arrange the tasting for her company. So she knew what he looked like, but every time he had come up in conversation she had quickly changed the subject. That meant she was jealous, and for Valentina to be jealous of me was a completely new experience.

It was also an arousing one. So many times before it had been all too obvious that my boyfriends weren't worth a second glance from her. She had always tried to be nice about it and it wasn't her fault, but it had always put me off and, in the end, made the sex unsatisfactory. I know it's bad, but her jealousy made what Michael and I had done even better.

I was thinking about it all the way home, with my imagination working over memories and thinking up little fantasies. First it was just about her being with the two of us, perhaps in a restaurant, until he and I had to go. I could use the phrase she had used to me so, so many times when she wanted to be alone with a boyfriend – 'private time'. I can't remember when I first heard those two awful words, but it must have been when I used to 'play gooseberry' on dates with Valentina. I could remember all of them – hanging on after school and watching her with Andy Dawtry, the best-looking boy in the entire sixth form, as they got ruder and ruder. Finally she'd chirped up, oh so sweetly, 'Private time, Chrissy.' Off I'd gone, home, on a cold, damp bus.

Then there was Simon Straw, who I'd fancied so much, and who I'd taken my top off for, only to discover he was completely besotted with her. I'd been with him for a week before he'd dumped me for her. I'd been cold to her for another week – sulking, she'd called it. Then she'd explained ever so sweetly how he had only gone out with me to get to her in the first place and we'd made up. The three of us had even gone out to see a film together one night. The only way home had been in his car, so after 'private time, Chrissy' and being booted out of it, I'd had to wait in the freezing cold while they made love on the back seat.

The only one that brought a smile to my face was Robert Wall. She and I had been going ice skating together. She'd met him there, with inevitable consequences. Only when we'd driven out to a convenient car park afterwards and she had given me my 'private time, Chrissy', he had suggested a threesome. She'd slapped his face.

Now I could get my revenge. It would have to be timed to perfection, preferably when she was relying on him for a lift, or had to stick around for some other reason. Slowly the intimacy between Michael and me would grow, until finally my moment came, and I would deliver my line with such sympathy, such compassion, such pity, just as she always had – 'Private time, Val.' It would be perfect.

By the time I got home I'd worked myself into a fine state. I was even imagining situations where for one reason or another she couldn't go, but would have to wait while we made love. She'd hear everything, which was an embarrassing thought, but also a satisfying one. I could just imagine her frustration, maybe so strong that she'd have to slip a hand down her knickers and bring herself off, the way I'd done once.

It had been on a date with Simon, in his car as usual. They'd fixed me up with a blind date, a skinny ginger-haired boy whose name I couldn't even remember. Even he had obviously been more interested in her than me, watching them out of the corner of his eye as he struggled to get my bra undone. I might even have let him, but he had to be in by ten thirty. So I was left, again, standing outside the car as I watched Simon and Val by the orange light of a street lamp. She hadn't known I could see, and I'd been amazed by how rude she was, and how experienced. They'd gone head to tail ... No, she'd made him go head to tail, and lick her pussy while she sucked his cock. I'd had a fine view, of her lipstick-red mouth moving up and down on him. It had been too much. I'd been terrified of being caught, but I'd done it, well back in the shadows, my jeans undone, one hand down the front of my knickers, the other up my top, teasing my clit and a nipple until I came. It had felt so good, but afterwards I'd felt so ashamed. Now I wanted her to feel the same.

I knew that in reality she would probably have managed to put a stop to it somehow, but that didn't matter. As I sat down in an armchair with a cup of coffee, it wasn't reality that mattered. I didn't just want her to hear either. I wanted her to watch, as I had done with her and Simon. She would see everything, his lovely big cock, proud and hard for me. I'd suck him in front of her, showing off my affection and the intimacy between us. Maybe I'd even let him come in my mouth, just to show her that I was prepared to give him something she hated, something she never gave.

That was dirty, not just sucking his cock in front of her, but letting him come in my mouth. I undid my jeans, narrowing my eyes as my hand burrowed down the front. My pussy was soaking, my clit urgently in need of attention. I shut my eyes, pulled my top and bra up to spill out my breasts and began to masturbate.

She would be so jealous, and so aroused. I'd see the

desire in her eyes, strong and helpless. Maybe I'd even invite her, ever so sweetly – 'We don't mind if you do it, Valentina. We'll understand, won't we, Michael?' He'd agree. Her face would be full of shame, but she'd do it. This would be before he'd come, and I'd go back to sucking his cock. He'd be watching me, as he had on the golf course, indifferent to her as she shyly pushed down her knickers and bunched up her skirt.

Michael would mount me from behind as she began to masturbate, his hands on my boobs, murmuring sweet compliments about my body as he fucked me, and ignoring her completely. She'd come first, with a little sob, as much frustration as ecstasy, just as he took out his cock to do his wonderful little trick. I'd let her see, hiding nothing of my body or my emotions as he brought me to the most wonderful, utterly fulfilling climax, cock to clit, rubbing and rubbing as she stared in envy . . .

I came, my head burning with the thought of Michael rubbing himself on my pussy, with Valentina staring, legs wide, everything on show, totally unable to control her feelings as she watched us.

My date with Michael was at Marco's in the King's Road. It would have been nice to go back home and change beforehand but Chrissy had spent so long choosing her outfit for the tasting that I'd be impossibly late. Men will wait half an hour, maybe an hour, but two to three is pushing it.

It was really irritating because she must have known that that class of shop simply doesn't stock things in her size. I mean, if anyone put a mannequin her shape in a shop window, they'd be laughed out of town. She'd made me feel bad as well because I'd not been able to tell her about me and Michael. I'd wanted to, but every time she'd mentioned him she'd been so full of enthusiasm I just hadn't had the heart. Of course, the longer I left it, the more it was going to hurt her, which was the last thing I wanted, so I knew I'd have to do it soon.

It was also annoying because she had put me in a difficult position when she really should have had more sense than to try for someone as upmarket as Michael in the first place. What she needs is a nice, steady man; someone ordinary, someone faithful, who will appreciate what she has got. Mark you, it didn't surprise me. She never could see herself as others saw her.

She'd been the same at school, always setting her sights too high and then getting hurt, time and time again. Most of them would date her a couple of times just out of a perverse fascination with her breasts. Boys are like that, they're always into extremes: the top team, the fastest car, the girl with the biggest breasts in school. It never lasted.

The truth is, she's a slut. She never did know when to hold back. She never did know when she wasn't wanted either. So many times I've had to drop hints that she should leave me and a boyfriend alone, but she always loved to listen to me having sex. Sometimes I even let her watch from a respectful distance, and there was one time, with some guy in his car, when I'm sure she sneaked a crafty wank over us, right there in the bushes! Sometimes I wonder if she isn't a closet lesbian.

What I had done was make sure she wouldn't be at the tasting. I'd been to the Home and Colonial before, and I know what they're like. She wasn't going to get in, so she wouldn't see Michael and there wouldn't be a scene. Cruel to be kind.

Michael was waiting when I arrived at Marco's. I was barely twenty minutes late, but I still got an irritable look from him. That was going to have to change, but for the moment I was prepared to put up with it and apologised, citing bad traffic and an incompetent cab driver as my excuse.

He accepted it, but still managed to give the impression that I should have been better organised. It was a bit like when we'd had sex, with him casually assuming that he would get what he wanted. I've known men like that before, too used to getting their own way, too selfish. He was going to have to learn that I don't work like that. With me, he would have to work around the way I am, and not the other way around. It was going to take work, but I'd get there.

Dinner was fabulous. Langoustine, turbot and tiny crêpes, all immaculately served. I didn't eat much as I wanted to leave myself plenty for energy for bonking afterwards, but I didn't stint on the wine. I even let Michael choose. After all, he was a professional and could be relied on not to try and make me drink some filthy house plonk all night. There was no nonsense about the bill either. He paid without a murmur.

So it was back to his flat for what I knew was going to be a night of just the best sex ever. I wasn't going to stand for any nonsense about who was in charge. He played it cool in the cab, which was just as well. There really is nothing worse than being groped in the back seat of a taxi with some oik from the East End leering at me in his rearview mirror.

In his flat it was a very different story. We were

kissing as soon as we were through the door, and I had his tie and jacket off in double quick time. That's where I halted it, determined to teach him a little respect. My men do things for me, not the other way around. I told him to strip and to fetch me a drink, in that order. He hesitated, but just for a second, and I knew I'd won. I walked over to the sofa, then settled down to watch.

He was magnificent. Not that he knew the first thing about how to strip for a woman, but his body more than made up for that. The tough, rebellious look on his face was great too, as he obviously thought it should be me stripping for him. I don't do that, but he wasn't to know. He would ask though, I was sure of it.

First came his shirt, the buttons and cuffs undone, and peeled off to reveal his smooth, well-muscled torso and arms. His trousers followed, unfastened and dropped to the floor, only he had made the most elementary mistake and forgotten to take his shoes off, which made me giggle and hardened the look in his eyes. He kept on, though, rather awkwardly removing his shoes, socks and trousers to leave him in just briefs, which did very little to hide the size and shape of his already half-stiff cock. That was when he decided to ask for me to return the favour.

'Now you.'

I wagged a finger and pointed to the floor between his feet. He smiled and shook his head. I repeated the gesture a little more firmly.

'All the way, Michael, and get me that drink. Then it's my turn.'

He hesitated, nodded, his hands went into the top of his briefs and down they came, to show off his lovely big cock. I found myself licking my lips but held my poise, nodding towards his kitchen area. Kicking off his briefs, he went, giving me a delightful view of his tight hard buttocks as he walked across the room.

'Champagne?'

'Of course. What else?'

Again he nodded, accepting my verdict, and busied himself with the bottle, glasses and an ice bucket. I relaxed, content to be served. He was like the rest of them, very easily led, happy to do anything just so long as they thought they had a treat coming at the end. The knack, of course, is never to actually let them have the treat. Do, and they lose interest.

He made a very good servant, opening a bottle of Bollinger and pouring out the glasses with practised efficiency, and even putting it all together on a tray to bring it over. I was tempted to have him serve it kneeling, but something in his look told me he wouldn't be prepared to grovel quite that much, or not yet anyway.

I took my glass. He made himself comfortable and gave a polite gesture to the floor. I answered him.

'No, Michael, I'm not going to do a striptease for you. I'm surprised you would even ask. Don't you have any respect for me?'

He was supposed to go into a flood of apologies. He simply shrugged and took a swallow of his champagne. For one moment I felt my grip slipping, but I reached out to press my talons to his leg and he was all attention again, shifting position to let me get at his cock. I ignored the offer and continued to run my nails gently up and down his leg. He gave no response, but his cock did, twitching slightly as it began to expand. I met his eyes and let my tongue flick out to touch my lips. My hand went a little higher, to tickle his balls and make his cock stiffer still. He took hold of it, as eager and as easily led as any other.

Nothing more needed to be said. I stood up, to throw one leg over his naked body. As I sat myself down on him his cock pressed against my panty crotch. I reached down to pull aside my panties and take him in, his cock seemingly still swelling as it filled me.

I was riding him, the way I like to have a man, with me on top, clothed, or as much clothed as it pleases me to be, and him naked underneath me, with his cock at my disposal. There was no need to hurry either. Michael was now as obedient as a puppy dog, just pushing gently up into me as I picked up my champagne glass once more. He was watching me as I sipped the pale golden fluid, his eyes feasting on my breasts and waist, full of longing. He wanted my dress off, obviously, and I was sure he was going to ask and provide me with the delicious thrill of denying him. I put the glass down, as if I was going to do it, but stopped, determined to make him ask.

He didn't, but picked up his own glass and took a leisurely sip. I began to move on his cock, wriggling my bottom. He swallowed hard, took another sip, and put the glass down. I reached down, to rake my nails across the hard, smooth muscle of his chest. He began to push harder into me. His hands found my hips and I was being bounced on his cock, suddenly breathless. I gasped for him to stop, that I was not ready. His grip tightened. He rose as easily as if I weighed nothing at all. One hand cupped my bottom, another came around my back. His fingers found the nape of my neck and my bottom hole at the same time, tickling both. I gasped out, trying to tell him not to be dirty with me, only to have my mouth stopped with a kiss.

Then I was down on the sofa, squirming underneath him as he pumped into me with incredible energy, his cock moving in and out so fast it left me dizzy, my breath coming in short hard pants. His mouth went to my neck, but still I couldn't speak, only gasp and moan, even though he had his finger well up my bottom, which I hate.

No, I don't hate it exactly. It's just that it's too intimate, too dirty, to let a man touch me there, even to look at it. When it happens though, and it does, it's just too much. I can't help myself, for all I never want to, and I couldn't now. Michael didn't care anyway, playing my body for pure, physical excitement alone, without a thought for my dignity.

His cock came out at the same time as his finger and, for one panic-stricken moment, I wondered if he was going to put his cock up my bottom hole, and if I would even try to stop him. He didn't, simply whipping my panties off under my skirt and flipping my legs high, to hold me by the ankles as he entered me again. Now he was completely in control of my body, pumping faster than ever, so that all I could do was lie there and clutch at the fabric of the sofa as we fucked. No, as he fucked me, using me like a doll without the slightest thought for my needs, just as he had done before.

I thought he was going to come and just leave me there or try to make me masturbate in front of him. Then he was out, his cock was against my sex, and I knew exactly what he was going to do. I just surrendered. My knees came apart, spreading my sex to him, my bottom too, showing everything. The bastard watched too, letting his eyes run slowly from my face to my bum and back, over and over as he rubbed himself on me, my clitoris bumping back and forth under the firm flesh of his cock. His knuckles were rubbing on me too, but I was so close to climax I never even realised what he was doing until I felt a gush of hot fluid spurt out over my sex.

He had come on me, but it didn't stop him, his cock just moving faster as he milked himself over me. Suddenly I was coming too, coming on my back, spread bare for him, showing everything, as he took complete control of my climax, holding me on a plateau of ecstasy. Even when my sex had become unbearably sensitive he kept on, leaving me screaming and clawing at the sofa, out of my mind with pleasure.

3

The day of the tasting I spent the entire afternoon getting ready. A long soak in the bath, a visit to the hairdresser's, and plenty of time getting dressed. There seemed a fair chance I'd be going home with Michael, so I chose a tailor-made bra with plenty of lace and plenty of support, very loose French knickers, which I always feel make the best of my bum, stay-ups and three-inch heels to lift me to five foot four. The trouser suit looked a bit plain, and concealed my waist so that I actually looked bigger than I am, but Valentina had been adamant it was the right thing for the club. She was bound to have a go at me if I wore anything else, so I went with it.

I took a cab to St James's, picking Val up on the way. She looked gorgeous as always, incredibly chic and just a little daring, so that I wondered if she hadn't overdone it for the club. She just laughed and told me she'd get away with it.

Sure enough, she did. There was a doorman sporting a long crimson coat with brass buttons, like something out of the eighteenth century, standing on the club steps. He bowed politely to Valentina, a gesture she ignored completely as she sauntered into the club, but put out his arm to stop me.

'Excuse me, miss, but you can't come in like that.'

'Like what?'

'Improperly dressed, miss.'

'Improperly dressed?'

I glanced down, expecting to find my zip wide open or my knickers showing through a tear. There was nothing wrong. He went on.

'In trousers, miss.'

'Trousers? What's wrong with trousers?'

'No women in trousers, miss. Club rules.'

'No women in trousers? Why not? That's silly!'

'Sorry, miss. Club rules.'

'Look, I didn't know about rules. Can I at least speak to my friend? Valentina! Val!'

She had disappeared. The doorman stood in frozen immobility.

'I ... I'm attending a wine tasting with Michael Callington. Surely I can come in for that?'

'Sorry, miss. No women in trousers.'

'But...'

I gave up. I hate arguments and it was obvious he wasn't going to budge. Suddenly I was close to tears, only for my hope to revive as a stern-looking, silver-haired man strode out of the club – Michael's father. He surely could handle the doorman. I gave him my sweetest smile.

'Major Callington?'

'Ah, Christina, my dear. Come for the tasting?'

'Yes, only I can't get in because I'm in a trouser suit. Perhaps you could explain?'

'Nothing I can do, I'm afraid, my dear. I'm not even a member.'

'Oh.'

'Well, never mind, I was just on my way to my own club, around the corner. Join me.'

'But...'

I shut up. He'd taken me by the arm and was steering

me along the street. There was really nothing else to do, and I've always been one to go with the flow anyway. Besides, if I was with him, there had to be at least a chance of meeting up with Michael later on. So I let him lead me along the street and across a square to a building much like the one we'd just left. There was another doorman in livery, but this one just nodded politely.

Inside it was quiet, with only the faint buzz of conversation and the occasional clink of glassware from a room towards which the major was steering me. It was a dining room with delicious cooking smells mixing with those of wood polish and antiquity, and dust motes dancing in the evening sun that was streaming through the windows.

'You'll have some dinner with me? At least we'll get something worth drinking here.'

'Worth drinking? Aren't Michael's wines good quality then?'

'Good enough, I dare say, but he has this obsession with Australia . . . Yes, Ivan, for two.'

The waiter he had addressed bowed and led us towards a table somewhat apart from those already occupied. I was wondering if the man thought Malcolm Callington was playing sugar daddy to me. The idea sent the blood straight to my face, and when I was sent towards my chair with a gentle pat on my bottom my embarrassment grew stronger still. I was going to say something, but Malcolm Callington went on as if nothing had happened.

'I dare say he'll grow out of it. We'll have the asparagus, I think, and a bottle of Crémant. The pigeon are good, or maybe duck . . . no, pigeon, and Burgundy, of course, perhaps a Morey.'

He went on, never once pausing to consult me or ask if I might be vegetarian, or allergic to something, or even if I liked it. I was glad to be rescued, and I do like assertive men, but it was irritating. Still, I think I would have said something if he'd been just a little less sure of himself, or if he hadn't been Michael's father. Not that he let me get a word in edgeways anyway, and our starter had been served before he asked me a question.

'So what d'you do with your time? Secretary or something?'

'Well, no ... nothing really ... I ...'

'Splendid. I approve of that in a woman. Shows you've got your own mind. Why women have to go rushing around after careers nowadays I can't understand. After all, everyone knows they're likely to drop the whole thing to go and have babies at any moment. That's what makes such a nonsense of it, you see. No matter what these types say about equal opportunities, it will always be the women who have the babies.'

'Well, yes ...'

'It's nature. There's no getting around it. So where's your family from?'

'London, really. Mum came from Wisbech.'

'The Fens, splendid. Michael's a blue, you know, I expect he told you?'

'No.'

'Always did hide his light under a bushel, that one. Damn good sportsman, Michael, and very much a wet bob. So was I, in my day. That's what brought Pippa and me together – Pippa's my wife, you know – that, and swish.'

He laughed, went suddenly quiet, then spoke again, in a low, serious voice.

'I take it you're ... hum ha ... a fan yourself? I mean, if you're a friend of Michael's?'

I had no idea what a 'wet bob' was, or 'swish', except that they had something to do with sport. I nodded anyway. Suddenly he was smiling again, absolutely beaming in fact.

'Splendid, splendid! That's what I like to hear. I knew you had bottom, ha ha! Look, er ... I hope you won't think I'm being too forward or anything, but as it happens, we're taking *Harold Jones* up to Norfolk. You should join us.'

'Harold Jones?'

'The yacht. Just a small party, of course. Pippa, that's my wife, as I was saying, Tilly who's her sister, and Michael. Family, really, but you should come. You'd be very welcome.'

'Well, yes ... I mean, thank you. I'd be delighted, of course, but are you sure that's OK, if it's a family holiday?'

'Absolutely. Pippa's insisted on renting this whacking big cottage at Hickling Green, so there's plenty of room, and I could always do with an extra hand.'

'I ... I really don't know all that much about sailing.'

'Oh, you'll pick it up soon enough, what you need to anyway, so long as you don't mind a little deck scrubbing, fair turns in the galley and a spot of swish.'

He took a swallow from his glass, turning his attention to the wine for a moment before looking at me expectantly. I wasn't at all sure what he was talking about, but the chance of sharing a boat trip with the ebullient Michael was far too good to pass up.

'Thank you, I'll come. That's very kind.'

'Splendid. We'll get along famously, I can see.'

'How long will we be staying?'

'Oh, a month or so, I would suppose, to get a decent piece of the summer before the schools break up and it gets crowded. We usually try to get a house party together every year.'

'Will Michael be there all the time? I mean, his business...'

'Business? More of a hobby really. After all, a fellow has to do something with his life. He was never very keen on the army, and I don't suppose the Church would have had him. No, I'm surprised he hadn't invited you himself. He speaks very highly of you.'

I was beginning to realise just how rich the Callingtons were. There was no charge for the tasting, yet Michael had booked a huge room and opened at least two bottles of every wine he was showing. There no pressure to buy at all, while his customers all seemed to be friends of his or city types, without a restaurateur or a commercial buyer in sight. Obviously he was not in it for the money.

There were about a hundred wines, mostly Australian. I had no intention of trying them all, which was what most of the guests seemed to be intent on. Certainly I had no intention of buying any when my relationship with Michael would shortly be guaranteeing a steady supply of the best for free. I had to look vaguely willing though, and not crowd round Michael too much in case he thought I was clingy. So I sipped a glass of the most expensive and drinkable of the sparkling wines and made small talk with his customers.

They were a pretty dull lot. Most were public-school boys, others presumably his Cambridge friends, or both.

All of them seemed to be at least passably well off, and a few were good-looking, and might even have been of interest had Michael not been there. I was beginning to think more and more of him as a serious prospect, so the last thing I wanted to do was earn myself a reputation for being easily available. Getting off with any of his friends was clearly out of the question, and even flirting with them not good. I was regretting shagging him, though, in a way, and hoped I hadn't lost all of my mystery.

So I stayed on my best behaviour, polite but cool to all the men who spoke to me, for about ten minutes. Then a girl walked in. She was hard to miss, straight out of the pages of *Vogue* – tall, dark, languid, and wearing something from the latest Firidolfi collection. Not only that, but she was absolutely dripping in jewels, and only a couple of years older than me, if that. She walked up to Michael, as cool as you please, kissed him and pinched his cheek, a gesture so casual, so intimate, that there could only be one possible explanation. She was his girlfriend, even his wife.

Nobody does that to me, nobody. My first instinct was to march straight over and tell her all about him and me, and about him and Chrissy Green into the bargain, then deposit a glass of red wine down his shirt front. I even started to walk towards them, but then I started to think about the flat, and the yacht, and the casual way in which he spent money. She couldn't be his wife anyway. His flat was strictly masculine. So she was a girlfriend, a sister even ... No, the way they had greeted each other was wrong for a sister, and he still had his hand resting lightly on her shoulder, her bare shoulder. They didn't look all that alike either. She had to be a girlfriend, but it was no time to give him a dressing down. She turned as I approached, all smiles.

'Hi, you must be Valentina. I'm Pippa. Michael has told me so much about you. What a pretty dress, and you're so right not to wear too much jewellery. I feel completely overdressed.'

For a moment I didn't know what to say. What had Michael told her about me? That we'd bonked each other's brains out? Not likely, unless they were swingers and the bastard was hoping to get the two of us into bed at the same time. If so, there was another lesson he was going to have to learn. I do not share my men.

Even if he'd just told her I was a friend she had a cheek. She couldn't be more than two or three years older than me, but she was talking down to me, as if it wasn't perfectly obvious that I couldn't afford the sort of stuff she had on, all of which she'd probably have screwed out of Michael, literally. Two could play at that game. I answered her.

'Not at all. Jewellery is like wine. In good taste when the bottle's older.'

She started a little. Michael gave a nervous laugh. I went on happily.

'Talking of old wine, Michael's doing a tasting for my company, some wonderful things. He showed me the whole range. That's how we met . . . at his flat.'

'Yes, he mentioned that you worked. I think you're frightfully clever, all that computer stuff. I know I'd just get bored and make the most awful mistakes all the time.'

'Excuse me.'

The last comment was Michael, making a hasty departure. I forced a smile, although what I wanted to do was scratch the little bitch's eyes out. I kept my temper, just about, and tried to give her back a bit of what she was dishing out.

'Well, I think a woman should have a career nowadays, if she's capable. I like to be the equal of the men I meet, otherwise they're likely to think I'm just a gold-digger. You know how it is.'

She gave the same little start as before. She just was not in my class. A moment later she had given up the unequal contest.

'Quite. Well, I must find out what's become of Malcolm. He was here a moment ago, I'm sure. Nice to meet you.'

She turned away. Round one to me.

Making her feel small was all very well, but it wasn't her attitude I needed to change. If I'd been considering Michael as a serious prospect, now I absolutely had to have him. Nobody treats me as a casual shag, and even if it meant letting him have his way in bed it would be worth it. After all, once I'd got him firmly on my leash it would be a very different matter. I'd be able to pay it all back, nice and slowly.

I turned my attention back to the wines. She'd disappeared, and he was busy opening bottles and so forth. I made for the reds and poured myself a large glass of Shiraz, which earned me a disapproving look from some stuffed shirt next to me.

The walls were covered in paintings of various military sorts killing each other, and I pretended to study one as I mulled over the situation. Obviously she was his girlfriend, and had been for quite a while to have accumulated so much tinsel. He had to be getting bored with her, or he wouldn't have done what he did with Chrissy Green. So there were cracks in their relationship. Maybe he felt she was too demanding? I could see that, but I didn't want it to be true. I wanted him to be truly generous.

That thought set me off on a new tack. He hadn't given me any presents at all, not one. Obviously it had been a bad mistake to give in to him so easily. I should have made him wait, and now he was going to be thinking I was cheap. Well, it wasn't going to stay that way. Before he so got much as a peep at my breasts I wanted . . .

No, that wasn't the way to go about it at all. It was the way she was playing it, obviously, and he wanted something different. It made perfect sense, and even explained why he had bonked Chrissy Green. She was certainly different. For a start she was a slut, and would never have thought for a moment of holding anything back to gain an advantage. She's cheap too, not just for sex, but in general. Her idea of a present was a bunch of roses and a box of chocolates – that's the sort of roses you get from dodgy eastern European types at traffic lights, and the sort of chocolates you buy in cut-price supermarkets. Her idea of a night out was a film, a curry and a shag over the back seat of a car.

I was not going to behave like her, not for anything. For Michael I was prepared to put up with plenty, but there are limits. Still, I could put up with letting him go on top, and even some dirty stuff. I could do without decent presents for a while. That way he'd quickly come to see how much better I was, and in no time he'd be as faithful as a puppy, like all the others, and she'd be history. Until then, I was going to be Little Miss Nice.

* * *

It was impossible not to like Malcolm Callington. He was a bit crusty, and I could see he fancied me, or at least my chest, but he didn't try anything and stayed polite and friendly. He had all his son's self-assurance as well, maybe more, and had clearly been just as good-looking in his day. I had to admit that, in different circumstances, if he hadn't been married and I hadn't been so keen on his son, then maybe, just maybe, I'd have been interested.

I could just imagine Valentina's reaction. She would tease me mercilessly for going with an older man, but I know her, and there would be jealousy underneath. It would be my own choice as well, and she likes to choose my men for me, or at least she always says the ones I choose for myself are completely inappropriate. He was upper class too, which I knew would annoy her.

He drank like a fish, sparkling wine first, then Burgundy, a half bottle of something sweet and sticky with pudding and a large brandy afterwards. I suppose I must have consumed nearly half of what he'd drunk, because every time my glass was even close to empty he would fill it up, and he always poured with a generous hand. By the time we left I was more than a little tipsy. When he took my arm again outside the club I let him, sure it was just old-fashioned courtesy and quite glad to be able to steady myself on him.

When we got to the Home and Colonial the wine tasting had finished. There was no sign of Valentina, but Michael was standing on the pavement talking to a very pretty dark-haired girl in fur. They were standing pretty close, and my heart jumped at the sight, only for Malcolm's introductions to leave me feeling silly.

'Ah, there you are, Pippa. Christina, meet Pippa, the

wife. Pippa, Christina. Damn beadle wouldn't let her in, so I took her to the club for a spot of dinner. Michael, you've been hiding the pretty ones from us!'

He sent me towards Michael with a pat on my bottom. For one instant what I was sure was a possessive spark showed in Michael's eye, then he replied, 'I was wondering what had happened to you, Chrissy. Thanks for looking after her, Dad.'

'My pleasure.'

'Didn't Valentina tell you what had happened?' I asked.

'No, she didn't say a word.'

'Oh. Is she still around?'

'I don't think so, no. I think she left.'

'Oh.'

'Stuck for a lift?'

'Yes . . . I mean, if it's no trouble. I'm in Islington.'

'My pleasure.'

Malcolm Callington was grinning like a wolf, and I could see exactly what was going through his mind. Pippa was no better, giving me a sly wink as they turned to their car, a huge deep-red Jag. That left me alone with Michael, and suddenly as dizzy with arousal as with drink.

I snuggled into him. He didn't resist and that was it. I'd have asked then and there to get down to it if there hadn't been so many people still about. As it was we went to his car and drove east, through the bright lights of the West End, then quieter streets. It had been a while since I'd had sex in a car, and I do like it, with that delicious thrill of wondering if someone's peeping in. I almost asked him to find some quiet alley, but at Upper Street we came back into glare and bustle and the moment was lost.

'Whereabouts?'

'I'll direct you. Turn down the Essex Road.'

He nodded, and turned. I had to do it. Not to would have been silly. I told him to turn, once, then again, towards my house. The third time it was down a long road between old warehouses and the canal. The fourth it was into an alley. I told him to stop. He looked puzzled.

'Here?'

'Yes. It's perfect.'

I had undone my seat belt, and smiled as I turned to him. He chuckled and reached out to stroke my cheek, my neck, the curve of my breast. I sighed as his finger brushed my nipple. My blouse came open, my bra came up and my boobs were bare, showing to him, and the night outside the car. For a moment he looked surprised, but not for long. Reaching out, he took them in his hands, to knead them softly and run his thumbs over my nipples. I just closed my eyes in bliss, letting him enjoy my breasts as he pleased. His mouth closed on one nipple, sucking on the stiff bud of flesh to tease the tip with his tongue. I pushed out my chest, pressing my flesh to his face. A hand found my trousers, opening the button, slipping inside and down the front of my French knickers.

I just lay there, purring happily to myself as he fed on my breasts, kissing them as he moved from one nipple to the other, and back, and all the while teasing my pussy. I wanted his cock, but I wanted to surrender more, to let him do as he pleased, in the sure knowledge that he would take his time with me and bring me to climax.

Sure enough, he was in no hurry at all. I never even realised he had released himself from his belt until a weight shifted on to me. Then my seat was being wound slowly down and his kisses were becoming more intense. He began to masturbate me, slipping a finger up into my pussy briefly before finding my clit. I put my arms around him, holding him to me as he toyed with me, bringing me closer and closer towards orgasm.

When it came it was so sudden, and so good, long and sweet, my body tightening against his, utterly abandoned and utterly under his control as he worked his magic on my tits and pussy. At the very peak he put his mouth to mine, kissing me so passionately, and still kissing me as my climax faded to leave me purring and content on the seat.

I didn't even know he'd got his cock out, and one of the delicious thoughts that had been going through my head as I came was of how I would repay the favour by sucking it for him. I was never given the chance. No sooner had his mouth left mine than I was being rolled over, his strong arms turning me bum up on the seat so quickly I barely had a chance to let out a squeak of surprise.

The next instant he was on top of me, my trousers were down, my knickers followed, and I was bare. He began to feel me, stroking and patting my bottom, to fill me with the urge to lift myself for penetration. I couldn't, I was trapped, helpless beneath his weight, but that only made it nicer and my need stronger. The fondling grew rougher, the slaps harder, until I'd begun to wonder if he was kinky, and was going to spank me.

It stopped though, suddenly, and then his hard, hot cock was pressing between my bare cheeks. I was wet with my own juice, and as he pushed his cock down it pressed to my bottom hole for a moment, filling my head with thoughts of being buggered. I squeaked in protest, but he had already gone lower, and the squeak turned into a gasp as my pussy filled with cock.

He began to fuck me, pumping away at a furious pace, his hard muscled belly slapping on my cheeks as if I really was being spanked. It left me breathless, panting into the seat, with my head full of images of the way he'd made me come, of how we were, of how we'd look if anyone saw. I was bare breasted and bare bottomed, my tits squashed underneath me, my trousers pulled down, my French knickers inverted around my thighs. He was in me, fucking me, the man who had made me come, the man who played my body so beautifully. I was desperately hoping someone had seen, and that it could have been Valentina, when suddenly his cock was out of my body and the crease of my bottom was wet with hot, male come.

I didn't even think. As soon as his weight was off me my bottom came up. My finger went to my pussy and I was masturbating, rubbing at myself in a desperate need for orgasm, naked and rude and wanton in front of him, in front of anybody, just so long as they knew I was his. I screamed out his name as I came, in absolute ecstasy, high on my exposure, high on my fucking; high on Michael.

4

The only sensible thing to do had been to leave before the end of the tasting. I could have forced Michael to choose who he was going home with, but it would have been risky and might not have gone the way I wanted. So I went home.

I expected Chrissy to be waiting for me outside, but she wasn't there. That was annoying, because now I had the perfect way of letting her down gently about Michael and leaving myself a clear field. I'd have taken her for a drink, sat her down and told her about Pippa. She'd have been upset, but she'd only shagged him once, so it was no big deal. She was used to losing boyfriends anyway.

That way I'd come out smelling of roses. When Pippa got the boot I'd be able to hint that I'd done it at least partly for Chrissy's sake. She would be more grateful and more generous than ever, and wouldn't need to know that I'd had sex with Michael before telling her about Pippa. It was perfect.

What wasn't perfect was her not waiting for me. I was starving, but had to make do with a salad in a pizza bar before taking the tube home. All the way I was trying to look on the bright side, and imagining how satisfying it would be to see the look on that bitch Pippa's face when she found out I was with Michael. It wasn't easy, when I could be fairly sure he was bonking her back at his flat at that very moment, and I could have done with Chrissy's chatter to keep my mind off it.

It was worse at home, watching telly while thinking about Michael and Pippa. I was feeling pretty horny and drunk. I even considered rubbing myself off, but it would have been too demeaning with the two of them probably at it at the same moment. I prefer to leave that sort of stuff to girls like Chrissy anyway. I don't need it.

I did it anyway. I didn't want to, but it was the only way to get to sleep, the urge was just so strong. For a while I just played with my breasts, telling myself I would drift off eventually. I didn't, and before long I'd given in. My eyes closed, my fingers slipped down my panties and I was doing it, as I thought of how it had felt with him, on top of him, his cock inside me, riding him...

My excitement grew quickly, my thighs coming up and open, my fingers dipping into my pussy before returning to my clit. I was going to come at any second, my head full of dirty thoughts: of how I'd ridden him, of how he'd stripped for me, of how I'd made him serve me, of being taken, turned over, mounted, fucked vigorously and brought to orgasm under his cock as my self-control snapped. I was calling him a bastard as I came, and even at the peak of my orgasm it was impossible not to think of what he was probably doing with Pippa at that very instant, leaving me feeling angry and ashamed of myself. Before I went to sleep there was one thought uppermost in my mind. I needed another date with Michael, and soon.

If I hadn't been entirely sure about Michael before, now I was certain. I was in love.

He hadn't dropped me home. He'd come home with me. The rest of the night had been bliss. I lost count of the number of times we made love, Michael always forceful yet tender, always in control, yet so considerate of my needs. He gave me more orgasms than I'd had in a year – not counting playing with myself – with his fingers, with his tongue, and best of all, with his wonderful, beautiful cock. With him there were no inhibitions. I did it naked, with the light full on, on my back, on my side, bent over, but mostly kneeling for him with my bottom pushed well up, which made me giggle because it was so deliciously rude. He had stamina too, like no other man I've met, rising to the occasion every time.

When I finally went to sleep it was with my head on his chest and his arm around me. Outside it was already getting light, and I slept contentedly until late morning. I am not normally a morning person at all, but when I woke to the feel of him gently guiding my hand to his already erect cock, I was more than happy to oblige. I went down the bed, to take him in my mouth and suck until he came to orgasm, and swallow too.

Unfortunately he had to sort out the mess from the wine tasting, and left after a quick coffee. Afterwards I was floating, and it was only as I watched his car disappear down the road that I realised I'd completely forgotten to tell him about being invited on board the yacht. I decided not to so that it would be a nice surprise.

I wanted to tell the world, but most of all I wanted to tell Valentina. I could guess what had happened to her at the tasting. She'd have gone home with some good-looking young man. It had happened so many times before when we'd been out somewhere together, and so many times I'd been left on my own at the end of the evening. This time I didn't care. I'd done the same, and with simply the finest man there could be.

It was no good ringing her at work because she was never able to talk for more than a few minutes and the company had a very strict policy on personal calls. So I called her that evening, only to find that she was as keen to talk as I was.

'Valentina, hi. Chrissy.'

'Chrissy, hi. What happened to you last night?'

'The most wonderful thing, that's what happened. I met Michael after the tasting. I was with him last night, all night.'

'Michael? Michael Callington?'

'The very same. Val, it was wonderful. He is so good, so loving and so horny. You wouldn't believe what we did! It was in his car first, he was that horny. Then back home I said I'd make coffee, and he just picked me up and put me on the kitchen table, and had me like that. He's so strong! He just lifted me up as if I weighed nothing! He did it again in the bathroom, with me bent over the loo, so rude! And in bed ... oh, in bed, Val, he was so, so good. And he is just obsessed with my body, and he loves my bum! I don't know how many times we did it, but I have never, ever come so often in one night. Val, he is just so wonderful, the best, simply the best. Aren't I just the luckiest girl in the world?'

She didn't answer, which was just so satisfying. I don't mean to be nasty, but I have always, always had second best to her, and at last I was with somebody worthwhile, somebody she could not possibly say was anything but first rate. I went on.

'And I've been invited up to Norfolk with him. We're going on his father's yacht, the *Harold Jones*, next weekend, only he doesn't know yet, so don't let on when he does the company tasting for you. I want it to be a surprise. They've taken a cottage apparently, in Hickling Green, and we'll be there, and on the boat together and everything. It's so romantic! You must come and help me choose a swimsuit. I haven't had a new one in years. Do you think I can get away with red or –'

She interrupted.

'Sorry, Chrissy. I'd love to talk, but I have to go. I feel ill.'

The phone went dead. For a moment I stood there, holding the receiver and feeling disappointed, an emotion that lasted as long as it took me to remember another friend's number.

I just couldn't bear it, talking to her, not when she'd shagged Michael Callington. So I'd pretended I felt sick and put the phone down. It was enough to make me feel sick for real! I mean, Chrissy Green, fucking Michael Callington while I was lying in bed frigging off over him!

That was the sort of thing she did, not me, not Valentina de Lacy. She was just so soppy about it as well, like a teenager with her first crush on some spotty-faced schoolboy; truly pathetic. Only this wasn't a schoolboy, and he wasn't spotty: this was Michael Callington. Thinking of him with Pippa was bad enough, but with Chrissy it was almost unbearable. I mean, how could he have done it? Why would he have wanted her after me? OK, so I'd left, and maybe it was just a case of any port in a storm, or 'any cunt when drunk', as one of her more common ex-boyfriends used to say.

I could have accepted it if he'd just fucked her in the

car. He hadn't. According to her he'd fucked her in the car and he'd fucked her in the kitchen. He'd fucked her ... no, fucked was the wrong word. There was a better one – porked. Porked was right for Chrissy; it suited her. She was a pig – a little, fat, greedy pig.

She didn't deserve him. She didn't even appreciate him, not properly, not the way I did. I mean, there are some basic rules in this world, which we all need to stick to if things are going to work. Some people are more attractive than others; it's just the way we are made. Some are tens, some are zeros. Tens should stick with tens, and zeros should stick with zeros. Michael Callington was a nine ... no, Michael Callington was a ten, no question. Chrissy Green was maybe a five, average ... no, more like a four. Fours did not go with tens.

I'd explained it to her so many times, but it never seemed to sink in. Always her relationships ended in disaster, and this one would be no different. That didn't make me feel any better. In fact, it made me feel worse, because I knew it would be me who was left to pick up the pieces, as always.

One thing I could be sure of: he was not going to leave Pippa for her. I'd meant to tell her and that would have been that. Down to earth she'd have come, with a big, squashy bump, right on her fat behind. Now I wasn't so sure if I would. No, I wouldn't. I'd let her get a bit deeper in, and then this time maybe the lesson would finally sink in. There would be some radical histrionics when it did, but it would be worth it.

It wasn't going to stop me making my play for Michael either. I mean, just because the stupid little pig was going to make a fool of herself, why should I back down? It just wasn't my fault!

So I rang Michael. It took an effort to sound nice when I knew he was bonking not only Pippa but Chrissy behind my back, but I managed. The company tasting was on Thursday, but I wasn't content to wait until then, and suggested Tuesday evening. He accepted, without so much as a tremor in his voice.

He was an absolute bastard. I mean, he seemed to think it was perfectly OK to keep three girlfriends on the go at one time – or maybe more, I didn't know. I suppose because he was so good-looking he was used to women coming on to him, but there was no need to be such a pig about it! Mark you, that's men all over.

The date went well enough, dinner at La Tourangelle, then back to his place for our night of passion ... Or that's what I thought until he parked the car in some industrial backwater in the East End. It was obvious what he wanted, and why. He'd had Chrissy in the car. Now he wanted me.

That was not good. It had been a long, long time since I'd had sex in a car, three years at least. Even then it had only been because there was nowhere else to go. It is uncomfortable, it is undignified, and as likely as not there is some dirty old man getting off over you in the bushes.

There weren't any bushes, but that was the only saving grace. As I slid my panties off under my skirt I was feeling seriously fed up, and terrified that some-body would come past. It was just the sort of place another couple might come for a quick one up against the wall – another thing I hate. Or it might be some drunk relieving himself, or the police.

I couldn't refuse though, not when Chrissy had done it. For all I knew Pippa did too, and I already knew that he was not the sort of man who could be given a quick lecture on how to show a woman respect. He could pick and choose, and if I was going to be his choice . . .

So it was off with my panties and down on his cock, sucking him hard with our seats back to provide plenty of space. I wanted it to be quick, so I played with myself while I did it, trying not to show too much with my skirt pulled up just far enough to let me get my hand in. I was embarrassingly wet, but at least that was convenient.

He obviously liked it, because he was rock hard in no time. That gave me an idea, to let him come in my mouth and get it over with. I made a pussy of my lips and began to work on the head of his cock, something that gets most men there in seconds. Not Michael Callington. He simply sighed in pleasure and began to stroke the nape of my neck.

It would have been very, very easy to get carried away, with a big cock to suck and my fingers on my sex. Only the constant shift of light outside the car stopped me, as every time the patterns changed I glanced up, expecting to find some grinning pervert peering in at us; that or a constable.

He didn't seem to care at all, just enjoying my efforts to make him come, but without any sign of actually doing it. In the end I gave up and lay back, smiling at him as my thighs came open after a final nervous glance at the windows. He smiled back, reached out, and simply lifted me bodily on to his cock.

My mouth came open to protest, but my sex was full before I could find anything to say. He was just so strong, lifting me as if I was a doll and popping me on. He'd pulled my skirt up too, as he did it, to leave me in a hideously embarrassing position, with my bare bum stuck up in the air and my cheeks spread. He began to move inside me immediately, which felt so nice, but I was struggling to cope. And all the time I was thinking of what anyone who peered in at the windscreen would see. It wasn't just my bare bum either, but everything, my bottom hole and, worst of all, his great big cock going in and out between my sex lips.

I couldn't stop it though. He was holding me and nibbling my neck and pumping into me with short, hard strokes, on and on, until I was dizzy with it. Eventually I just hid my face in his shoulder, my embarrassment warring with my pleasure, and so, so thankful that nobody I knew could possibly catch us.

When he stopped and reached down for his cock, I knew exactly what he was going to do. I couldn't stop myself. My bum came up, into an even ruder position, if that was possible, the head of his cock went to my sex and he was rubbing himself on me. All I could do was cling on to him, my head spinning with pleasure. Bum up like I was, I felt ready for entry again, so ready I wanted another man to mount me, to slip his cock in up me as Michael made me come, to fill my body right at the moment of orgasm, even up my bottom as Michael fucked me . . .

I just couldn't help it. As I started to come I imagined being caught by a policeman, a young, horny policeman, one whose duty came well behind the chance to mount a girl with her bottom spread for entry. He'd pull open the door, climb on before we could react, and just fuck me, hard and deep as Michael brought me off on his cock . . . no, bugger me, taking advantage of my dirty pose, of my helpless excitement, using me, a total stranger taking me in the dirtiest way.

As I came I yelled out, then bit on to Michael's jacket, struggling to control myself. It was hopeless. I was squirming my bum about, rubbing on him even as he was rubbing on me, thinking over and over of how easily and how rudely I could be taken from the rear in my position.

It was a good orgasm, a great one really, but no sooner was it past than all my fears of being seen came rushing back. I climbed off, indifferent to whether he wanted to come or not, only to discover that he had as I pulled my panties back on. It got worse when I sat down. My panties were full of it so that it felt as if I'd wet myself. Somehow my skirt and blouse had become twisted as well, making it really uncomfortable.

For some reason I just couldn't get it right in the car. It was fairly dark outside, with just one dull orange street light a good ten metres away, and as we hadn't seen anybody at all I risked getting out to adjust myself. I was just pulling up the second stocking when a figure stepped out from a doorway, right next to me. My heart jumped straight into my mouth, and only came half-way back down when I realised it was a girl.

Her profession was all too obvious. A red leather miniskirt, fishnets, high heels and a black leather jacket with the zip half down at the front to show off her cleavage. She had a lot of dyed blonde hair, a lot of make-up and a lot of attitude. She spoke first.

'Thought I didn't recognise the arse. You on a call?'

It didn't take a lot to work out what she was talking about. I couldn't speak for indignation, and my face began to burn as she went on, 'So how much d'you charge for that bizarre stuff?'

'I ... no, you don't ...'

It was pointless. I could hardly speak and there were no words to express my feelings anyway. She thought I was a call-girl, a tart. She'd seen my bare bum too, and Michael's cock going in and out, and him frigging me off.

It was unbearable. My face was so hot I felt it was going to catch fire as I scrambled back into the car. Michael had tidied himself up and was winding the seat back. He laughed. Obviously he thought it was funny. I snapped at him, 'Just go!'

I caught the prostitute's voice as I slammed the door.

'Too good for us, are we? Fucking stuck-up bitch!'

She spat, right in the middle of the windscreen, even as Michael let the clutch out. He had to turn, and as he manoeuvred she was screaming abuse at us, calling me a whole string of filthy names and laughing at me. Her last comment was yelled at the top of her voice, and it really got to me.

'Your cunt don't look no better than mine with a cock up it, you stuck-up cow!'

She had seen everything. Maybe she had watched from start to finish, seen me fuck, seen me come. It was mortifying, but Michael just seemed to think it was funny, something that could be laughed off. He tried to make light of it as we drove back, but finally it sank in that I didn't want to talk.

He drove to his flat anyway, never even suggesting that I might like to go home. I felt numb, and badly in need of a drink. So I put up with it, despite having decided absolutely firmly that there would be no more sex for him that night, or ever, not after what the bastard had put me through.

When I'm in a bad mood I like people to know it, and I like them to give me space. What I wanted Michael to do was pour me a large brandy and leave me to my thoughts while he hung around out of sight, there if I needed him but not in my face. What he did was pour about four shots of brandy into one glass, then take another for himself. He was supposed to look concerned as I went to sit down. He smiled happily and suggested coming out on to the balcony. I shook my head, making it quite clear that I needed a decent amount of attention paid to my feelings. He shrugged and walked into his bedroom.

It really was too much. He just wasn't taking my feelings seriously, as if it was no big deal that some tart had watched us shag and then mistaken me for a call-girl. I mean, me! Unfortunately there was a nagging voice in the back of my head trying to remind me how well off he was, and about Pippa, and Chrissy. If the same thing had happened to Chrissy she would have laughed with him, the little slut. Finally I went out to join him on the balcony, my pride swallowed. He was looking at the yacht. He spoke immediately.

'Beautiful, isn't she?'

It was the chance I'd been waiting for all evening, to bring his holiday into the conversation without a hint that I already knew. I agreed.

'Yes, beautiful. I don't suppose you get much time to take her out though?'

'Oh, a fair bit. We're off up to Norfolk at the weekend, as it goes.'

'Norfolk?'

'Yes, just sailing slowly up the coast, then spending a few weeks on the Broads until the crowds start to build up.'

'A few weeks? What about your business?'

'Oh, Graham can take care of things there. I like a long summer break anyway.'

So he was that rich.

'It sounds wonderful. Romantic.'

I moved a little closer, pressing against him. His arm came around me. He was supposed to take the bait, but took a sip of brandy instead. He laughed.

'Hardly romantic, no, not the way Daddy likes to sail. It's all hands on deck, and woe betide anyone who makes a mistake! Do you sail?'

'No. I get seasick.'

'Bad luck. You'd get used to it. Still, you don't come across as the sort who likes it rough.'

'I'm not. I like it gentle, feminine.'

'Pippa loves it, as rough as it gets.'

That was too much. He could hardly expect me not to protest.

'Michael. Is it really fair to mention Pippa, so soon after we've made love?'

He gave me a puzzled look, as if it was the most natural thing in the world to swap innuendo about one girlfriend with another. It just wasn't right. Perhaps she was his sister after all, or an ex. I had to know, but I didn't want to leave myself looking foolish or to pressure him. Valentina's rules for dealing with men – rivals: the one who puts the pressure on gets dumped.

'She's very beautiful.'

His answer gave me mine, and more.

'Gorgeous, absolutely, and she's ever such fun. The two of you should get to know each other properly. She'll be on board the yacht. Maybe you should come with us?'

No man calls his sister gorgeous ... well, very few. She didn't sound like an ex either. My first suspicion had been right. They were into swinging and they wanted me to join in, 'just sailing slowly up the coast', just the three of us ... no, four, because Chrissy would be there too. That really took the prize. I mean, the sheer cheek of the man! Not content with trying to get me into the sack with his dirty-minded girlfriend, he wanted Chrissy too. Well, if he imagined for one second that I was going for that sort of thing he had another thought coming. I opened my mouth to speak, then shut it again, suddenly remembering that Chrissy said her presence on the boat was going to be a surprise.

I wouldn't go for group sex, but I had a nasty suspicion that Chrissy might. Not that she'd actually ever done anything like that, not to the best of my knowledge, but there was no question that she got off on hearing me with men, watching even. Maybe all the time she had been wanting to join in? It was possible and, after all, she knew how I felt about that sort of thing and so would never have dared ask. If Michael managed to set up a cosy little ménage à trois with Pippa and Chrissy, I could see where I was going to be – out in the cold.

For a moment I considered dropping the whole sorry mess. I could tell Michael exactly what I thought of him, and of his dirty girlfriend. I could also put a spoke in his plans for Chrissy. Unfortunately I knew his reaction – he'd laugh.

So would Pippa. I could just imagine the two of them, probably in bed, having a good giggle over the whole thing at my expense, even making out that I was some sort of prude because I wouldn't join in their perverted little games. It was so galling it didn't bear thinking about. That wasn't all.

God knows there are few enough decent men around. If they're good-looking then they're either married or poor or divorced with kids, or gay, or some horrible combination of all those things. When I finally found one who seemed just right, or at least close enough for me to mould him, he turned out to be a pervert! It was not fair, but I do not give up that easily.

5

I said I'd come to Norfolk. What else could I do?

That didn't mean I was going to be doing any sailing, not if I could possibly help it. My first problem was getting the time off, but I managed that, even though it meant flirting with the balding old greaseball who runs our personnel department. Fortunately he was an ordinary man, not like Michael, and putty in my hands. I got two weeks at the expense of a couple of colleagues whose lives were too boring for it to matter anyway.

Next I had to do my best to get Michael to drive up and to forget the yacht. By the morning of the company tasting I had it all worked out. I had already pleaded seasickness, and he did want me to come, so I could lay that on a bit more. I would then offer to get the cottage ready if he drove me up, a generous gesture he would appreciate. It would also leave me ready and waiting for him in the cottage when he arrived with Pippa, or so he would think.

So off we'd go, on the Friday evening, and inevitably he would stay over. By the morning I would have him eager to stay with me, alone, or I'd lost my touch. It meant a big sacrifice for me, something I hadn't done for years, and which was strictly against the rules for all that I could never help enjoying it. It would be worth it. Whatever he said about Pippa's love of sailing, she didn't look the type to be able to handle a twenty-metre yacht up the coast of East Anglia on her own, while Chrissy would just get in the way.

That would leave me in the cottage with Michael, and hopefully with Pippa furious with him for deserting her and Chrissy furious with him about Pippa. There was a fair chance that they'd be furious with each other too, that or end up shagging to console each other, which was just funny.

OK, so there were plenty of ways it could go wrong and I needed a big slice of luck, but it was the best I could do with so little. As for luck, that's something I've always had, and if it deserted me I could make my own.

It worked a treat. The tasting was a huge success, which made me Miss Popular in the office, and afterwards everyone from the girl who distributes the post to our sole female partner was cooing and ahing over Michael. I stuck firmly by his side and soaked up as much of the praise as I could.

He'd drunk very little and talked a lot, so he was sober as we drove back. I was tipsy, but pretending to be a lot more than tipsy, which made it seem all the more truthful when I spun my line. He swallowed it and we were leaving for Norfolk in the morning, as simple as that.

I wanted to get the full effect of my sacrifice, so held off that night, simply letting him lead. I even stripped in front of him, not a full striptease, but teasing, which earned me a hard cock and a good fuck on the sofa before we'd even gone to bed. Once in the bedroom he enjoyed himself thoroughly with me, on my back and on my knees, sideways and up against the wall, but always with him controlling me, the way he liked it. I even willingly sucked his cock after he'd been in me and took his balls in my mouth, which I won't normally. I even broke one of my own rules and let him come like that, over my face and in my hair. It was pretty gross but it was worth it, providing the perfect excuse for a long clean-up. By the time I finished he had gone to sleep, allowing me to sabotage his mobile phone at leisure.

That was three in the morning, but he was up bright and early, bustling about the flat and making coffee. I tried to tempt him back to bed with the offer of a nice leisurely suck of his cock, but he wasn't having any of it. He seemed to want to get to Norfolk in time for lunch for some reason, and was pointing out that we needed to get going so that we could pick my things up from my flat. I was in no mood to argue, and let him hustle me into the shower and then into my clothes.

I had everything packed and ready, but hung around a bit at my flat to give the illusion of being busy, and to waste time. Then we were off. Michael drove with a complete indifference to speed limits, doing over a hundred most of the way up the M11. By noon we were not only in Norfolk, but well off the main road, in some huge forest. He parked on a track. I could see what was coming.

We'd stopped at the entrance to a path leading into the woods, a very muddy track. There were lots of trees, lots of green, lots of birdsong, the usual sort of stuff. He was looking around as if he'd just been given a free choice in a designer store. I hid a sigh. He spoke.

'I used to drive down here sometimes when I was at college. I think it's one of the most beautiful places in England.'

He held out his hand. I took it and let myself be led down the track. I could see what was going through his head, thoughts as dirty as they were romantic. Sure enough, they were.

'So secluded too. That's one of the wonderful things about East Anglia. It's never too crowded, except by the coast, of course, and even there you can find private places if you look. Yes, I used to come out here whenever I got the chance . . .'

No doubt with some soppy undergraduate so that he could shag her senseless where there was no chance of her squeals drawing attention.

'It's a great place for running too. I always find I can think most clearly when running, especially somewhere like this. Do you manage to get out to the countryside much? I suppose it must be difficult with your job?'

'Now and then. I like the North Downs, there are some beautiful walks there.'

None of which I'd ever been on, but Chrissy had and I'd been given the lecture and seen the slides.

'You're right, and some wonderful views. Not so secluded though. Here, we could be together all afternoon and not be disturbed.'

I knew what for too. So did he.

'There's something particularly fine about making love outdoors, don't you think?'

'I do.'

'It feels so natural, and it's a lovely day, hot but just fresh enough.'

'You're right, beautiful.'

My true thoughts were very different, of mud and wet grass and bugs and midges and big squashy caterpillars. If there's one thing I hate worse than sex in a car it's sex outdoors. There's not only the risk of getting caught, but it is so uncomfortable. Even on top I always find I'm kneeling in something disgusting, or on an ant's nest. Go underneath and those same ants are crawling around in between my bum cheeks. It was one more black mark, but I put up with it, consoling myself with the thought of the time we'd spend there.

He led me deep into the wood, where at least the chances of getting caught seemed extremely remote. There was a glade, which he obviously knew, carpeted with long, fine grass and shaded by two huge trees, oaks I think. It wasn't as bad as I'd expected, but I was still pretty fed up, until he began to undress and my hormones kicked in.

Whatever the situation, watching him strip was worth it. His body was so good, all smooth golden skin with hard, powerful muscle working underneath. Knowing how strong he was made it all the nicer, and I just stared, drinking in the sight until he was stark naked and stretching in the dappled sunlight.

I thought he was going to want me to strip for him, but he came close in order to kiss me. As our mouths met his hands found the buttons of my blouse. One came open, and a second, before I had hugged him to me, kissing open-mouthed with the firm bulge of his cock pressed to my belly. He stopped and took my wrists to lift my arms, very gently, and place my hands on top of my head. It was a really domineering gesture, and sent a little rebellious jolt through me, but I kept them there, playing his game.

He continued undressing me and began to kiss my flesh as it came bare. It was my blouse first, the buttons undone one by one, with his mouth tracing a slow line down the front of my neck, between my breasts and across my tummy. It was so slow that by the time his lips reached my navel I wanted him to pull down my skirt and panties and bury his face in my sex. He didn't, but stood again, to gently ease my blouse off my shoulders and arms, kissing every inch of skin as he did it.

The urge to grab was getting stronger and stronger, but despite myself I was beginning to enjoy the game. I knew how I'd feel when he'd finished, and as he peeled my sleeves off I let him put my hands back on my head without complaint. My nipples were aching to be kissed, and I thought he would do my bra, only to have him go down again. My skirt was undone, and eased down, his lips working over the skin of my hips, my belly, right to the edge of my panties, and my bottom.

As his tongue traced a slow line down the crease of my bottom I really thought that was it. His cock was almost hard, and I thought he would bend me forward, pull my panties aside and lick me from the rear, then fuck me. He didn't, contenting himself with teasing my bottom with his tongue before he set to work on my legs. My stay-ups were peeled down, one at a time, ever so slowly, with his lips working away all the while. I stepped out of them for him, and my shoes.

For one moment he was kissing my feet, and I thought how immensely satisfying it would be to make him do that, on his knees, before licking me to heaven. Then he stood up again, his hands found the catch of my bra, and he began nuzzling one of my breasts. A second later my cups had come loose and off, and he had taken a nipple between his teeth, ever so gently. I shut my eyes, sighing with pleasure as he suckled on me, moving between my breasts until both were aching. He held them too, cupping them in strong, male fingers, really taking his time, until I was growing truly desperate for his cock.

Finally his hands went into the waistband of my panties and I knew it was going to happen. Down they came, eased off my hips, to my knees, to the ground. I kicked them away, giggling, nude, and really enjoying it, everything forgotten but what Michael was doing to me. His face went to my sex, his tongue burrowed in among the folds and he was licking my clit. That was it. I could no more keep my hands on my head than fly. I reached down, pushing my fingers into his hair, to pull his head in. His licking grew firmer. His hands came up, to take hold of my bottom. Fingers slid up between my cheeks, penetrating me, and working inside my body. He'd put one into my bottom, but I didn't care, lost to everything but my physical sensations as he brought me towards orgasm, licking and probing until my muscles started to tighten in his face and I was there.

I think I would have collapsed if he hadn't been supporting me. It was so good, so long too, under his control, so that it didn't stop even when I would have had to take my finger away. By the end one of my legs was shaking uncontrollably, and my body was wet with sweat and my own juice.

He laid me down in the grass, supporting my body in his hands. My thighs came up and open. His hand went to his cock and he was on me, rubbing himself against my sex, then inside, the full, firm length of his cock slipping into me. It never even occurred to me to resist being mounted, I just let him, putting my arms around his neck as he took off at his usual furious pace.

As always it left me gasping and breathless with

pleasure in an instant. As always he took his time, thoroughly enjoying me. After a while he turned me over into his favourite position, with a good view of my arse as he slid himself back up me. His big hands took hold of my hips and we were fucking again, fast and furious, with my breasts swinging in the grass and his front slapping against my cheeks.

I wanted to come again, and I knew that if I was going to do it, to surrender my bottom, the time was now. He had to want it, I was sure, the one thing he dared not just do. I pushed up my bottom against him. He went into a flurry of pushes, harder and faster still, knocking the breath from my body. As he finally slowed I found I could speak again.

'You can ... you can do it, Michael ... if you want.'

There was no awkward moment, no embarrassing, breathless conversation. He knew, just as I knew he wanted it. He stopped. His cock left my body, pulled slowly free and lifted, finding my bottom hole. I put my face in the grass, telling myself it would be worth it as we began to push together, and moaning as it began to go up.

He gave a long, satisfied sigh as he pushed into me. I bit my lip, trying to tell myself I wasn't enjoying it. It was a lie. It felt horribly dirty, but so good. I wanted to come more than ever, and with a last flush of shame and guilt I reached back to find my sex. He pushed in, deeper, as I began to rub. That was it, done. I was being buggered, and outdoors into the bargain, and I was enjoying it.

I just let myself go, because I couldn't stop it. He was in me, all the way, and I felt full up, right to my capacity. It was only going to take a few more touches and I would come with a cock up my bottom for the first time in years.

It wasn't his first time either. He knew just what to do, slow and easy so he wouldn't hurt me, and all the while holding me firmly by my bottom. That was what really got to me, in the end, being held like that, his hands so strong, so sure, soothing me for what I was doing, and how dirty I was being. That let me come. The last of my regrets and inhibitions just slipped away as I rubbed myself to a long, glorious climax with my eyes tight shut and my free fingers clutching at the grass, my whole being focused on the cock inside me.

He held me as I did it, just moving slowly inside me until I was good and done. Then he told me it was time and I knew he was going to come up my bottom. I didn't even try to stop him, staying down, surrendering to him as he began to push harder and faster. I began to gasp. My hands clutched tighter still, into the soil. It began to hurt. I gritted my teeth against the pain. He grunted, drove hard up me one last time, and stopped. He'd done it.

It was a good ten minutes before I could really get my head around what we'd done enough to talk. By then we were lying together in the grass, still naked, with my head on his chest. My bottom felt sore and I was feeling a little resentful, but I was not going to waste my sacrifice. I spent a moment getting my thoughts in order, then spoke.

'Michael?'

'Yes.'

'You do realise how special that was to me, don't you? It's not something I would normally do with a man, but I knew you wanted it.'

'Thank you ... How did you know?'

'Oh, just from the way you are. OK, I like it too, but it's special, private ... very private. Look, seriously, it's not something I could ever share with anyone else, and I mean anyone. Not Pippa, not anyone.'

'Good heavens no, of course not!'

'Good. I'm glad you understand. I really mean that, yes?'

'Yes, of course. Absolutely.'

'You can do it again, but only when we're alone, really alone. I don't just mean alone like in bed together. I mean completely alone. That's why I let you just now.'

'I see. I think.'

'Of course you don't, you big silly man. Men never understand how sensitive women are about these things.'

He didn't answer. I began to stroke his chest, just gently running my nails over his skin. After a while I spoke again.

'We'll be alone tonight, in the cottage, won't we?'

'Tonight? This evening, yes, but I really have to get back –'

'Tonight, Michael, in bed, just the two of us, without a care. I need to be held too, after ... after that. Please?'

'But I have to be with the yacht by ten thirty.'

'Michael ... please? Pretty please?'

'Well ... I suppose I could leave early in the morning.'

I didn't answer. I just gave a satisfied purr as I cuddled into his chest. Something ticklish had begun to explore my foot, but for once I didn't care. I was smiling. I'd known he wanted it, from the first. At heart, all men are dirty little boys, and Michael Callington was no different.

Malcolm Callington was absolutely clear that I had to be at the yacht by ten thirty on the Saturday morning. They left with the tide, and that was that, Chrissy or no Chrissy.

There should have been no difficulty at all, but as it was I nearly didn't make it. I'd been too excited to sleep properly, but ended up oversleeping. From then on everything went wrong. First it was the cat. One of my neighbours had agreed to look after him, but she wasn't in, and I ended up having to push some money, keys and a note with instructions through their front door. Then it was one of my bags, which I'd had for years, but chose the exact moment I picked it up to split wide open, spilling knickers, bras, tops and just about everything else all over the floor.

I called a cab, to be told there was a forty-five minute wait time. So I dragged myself down to Highbury corner with my luggage, but every black taxi seemed to be full. Finally I took the tube, spent nearly half an hour sitting in a tunnel outside King's Cross, and got lost trying to find my way from the station to Michael's flat. When I did get there I realised that I had no idea of how to get to the back. You'd have thought it would be obvious. It wasn't. It was a warehouse conversion, with others to either side. I tried the underground car park and nearly got lost again.

Finally I found the way, a cobbled alley leading off the main road, with no link to Michael's road at all. There was the yacht, her tarpaulins off, with someone untying her: Pippa. I ran, staggering under my bags and trying to wave at the same time. She saw me and paused to stand with her hands on her hips, shaking her head as I approached. Malcolm appeared on deck, then someone else, a woman, as I reached Pippa, gasping out my apologies.

'I'm sorry ... the cat ... trains ... everything ...'

Malcolm had come to stand at the rail of the yacht. He laughed.

'Well, we'll let you off this time, shall we, girls? Come aboard then, and get your gear stowed. Tilly will show you where.'

I smiled at the other woman, who had to be Tilly – she looked a lot like her sister: tall and dark and very pretty. She smiled back and helped me to climb on to the yacht, then took me down below decks and helped me sort myself out. I was feeling less than sure of myself, especially after she had put me in a lifejacket. So I did as I was told, all the while wondering where Michael was.

There was a shudder as the engine started and I realised the answer. We were underway, edging gently down the little creek behind Michael's flats and out into the Thames, with Tower Bridge to our right and a wonderful view of the city. Pippa and Tilly were on deck, and busy doing all sorts of things I didn't understand. So I kept firmly out of the way, happy to just admire the view as we moved slowly out along the river and east, with the towers of Canary Wharf high above us.

At last everything seemed to be in order, but there was still no sign of Michael. Malcolm was in the wheelhouse, and I joined him, to thank him for the invitation. He spoke first.

'Thought we'd lost you there, girl. Glad you could make it.'

'Thank you. It's ever so kind of you to invite me.'

'Not at all. My pleasure.'

'Michael will be surprised, won't he?'

'Michael? He's not aboard, my dear. In fact, I've no idea where he is.'

6

I woke to bright sunlight. Michael lay beside me, asleep. A glance at the clock showed the time – eleven twenty-two. Clever Valentina.

There was a welcome pack in the kitchen. It included coffee, something I needed very badly. I climbed out of bed and made my way downstairs, waddling slightly.

It had been quite some night. Following our dirty little escapade in the forest we had found a country pub and taken a leisurely lunch. Afterwards we had stuck to the back roads, zigzagging slowly across Norfolk until at last we had reached Hickling Green. The cottage wasn't in the village at all, but down a long track that ultimately led nowhere. It was all a bit rustic for me, but undeniably beautiful, with the house set on its own in a walled garden and a view over a huge, reed-fringed lake from the upper storey.

By then I'd been tired, while the wine I'd had at lunch hadn't helped, so I'd gone upstairs for a nap while Michael brought everything in from the car. It had been hot and stuffy, so I'd stripped down to a T-shirt and panties and lay on top of the bed, falling asleep in no time.

I'd been awakened by the feel of Michael's lips on my bottom. He'd been kissing very gently, with my panties eased a little way down to let him get at my cheeks. I'd made no move to stop him. Slowly I'd woken up, coming from sleep into a pleasantly drowsy erotic haze. Before long my panties had been pulled off and my top rolled up over my boobs. He had licked me, long and slow, until I was close to orgasm, with my fingers tangled in his hair and my sex pushed into his face.

He had stopped, leaving me right at the edge, and mounted me. We'd fucked for ages, before he went back to licking me to a truly glorious climax. By then he'd had a finger up my bottom, and before I'd even come down properly he had replaced it with his cock. I'd taken it moaning and shivering, with my legs rolled up to let him get inside me. Ten minutes later he had come up my bottom for the second time that day.

The third time had been in the early hours of the morning. We'd had sex twice more, and as he'd stayed firmly in charge but hadn't tried it, I'd assumed he'd had his fill or was taking mercy on my already sore bottom. I was wrong. Just when I thought it was safe to go to sleep I'd felt his cock growing between my bottom cheeks. I'd opened up obligingly, only to have a spit-wet finger introduced to my bottom hole, then his cock.

It was quite a memory, enough to send a shiver right through me each time it came back. There was resentment too, for all the pleasure, at the way he just assumed he could do it, and at the way he quite obviously didn't feel any guilt at all. I pushed the bad emotions back, telling myself it was in a good cause, and that that excused it.

There was bread, so I put a couple of slices in the toaster, and after a moment's hesitation decided to treat myself to butter and jam. After all, it looked like I was going to need all the energy I could get. I was just buttering the toast when I heard him coming down the stairs. Even though it was as much his choice as mine to have stayed up shagging all night, I half expected

him to be angry, even to expect some sort of explanation. He wasn't and he didn't. There was a substantial
bulge beneath his dressing gown, and the grin on his
face told me exactly what he did expect. I tried a heavy
sigh.

It didn't work. He came up behind me, his cock
pushing between my bottom cheeks as his hands found
my breasts. I let him play, my nipples quickly popping
out under his fingers. He chuckled, and reached down
to pull up my top. Suddenly my breasts were out,
offering a fine view to anyone in the garden. He took
them in his hands, bare now, and went on kneading. It
was nice, but I was terrified someone would see.

'Come on, Michael, that's enough.'

'Oh, nonsense, I'm only just starting.'

He let go of my breasts. His hands found my bottom,
kneading, then spreading my cheeks to let a finger
between them. His lips found my neck as he began to
tickle my hole.

'Michael, don't be dirty . . .'

'That's not what you said last night.'

'I know, but we're in the kitchen! I'm trying to make
toast!'

I was also trying to keep the giggle out of my voice,
but it was impossible. It just felt too nice.

'Oh, go on then, you dirty so and so, but you're not
. . . not doing that to me, not here.'

'Doing what to you?'

'You know . . . that . . . what we did in the forest, and
last night.'

'I don't know what you're talking about.'

'Stop it, Michael! You know perfectly well what I
mean. Putting your cock where your finger is right
now.'

'What, here?'

I gasped as his fingertip popped inside me, just a little way, but enough to give me a shock. He pushed deeper in, and I gave a little involuntary gasp. He chuckled and began to ease it in and out.

'No, Michael, please, not here!'

His hand reached around me, one finger dipping into the butter pat.

'Michael!'

He just chuckled, put a hand between my shoulder-blades and, gently but firmly, began to push me down over the table.

'No, Michael, not again. I'm sore!'

'That's what the butter's for.'

'But, Michael! What if someone comes, the landlord or . . .'

'The landlord lives in Norwich. Now ssh.'

'Michael, no! Not . . .'

I broke off with a sigh. His buttery finger had found my bottom hole, replacing the other to slide deep up me, probing. He gave the dirty little schoolboy chuckle I was coming to recognise so well. I couldn't stop him, but there was as much resentment as lust in my head. He was impossible to control, and so demanding, yet he made me want sex like no other man. But that did not mean I wanted to be constantly shagged up my bottom.

'No, Michael, please! Can't we just . . . just be normal?'

'Hmm . . . OK.'

It was just so casual. I hadn't even realised he'd opened his dressing gown, and then his cock was at the mouth of my sex, and then inside me, just pushed rudely up from behind. I went down across the table, one tit squashing down on the buttery piece of toast I was about to enjoy for breakfast, and we were fucking over the kitchen table. His hands closed on my hips as he sped up, and I couldn't have moved if I'd wanted to. He was so fast, so strong, pushing in and out with demented energy. It was so dirty too. I could feel the butter melting in my bottom hole, warm and greasy as it trickled down to where he was pushing his cock in and out. I knew what he wanted to do, what he really wanted to do.

He did it. Just as soon as I was in breathless, abandoned ecstasy, out came his cock, straight to my bottom hole. I gasped in protest, and tried to rise. It was already too late. I was too loose, too buttery to stop him. The head of his cock was quickly inside. The rest followed, pushed slowly up as I panted out my feelings into the tablecloth.

Inevitably he took his time, easing himself in and out and all the time fondling my bottom cheeks, holding them apart too, so he could watch as his cock moved in my body. I was burning with resentment, and trying to tell myself I hated him, but it didn't work. It felt too good, not just what he was doing, but being so firmly controlled by him. Even as I tried to tell myself that my surrender was just a tactic to get rid of Pippa and Chrissy, I knew it was a lie. I wanted him, and I wanted him to treat me the way he did.

My last twinge of bitterness came as he curled his hand under my tummy to find my clit. He was playing with me as if I was a toy, masturbating me to keep me sweet while he buggered me, even just so that I'd tighten on his dirty cock. Then he had found it, and all such thoughts were forgotten.

He brought me off, rubbing and flicking at it, and never once stopped moving inside me. Soon I was clutching at the table and squirming my bottom on his cock, trying to get him deeper, to get more friction, anything to make the experience dirtier, harder. I was fantasising too, imagining being watched again, with some leering old pervert staring at me being buggered. No, worse, some thoroughly respectable village matron, her eyes round in shock as she watched me, bottom up over the table as Michael's big cock slid in and out of my hole. With that, I started to come, and I started to talk, babbling out a string of dirty demands over which I had no control whatsoever. His response was to grunt, push deeper and to come up my bottom.

It was right at the peak of my orgasm. I just went wild, screaming and banging my fists on the table and calling him a bastard and telling him I loved him. He was jamming himself deeper and deeper into me, and all the while rubbing at my clit. I could feel myself tightening on his cock, only it wasn't in the right place, not where it should be. He'd buttered me and he'd put it up my arse, where no man should even dare think of putting his cock, only he had, and now he'd come up there, and, and ...

He'd made me come too, and I'd wanted it, and I knew that I'd surrender the next time, and the next. As my climax came down it left me feeling defeated. Slowly my resentment rose back up over my ecstasy, until it was my main emotion. He had used me, utterly. I was a mess too, sweaty and dishevelled, my bottom all sticky, one tit covered in butter and crumbs. Michael just grinned, obviously enjoying the view. For one moment I forgot myself.

'Did you have to do that?'

He looked taken aback.

'You enjoyed it, didn't you? I thought you said it was a special thing for you.'

'I ... it is ... I do like it, Michael, but really, that's the fourth time since yesterday!'

'Well, I have to make the best of it, as it's so private for you. After all, in three or four days Dad and Pippa and Tilly will be here.'

I stayed firmly out of the way while the others set sail. I didn't even understand what they were talking about, much less what they were doing, but it all seemed to work. We were well down the river, past the barrier, with a lot more space and bits of marsh and decaying wharves along the bank as well as houses and modern quays when Malcolm called us together. He looked thoroughly pleased with himself, but his voice was more than a little stern when he spoke.

'You all know how things work, but just to run it over for Chrissy's sake. I'm the captain, and what I say goes, pronto. Pippa's the mate, Tilly able seaman. Chrissy, you'll learn soon enough, I dare say, but until you do, you're to do as you're told and stay out from under everyone else's feet, or else. Do I make myself clear?'

'Yes, sir.'

Pippa and Tilly had spoken in chorus, and as if they were a couple of schoolgirls being put in their place by the headmistress. It was obviously deliberate impudence, but I knew Malcolm meant it about doing as we were told. I liked his attitude though, stern yet playful. I'd nodded, but he fixed me with a gimlet stare as he went on.

'Bottom of the ladder, my girl, that's where you'll be, as galley slave.'

It was impossible not to smile, and to join in the game.

'Yes, sir.'

Tilly giggled. Malcolm gave a pleased grin.

'Good. Well, I must say I'm looking forward to this immensely. We'll be calling in at anchorages every night, civilised fashion, and with a bit of luck we'll get a decent run. Usual rules, and Tilly can fill Chrissy in as we go. Any questions?'

The girls shook their heads and answered in chorus again.

'No, sir.'

Not wishing to look silly by asking what were sure to be obvious questions, I did the same.

After that I even began to feel OK about Michael not being there. Obviously something important had come up and he hadn't been able to make it, but if we were going to be calling in at anchorages every night, he would be able to catch up. Meanwhile I could enjoy the trip and let my imagination run on the joys of spending several weeks with him.

It was going to be great. We'd go boating, and to the beach, and for long walks, all activities punctuated by bouts of nice, rude sex. I love sex outdoors, with the air on my bare skin and the delicious thrill that comes with knowing we might be seen. After the way he had been in the car it was all too easy to imagine him just taking me. It would be somewhere quiet but not too quiet, with me laid down in the long grass for a good fucking just because he felt horny. Or it might be really risky, in the cottage with the others in the next room and me bent across a table or rolled up in a chair. Skirt up, knickers down and his lovely big cock slid in all the way.

That was in the future. For now, I couldn't even get in touch. I'd packed my mobile, but it wasn't there, presumably having got lost when my bag split. Malcolm didn't have one, and didn't seem to approve of them either, so that neither Pippa nor Tilly had been allowed to bring theirs. He was extremely bossy in other ways as well, behaving pretty much as if they were his servants. Neither girl seemed to mind though.

It had occurred to me to wonder about Malcolm and Pippa. He had to be pushing thirty years older than her. Watching her go about her tasks on the yacht, I began to understand. She didn't just not mind being told what to do by him, she actually relished it. In fact, it was almost as if it was something sexual for her.

I wasn't at all sure about their relationship with Tilly either. All she had on was her lifejacket, deck shoes and a skimpy green bikini that left most of her bum on show. Twice I'd seen Malcolm pat her, the same way as he had me, and in front of Pippa, who didn't seem to mind at all. Tilly just giggled.

Not that it really mattered to me, so long as she had no interest in Michael. She was friendly, without the slightest sign of jealousy or bitchiness, so it didn't seem likely. I couldn't very well ask straight out, but the way she spoke about him was more sisterly than anything.

Once I'd convinced myself that she wasn't a rival we got on really well. She was twenty-two, and still at university, studying English literature at Bristol simply for the sake of her education. She also knew the Callingtons well, and was more than happy to gossip about Michael. I knew he'd been at Cambridge, and I'd guessed he was public school. What I hadn't known was that he'd been together with a steady girlfriend for nearly five years, and had split up with her only that spring.

If she was happy to chat about Michael, she was

more than happy to talk about Malcolm and her sister. Pippa had been teaching at a school for which Malcolm was a governor, and they had been having an affair for over a year before Michael's mother found out, ending in a divorce. Apparently it had been quite a scandal, and Tilly was about to go into the juicy details when Malcolm called to her to help bring the yacht on to a new tack.

I watched them work, wondering if I could ever be as fast at the same tasks, or do them at all, and what outrageous behaviour on the part of Pippa and Malcolm had filled Tilly with such embarrassed delight. It had to be rude, and I was thoroughly looking forward to hearing it.

Given the way they were, it didn't surprise me when Malcolm ticked Tilly off quite loudly for fastening a rope in the wrong place, or possibly the wrong way. He made her do it again, and chided her for giggling, then said something I didn't understand at all.

'Our first for the trip, I think, Pippa.'

Pippa nodded. Tilly answered him.

'Just for that?'

'And for answering back.'

'Hey, that's not fair!'

'Protesting.'

'Oh, come on, Malcolm, not with Chrissy on board, not yet . . .'

He raised a finger and she went abruptly quiet. As she came back to the main deck she was biting her lip and looked almost as if she was going to burst into tears, which seemed a bit childish when he'd only told her off. For some reason she didn't seem to be able to look at Pippa either, and stayed put, sitting to one side looking rather forlorn and full of nervous embarrassment.

I was wondering what was happening, and why it mattered that I was on board. She was so obviously embarrassed that I could imagine it was something a bit rude, like having to take her top off as a forfeit. It was hard to imagine a man making a girl do something like that, or a modern man anyway, but Malcolm Callington was anything but modern, and I was sure he didn't give a damn for political correctness.

The idea was oddly titillating, and made me wonder if they would try to apply the same rule to me, something that put an immediate knot of apprehension in my stomach, and something else. Certainly it was just the sort of thing I could imagine Michael making me do, and if he had been aboard I would have been more than happy to comply, even in front of the others. Without him, I was not so sure.

Malcolm began to give instructions.

'Bring her in towards the Rainham bank and we should be able to find a soldier's wind. Ready about.'

Both he and Pippa moved quickly, hauling on ropes and turning the little winches they had until the *Harold Jones* was moving slow and flat, parallel to the bank. Only when the manoeuvre was complete did Malcolm speak again.

'Pippa, keep her steady. Chrissy, a little further aft if you want the best view. Right, young lady, let's be having you.'

I moved to where he had said. Pippa winked at me. Tilly had stood up, her face absolutely scarlet. Very slowly, she removed her lifejacket and deck shoes, placing them carefully to one side, which for some reason made Malcolm chuckle. Now in just her green bikini, she came over to where he had sat down, to stand with her back to me and her head hung down. Malcolm patted his lap, and it was only then that I realised what he was going to do – he was going to spank her.

I just watched, open-mouthed, unable to find words. Part of me still thought it was a joke, just a bit of rough and tumble, but it wasn't. He took her firmly by the wrist and pulled her down, across his knee, ignoring her protests and struggles, except to lock her firmly into place. Winding one leg around her calf, he twisted her arm into the small of her back, and she was helpless. He lifted his knee and her bottom came up, round and pink, with the green bikini pants covering very little, and one full cheek peeping out where they had pulled into her crease.

It was impossibly rude, impossibly demeaning, and he wasn't even in a hurry, going about the process of preparing her for the utterly humiliating and utterly inappropriate punishment as if it were an everyday occurrence. I felt so sorry for her, but I couldn't bring myself to intervene. Worse, a tiny, nasty part of me wanted it done to her, and wanted to watch, to watch another woman have her bottom spanked.

Then came the real shock. He took her bikini pants down!

He didn't even make a fuss over it, but just stuck a thumb in the waistband, popped them down and tugged the material out from between her thighs to make sure her pussy showed. He didn't stop there either. Once he had her bikini well down, he took a firmer grip on her arm and reached under her. A single twitch and her boobs were out, hanging bare under her chest, so that they began to wobble as he set to work on her bottom.

That was the awful thing. He just started, not warning her or lecturing her or anything, but just laying into her poor bottom, to set her cheeks jiggling and bouncing under his hand. She immediately went crazy, kicking and struggling and yelling, but she didn't stand a chance – he was just too strong. He was so calm about it too, so matter of fact, as if it were a perfectly reasonable thing to do, to strip a grown woman and spank her bare bottom.

Pippa did nothing, but just watched, with a cute little smile on her face, obviously not just content to see her little sister spanked, but enjoying it. That just seemed so cruel, worse than Malcolm, and from what they'd said, I was obviously supposed to enjoy it too. That was awful, because of what it implied they thought about me, and worse, because I did.

I just couldn't help myself. It obviously hurt like anything, and I could imagine the awful humiliation of it, spanked, and with her bottom bare, completely bare, with everything showing, and I do mean everything. Not that she tried to hide it. Her legs were really pumping, and she was bucking up and down with her thighs wide apart most of the time. Her bum cheeks were opening and closing to the smacks, so that I knew he could see the rude little hole between them. She was thrashing about with her arms too, and squealing like anything, in a full-blown temper tantrum. It was so rude, such an appalling, unspeakable thing to do to a woman, and I was enjoying it.

So was Malcolm, the stern look on his face gradually fading to be replaced by a pleased smile. He kept his eyes on her bottom too, obviously enjoying the thoroughly rude view, and even planting the smacks to make her cheeks come apart. He also made sure her whole bottom got an even dose, slapping his hand down all over the trim little cheeks until the whole bare moon of her arse was an even, glowing pink. He did her thighs too, which made her squeal even louder and kick with even more energy.

Malcolm delivered a final barrage of slaps to the tuck of her bottom and at last it stopped. He let go of her, but she just lay there, defeated, beaten, her legs still wide apart, with every rude detail of her pussy and bum on show to him and me. Her cheeks were red all over, even quite well down into her crease, and a few darker blotches showed where she was obviously going to bruise.

At last she stood up to squeeze her smacked bottom, her eyes shut, her mouth a little open. Then she had snatched up her bikini pants around her thighs and run for below deck, not even bothering to cover her bottom or boobs. Malcolm just chuckled, and called after her as she disappeared, 'Next time it's the rope's end for you, my girl!'

I expected Pippa to follow, but she didn't, to my amazement. After such a horrible experience Tilly was bound to need to be comforted, and for all my awful response I felt desperately sorry for her. I couldn't bear to stay on deck anyway, not with my nipples standing up as if I'd put corks down my bra, which was hideously embarrassing. So I climbed down after her, expecting to find her in tears.

She wasn't. She was kneeling in her berth, her bikini still down, and up, bare red bottom in the air, little round breasts squashed out on the bedding, one hand between her thighs, masturbating.

7

Pippa was Michael's stepmother. I had let a man use me as a sex toy. I had been buggered five times, and Pippa was Michael's stepmother.

It was just not fair! The idiot might have told me before, or stupid Chrissy might have done, because presumably if she was also coming up on the yacht then she knew too. In my anger I almost told Michael about her, but I managed to hold it back and went quickly upstairs to hide my emotions, and for a badly needed wash.

The whole thing was a complete mess. Not only had I done things with Michael I would never normally have submitted to, which I always hold back for when it really matters, but I'd been enjoying it, which was worse. Add to that having given my prospective mother-in-law several choice put-downs, and I was really in it, up to my neck. The only good thing was that after what Michael and I had done he was sure to have lost interest in Chrissy Green.

I would still have to put up with her moping about like a love-sick puppy. She was sure to do it, because she never did have the sense to see when she was not wanted. It had happened before, all too often, with her thinking she had some sort of right to a man just because she had met him first, or shagged him first, or let him feel her breasts in the back row of a cinema, or whatever.

So instead of two weeks of undiluted sex, I was going to have Chrissy hanging around me and have to be on best behaviour for Michael's stuffy old git of a father and his stuck-up bitch of a wife, along with Tilly, who Michael told me was Pippa's sister and would undoubtedly turn out to be another stuck-up bitch. I had spent almost my entire year's holiday too. It just was not fair!

I showered and washed my hair and put some cream on my poor smarting bottom hole. I really wanted to be alone and get my thoughts in order, so if Michael thought I was upset because he'd buggered me too often that was fine. It was about time he learnt some respect for me anyway, and that I needed to be treated properly and not like a slut.

As I sat on the loo seat and dried my hair I realised that it was the sensible thing to do anyway. Now he knew just how marvellous sex with me could be, he was sure to want more. So it was time to hold off, not completely, but just enough to bring home to him that my feelings mattered. A little show of temper now, and he would soon be running in circles to make me happy again, as eager to please as any other man.

Once I'd got him where I wanted him, I would have three days or so to make sure he was mine. In fact, the best thing to do was get some sort of commitment out of him before I let him bugger me again, or even admitted to the possibility. With Pippa around as a rival it would have been too risky. With only Chrissy to worry about it was perfect.

I went to the bedroom to dress, choosing a blue summer frock and sandals, to look alluring without being in the least bit tarty. Michael was still downstairs, cooking eggs. I went into the living room, deliberately ignoring him. He went on cooking eggs. I changed seats so that he could see me and would realise I was angry with him. He went on cooking eggs. He made toast. He had eggs on toast. He drank a coffee. Then he came in.

'It's a beautiful day. Shall we go rowing? There's a pub I know in Horsey. We could row down to Horsey Mere and get there for lunch.'

I looked up, wondering if he could really be that insensitive, or if he knew perfectly well how I felt and just couldn't be bothered to sort it out with me. I had a nasty suspicion I knew the answer, and that if I carried on sulking ... No, I wasn't sulking, I had every right to be angry! And the idea of rowing, sitting on a hard seat with the sore bottom I had sounded distinctly unappealing.

He was still just going to go off rowing without me. With a normal man I'd have given a frosty answer and he'd have gone off to spend a few hours fretting over me before coming back with his tail between his legs. I'd have been happily sunbathing. With Michael it was all too easy to imagine him spending the whole day rowing happily around the Broads without so much as thinking about me. I'd have been sunbathing, but not happily.

I said I'd go, determined to make my feelings felt while I was with him if I couldn't make him fret over me when I wasn't. He became more cheerful than ever and started getting things together while I pretended to read the book on haunted Norfolk I'd picked up.

The cottage had its own boat, a rowing boat. Fortunately, for all Michael's faults, he was not the type to expect a woman to share the physical work if she didn't want to. So I sat in the back as comfortably as I could manage and dangled a finger in the water while he moved us through a narrow channel in the reeds and out on to the open water.

His rowing was like his fucking, fast and furious with the occasional pause. The only difference was that the pauses were to allow him to take a bearing or admire some bird or other rather than rub me to a climax or turn his attention to my bottom hole. I let him get on with it, trying not to let the perfect summer's day make me too mellow, or the sight of his muscles working and the huge bulge in the front of his shorts make me too horny.

I failed miserably. It was too tempting, to think of what we could be doing, to put my carefully evolved plans for our relationship to one side, to find somewhere quiet and just fuck and fuck and fuck . . .

I could see he was thinking the same too. Not that he said anything. He didn't need to. His quiet smile and the way his eyes ran over my body said it all. It would have been so easy, with all the little islands of reeds just made for concealment and privacy. If the boat wasn't going to be the most comfortable place to fuck it would give me an excuse to go down on my knees and offer myself to be entered from behind . . .

What was I thinking? That was not what I did, not what Valentina de Lacy did. I mounted men in a bed with black satin sheets. I had men begging to be allowed a single kiss. I had men swearing off sex because next to me anything else was worthless. I did not show off my bottom to some overmuscled oaf so that he could fuck me from the rear in a rowing boat!

I steeled myself, waiting for Michael to suggest sex and absolutely determined that I would turn him down. I wanted more than that. I wanted to turn him down and have him beg me, and still turn him down. I knew he wouldn't do it. He'd just give his little self-satisfied smile and wait. As it was, he didn't even have the decency to suggest it so that I could turn him down. Good-looking men are often complete bastards, but he took the biscuit.

So we carried on, with Michael rowing and occasionally making some fatuous observation about birdlife or the boats we passed and me in the back getting gradually more turned on and trying not to show it. Beyond the lake the channel grew narrower, so that he had to pay more attention to what he was doing and less to my legs. He still rowed fast, twice missing big riverboats by inches without batting an eyelid, before turning into a yet narrower channel. It was all a wilderness of water and reeds and wet growing things to me, but he seemed enchanted. He also knew where he was going, because when he eventually tied the boat up and helped me out on to the bank we were just a short walk from the pub.

It was a typical country pub, inhabited by halfwits with incomprehensible accents drinking dark brown beer, but the food was OK and we managed to get a bottle of drinkable Chardonnay. It was cold anyway, and very welcome after the long row in the hot sun, and it helped to calm my feelings.

There was a line of dunes in the distance which Michael said marked the sea and a lonely beach, suggesting a swim. I pointed out that I didn't have my costume, to which he just shrugged and suggested going nude. I quickly disillusioned him of the idea, to my great satisfaction, despite the immediate and dirty images the suggestion brought up. He merely shrugged.

By the end of the meal I was feeling a little better. Pleasantly tipsy anyway. I was even thinking of sex once we got back to the cottage, and telling myself that for all his cool exterior he had to be at least a little bit flustered underneath, or at the very least puzzled. After all, I had said being buggered was special to me, and he had no way of guessing the real reasons for my anger. Puzzled is good with men. It keeps them off balance.

I'd been going about it the wrong way. He wasn't the sort to apologise and ask for sex, not unless he had good reason. The silent treatment had been wrong. Flirting was better. Then I could turn him down, or at least make him wait. I let him take my arm on the way back to the boat, just to get his hopes up. Even when he gave my bottom a squeeze as I bent to step into the boat I made no objection. I just curled myself into the back, making sure I was showing plenty of leg and maybe a hint of my panties.

He gave a smile of appreciation as he climbed in, but said nothing. There was a look of contentment, complacency even, on his face as he began to row. Obviously everything was right in his world, and I could just imagine his simple male thoughts. He had eaten a good lunch with a glass of good wine. He was doing one of his favourite things, with a beautiful girl as company, which shortly meant he would be doing another of his favourite things. The thought processes wouldn't have been much different in the Stone Age.

If he was puzzled by my behaviour, he certainly didn't look it. I lay back, making myself as comfortable as possible, and adjusted my dress to show a little more. It felt good, and my need for sex was getting strong again, but I promised myself I'd turn him down at least once. He was going slowly now, using just his arms to pull us gently through the water, as if we had all the time in the world. I gave him a lazy smile, hoping he'd respond, and put one arm over the side to dangle my fingers in the river.

The water was deliciously cool, making me wish I'd taken up his suggestion of a swim. It also made me realise I needed a pee, and I wished I'd thought of going at the pub. We hadn't gone very far, and I almost asked him to turn back but stopped myself. Valentina's rules for dealing with men – start talking to a man about bodily functions and the last of your mystique is gone. Wet your panties in front of him and you can kiss goodbye to more than just your mystique. That was what was going to happen, too, if he didn't get a move on. I held on anyway, willing him to hurry up as we crossed the little lake and started down the channel. He did the opposite, slowing, to let the boat drift in among the reeds. He put one finger to his lips and pointed behind me.

'Marsh harriers. One just rose over the reed beds to the left of the trees.'

I turned around. There was nothing to see, only water, reeds, trees and sky. I gave him a wan smile.

'Missed them, I'm afraid. Oh well, another time.'

'Wait a while. They fly up over the reeds, but they're seldom in the air for long, so you have to keep watching. They were almost extinct in Britain a few years ago.'

'Yes, but ...'

'Ssh.'

He pointed again. There was a flutter of wings above the reeds, some boring brown bird that I immediately wished completely extinct. He didn't start rowing again, but kept staring at where the bird had risen.

'I think there might be a pair. Let's wait a while.'

He didn't wait for my opinion, sticking an oar into

the mud to hold the boat still and staring vacantly out over the reeds. Time passed. No movement. I had to say something.

'Michael, do you think you could move on now?'

'Don't you want to see the harriers?'

'Not all that much, no, and ... Well, it'll be a lovely afternoon back at the cottage, warm and cosy, and just right for sex, don't you think?'

He chuckled, but that was all.

'Just a minute more.'

I tried another tack, sticking out my bottom lip.

'Don't you want to play?'

'I do, but why go back for sex? There's a little channel a little way along...'

'Not in the boat, Michael! I want to be comfortable. I want to lie back and have you take me in your arms, and kiss me all down my body...'

'Oh, I think we can manage that. There's a little grassy islet, completely hidden.'

'I don't really like it outdoors, Michael...'

'Oh, yes you do.'

'No, I ... OK, OK! I need to pee, all right?'

'Oh. Just do it over the side.'

'Over the side!'

'Why not? Nobody will see. If a yacht's coming we'll see the mast long before she reaches us, and we can hear motor cruisers.'

'You'll see!'

'Does that matter? I mean, after...'

'Yes, it does matter! How can you even say that? I mean, it's not the same thing, is it, sex and ... and bodily functions!'

'I don't see why.'

'Well I do! I'm a woman. I like a little privacy!'

'As you like, but it's a good three hours back to the cottage.'

'Three hours!'

'Easily. Once we turn up into Hickling Broad I'll be rowing full into the wind, and she's very light.'

'Oh, for goodness' sake! Find somewhere to pull into the bank then!'

He made a doubtful face. I could see the problem. There were thick reeds on both sides of the channel. If I climbed out I'd get wet, and it looked fairly deep and extremely muddy. I had to do something though, or I really was going to wet myself. He began to row again, fast now, making for where we could see a clump of willows sticking up above the reeds. Sure enough, they were growing on a little grassy mound.

It was in full view of the channel, but I had very little choice. He swung the boat around, bumping the blunt end against the bank. I grabbed a branch and scrambled out, glancing frantically from side to side even as I hitched up my dress. There was no sign of a mast, and no noise except a distant squeaking, doubtless the marsh harrier eating a rat.

I whipped down my panties and sank into a squat. Even as I willed myself to let go I realised that Michael was still watching, playing the dirty little boy again.

'Michael!'

'What?'

'Don't look, you pig!'

'You look cute.'

'For goodness' sake! Turn around, will you? I can't do it with you watching!'

He just chuckled, but swung the boat around. I let go, closing my eyes and sighing in pure bliss as the tension drained away. For one moment it actually felt quite nice like that, bare outdoors, until I caught the faint throb of an engine. Michael spoke.

'There's a boat coming, Valentina.'

'I know!'

I pushed for all it was worth, finished, wiggled and just managed to get my panties up as the white bow of the boat appeared around the curve of the channel. That still left me standing on the bank as it passed, a small cruiser with four people, all old, stuffy-looking and staring at me in what looked uncomfortably like disgust. I was sure they could guess what I'd been doing, and I was blushing furiously as Michael moved the boat close again.

I stepped on board, feeling thoroughly embarrassed. A moment earlier and they would have seen me pulling my panties up or, worse, in full flow. It didn't bear thinking about, and I desperately wanted to be back in my flat, or anywhere which wasn't green and wet and had proper plumbing.

Michael was rowing slowly again, but not quite so slowly as before. He had braced his legs apart to help, which left me with a prime view of his crotch. I couldn't help but look, and as I did I realised that he had a full erection, showing under his shorts as if he'd stuffed a sausage down them, and a big one at that.

'You dirty bastard!'

'What's wrong?'

'You've got a hard-on, over me peeing?'

'Sure, what do you expect? You're beautiful, Valentina, and you must admit, you were showing off.'

'I was not!'

He just chuckled, then laughed out loud, a reaction to the expression on my face. I nearly slapped him, but caught myself just in time and slapped the water instead, making a pathetic little splash, about two drops of which caught his leg, while a lot more caught me. He laughed again and smacked the oar into the water, sending up a great spray of it, all over me and the back of the boat. I was left gasping, my hair plastered to my wet face, my dress clinging to my breasts and tummy.

I stood up, furious, and started towards him at the exact moment the front of the boat ploughed into the reeds. My balance went, my arms flailing wildly, and then he had caught me and I was sprawled across his knee, bottom up. I hit out at him, but he just laughed and began to pull up my dress. I screamed out as my panties came on show.

'No! You bastard!'

He chuckled and patted my bottom. He had a firm grip on me, and for one truly ghastly moment I thought he was going to pull down my panties and spank my bottom, which really would have been the limit. Nobody does that to me, nobody, but I knew he could, and there was as much panic as anger in my voice as I screamed at him.

'Don't you dare!'

He gave his infuriating little chuckle again, as his hand found the waistband of my panties and I realised that they were coming down and that I was going to be spanked across a man's lap – an unthinkable degradation for a modern woman. Again I screamed, near to panic.

'No! I mean it, you bastard, no!'

He paused, my panties peeled halfway down off my bottom.

'No? Really no?'

'Yes, really no! What do you think I am!'

'Oh.'

He released his hold to let me move back. I sat down, carefully, and glared at him from the safety of my seat. I was burning with indignation, and for a moment I could find nothing to say. He was still smiling, and his cock was still hard in his shorts. Obviously he was a complete pervert, and I just knew that no amount of remonstration would make him feel the guilt he should have. I snapped at him anyway.

'You do not do that, ever! And look at me! You really are an utter bastard, Michael Callington.'

'So you keep saying. You look rather good, as it goes.'

His eyes went to my breasts. So did my hands, to find my nipples hard underneath the wet fabric. His hands went to his fly.

'Oh no, Michael, not here!'

'Why not? We're well into the reeds.'

He stood as his zip came down. His cock sprang out, fully erect, so hard the skin of the head was glossy.

'No, Michael . . .'

He came forward. I wanted to hit him. I also wanted to turn over and stick up my bottom. He was right over me, his cock sticking out towards my face. I caught his scent and my sex twitched in response.

'Bastard!'

His cock went into my mouth. I sucked, my eyes closed, my resentment of the way he treated me still burning in my head but pushed down under my sheer need. He chuckled, watching me suck and masturbating himself gently into my mouth. I lifted my bottom, still sucking away as I pulled up my dress. There was a last twinge of irritation with myself, and my panties came down, and off.

Michael sank down, his cock pulling from my mouth. His arms came under me, lifting me from the seat and rolling my legs up, to slide me smoothly on to his cock, cradling me as my sex filled. My arms came up around his neck and we began to fuck, the boat rocking to the motion.

I could feel my wet dress clinging to my skin as he bounced me on his cock, titillating at first, then annoying as my excitement grew. I let go of him, to pull it high and off, leaving me bare, stark naked in his arms with my sex full to the brim of his lovely big penis. He put a hand under my bottom, supporting me, one finger tickling in my crease. I sobbed as a fingertip found my bottom hole, teasing the sore flesh.

'No, Michael, not that. I'm too sore . . . I really am.'

His finger pushed into my bottom hole, but he kept me on his cock, pulling me close to kiss me, open-mouthed. He began to go faster, pushing up into me, to make my flesh quiver and set me gasping into his mouth. I clung on, surrendering again to the way he controlled me, to the overwhelming bliss of fucking with him completely in charge. His finger slid deeper up my bottom, his pushes grew harder still, rubbing my sex against his crotch. I wriggled, squirming my clit against the tangle of his pubic hair, and I realised that all I need to come was a little concentration.

I thought of how we were, me naked, him still clothed, out in the open air, my sex full of cock, my bottom stuck out with his finger up the hole. It was so dirty, and risky too, when a boat might go past behind us, separated only by a fringe of reeds. All it needed was for someone to make a mistake and the reeds to be pushed aside. I'd be caught, wriggling my bottom on a finger, my sex stretched wide on the thick pole of Michael's sex, fucking, nude and dirty . . .

The boat was rocking frantically to our motion, back

and forward, pushing against the reeds holding us in. I was going to come, and I knew he was too, at any moment, deep inside me. I had to get there first, with his cock still in my sex, still moving. My wriggling became frantic, my fantasy dirtier. I imagined getting caught, as I was, nude with both my holes full. It would be by the two old couples, all four of them staring in utter disgust, at the taut ring of straining pink flesh where his cock went into my body, at my open, penetrated bottom hole, at all of me, at me fucking in the nude, in the open . . .

I came, crying out loud as the orgasm hit me. Michael grunted, pumping into me with desperate energy, to take me to a new peak, and a third as his cock jammed to the hilt in my body and I realised he had come inside me. I held on, letting him finish, pumping his sperm into my sex as I rode my own climax, on and on, floating free, my eyes closed, mouths wide together, in glorious, mutual ecstasy.

He gave one final, hard shove and it was done. I just clung on, shivering against his body in the warm air, the reeds brushing against my bare shoulder as the boat slid free of the reed bed. Michael swore, letting go of me as he grabbed for the oars. I let go too, and sat down with a bump, sprawling in the bottom of the boat as we drifted out into the channel, my legs wide, my wet, just-come-in sex gaping to the entire crew of a large yacht.

My mind had been in a whirl of emotions ever since Tilly's spanking. I'd heard about people like her . . . like them. I'd never understood, or rather I'd never believed the women involved really enjoyed it. I mean, spanking hurts, and it's an unspeakably humiliating thing for a woman to have done to her. Tilly had been in pain, and she'd been humiliated, but there was no possible question that she had enjoyed it. She had masturbated over it.

For a second I'd just stared, watching her fingers move in the wet, fleshy folds of her pussy. Then she'd noticed, and smiled at me – a lazy, happy smile that conveyed the exact opposite of what I'd expected her to be feeling. She'd not only been masturbating over her spanking, but she was thoroughly pleased with herself.

I'd apologised and beaten a hasty retreat, feeling utterly confused. I wanted to be alone, but there was nowhere to go. Tilly hadn't even stopped when she had seen me, and there was the awful thought that she might have wanted me to watch to cope with as well. She might even have thought I'd come down to watch, or worse, to join in!

It was utterly mortifying, and set me scuttling red-faced back on deck, Malcolm or no Malcolm. As it was, he and Pippa had had to adjust our course because another boat was coming towards us, a huge barge-like thing with enormous sails. So they'd ignored me, which was exactly what I wanted.

Ever since then I'd been trying to come to terms with my own emotions. I felt shocked and vulnerable, and it was impossible not to wonder if I was expected to allow my own bottom to be spanked if I made a mistake, and what I'd do when the moment came.

I knew the answer, or rather, I knew what the answer should have been – a firm no. Unfortunately I wasn't so sure I really wanted it to be. I'd enjoyed seeing it happen to Tilly, it was no use pretending otherwise, and there was an insistent little voice in the back of my head telling me I'd enjoy it being done to me. I tried to deny it, to push it away, telling myself I was just being weak, and trying to accept what I knew might happen to me anyway by pretending I wanted it.

I'd done that before. Now I wasn't. Thoughts of how she must have felt kept coming back – as she was turned across his knee, as her bikini pants were taken down, as he began to spank her bare bottom. Every time I imagined myself in her place. At first it was with Michael doing the spanking, which at least allowed me to feel I would be keeping a little of my pride. That was how I discovered that I didn't want to keep any pride. I wanted sex with Michael. I wanted to be spanked by his father.

They seemed to have some idea of what I was feeling, because other than Pippa bringing me a cup of tea, they left me alone. Tilly had been a little embarrassed when she'd come back on deck, but no more than a little. She'd then gone to prepare lunch, leaving me to watch the magnificent view of the QE2 bridge as we slid beneath and to think about bottom spanking.

It was one of those things in Valentina's list of 'don'ts'. They were the sexual things a girl shouldn't do because it was disrespectful, and included anal sex, striptease, doggy position, bondage and spanking, along with a lot of other things I couldn't remember. Some of them I'd never understood, like striptease, which is just fun, and going in doggy, which I adore. I knew she was right, because men always seemed to worship her, while most of my boyfriends had been about as disrespectful to me as it is possible to be. John McLaren having me in the changing rooms at a squash court and telling me he had a dinner date with another girl while

I was actually sucking his cock clean came to mind. Valentina would have bitten him, but then it would never have happened to her anyway.

I'd always agreed with her about spanking. Not that it really had much to do with me anyway. It's one of those things dirty old men like to do to much younger women, and is only erotic in the sense that it turns the man on, like so many male fantasies. So I'd thought. It was impossible to think of Malcolm Callington as a dirty old man, but he was old enough, and Tilly was young enough. She'd enjoyed it though, more than he had really.

That made me think of how it could have been, if he'd wanted to come. He could have made her do it, kneeling on the deck with her bright red bottom stuck out and her boobs swinging under her chest as she sucked his cock, a really rude image. More likely he would have taken Pippa below decks and fucked her, a thought that sent a shiver right through me. I wondered if he spanked her too. The answer had to be yes. When he did, it would be in front of me, Pippa taken down across his knee, or both of them, side by side, bottoms bared for spanking . . .

I stopped myself, the blood rushing to my cheeks as I realised just how badly I wanted to masturbate.

8

Why me?

I'm the girl with a plan. I'm the one who knows what she wants and how to get it. I'm Valentina de Lacy.

I had the brains and I had the looks. I worked hard at school. I worked hard at college. I got into a profession full of rich men. All I had to do was marry one, either someone soft enough to let me do as I pleased for the rest of my life, or one I could divorce and leave myself rich. It had seemed so simple.

Life is never simple, as I'd discovered, as I was discovering with Michael Callington. He had seemed close to perfect, with his looks and his money and his easygoing attitude. Sure he needed a few changes, but ... Valentina's rules for dealing with men – men can be moulded, do it. Unfortunately, Michael Callington seemed to be an exception.

Again and again I'd tried to ease him into following my line, and really only just for sex, which is the easiest because the woman can always take the moral high ground. Again and again I'd failed and ended up playing the slut to him, and enjoying it.

It was impossible to so much as ruffle him. After the incident in the rowing boat I'd been furious. It had been awful enough just being seen, but to cover myself I'd had to go over on my knees, leaving my bare bottom stuck up towards the people on the yacht, and everything showing. Even when I had managed to make myself decent I'd discovered that my panties had fallen into a little pool of disgusting brown water that had collected under the boards. They were soaking and filthy, and I was forced to stay bare under my dress all the way back.

Michael just thought it was funny and told me to laugh it off. When I'd told him what I thought of him, he'd laughed at that too. We'd sat in stony silence all the way back to the cottage. Or rather, I had. He had rowed and admired the view and made the occasional comment on birds or boats.

Now, back at the boathouse, he finally condescended to recognise my feelings, although hardly in the way I wanted.

'Shall we walk into Hickling for tea, or are you going to sulk all day?'

'I am not sulking!'

He laughed, made quick work of tying the boat up, and stepped out into the sunlight, then spoke again.

'Do you know what my father would do right now?'

'No, and I don't want to.'

'He'd take you across his knee and give you a damn good spanking.'

'Well then, the old pervert would get a knee in his balls, and end up in court.'

He laughed again, but it was just that shade less confident, disappointed even. Twice he'd tried it, once by experimentation, once by suggestion. Twice I'd made my feelings clear. Now he knew for sure. There are limits, and having my bottom smacked was beyond them.

* * *

By late afternoon I was absolutely certain that I was going to get put across Malcolm Callington's knee and spanked, whether I liked it or not. Once I'd had my tea and Tilly's embarrassment had worn off, they had begun to make little spanking jokes and to tease Tilly about her red bottom. She all too obviously enjoyed the attention, and I realised that her embarrassment had been more because she'd run off to masturbate than because she'd been spanked.

It had left her, and Pippa too, in a state of nervous excitement that was obviously more than a little sexual. Tilly's bikini had worked up between her bottom cheeks too, leaving a lot of very pink flesh showing. She didn't seem to care, just the opposite in fact, pouting and making a big show of rubbing herself in response to their remarks.

From what they were saying it was obviously something which might as easily have happened to Pippa as to Tilly, and to me too, or so they seemed to assume. Malcolm was thoroughly pleased with himself, and I was sure he was turned on. After all, what man wouldn't be after handling a beautiful girl like that? All he had to do was turn his attention to me, and over I would go, knickers down, to have my bare bottom spanked in front of the others. I knew I'd struggle and kick, just like Tilly, and part of me was saying that if I really made a fuss he wouldn't go through with it. That was logic talking. Emotion was very different, apprehension mixed with a terrifying compulsion to surrender, maybe even to do something he could pick fault with, on purpose.

I didn't. I was on best behaviour all day, doing exactly what I was told as fast and as well as I could.

Nothing happened, but there was more than a little regret mixed in with my relief when they finally took the sails down and reverted to the engine to guide the *Harold Jones* into a creek. There was a pub, the Mainbrace, with a system of wooden jetties outside. We brought the *Harold Jones* in among the other yachts and motor cruisers and tied up.

It was apparently their usual anchorage on the first day out from London, and I'd been hoping Michael would be there. He wasn't, and when I tried to phone him from the pub I found I couldn't get through. That was both worrying and annoying, but Pippa told me that, like Malcolm, Michael didn't really approve of mobile phones and preferred to leave his off when away. I had to be content with that, and the possibility of meeting him the next night when we planned to moor on the River Deben, just past Felixstowe, where he could be sure to find us.

It was a beautiful evening and we decided to eat outside. Malcolm dealt with dinner with his normal mixture of efficiency and chauvinism, ordering for us with no more than a lifted eyebrow to check that I was happy to eat a crab salad. He chose the wine too, without any consultation at all.

The garden was quite crowded at first, and the conversation stayed general, with none of the little spanking funnies and remarks about bottoms they'd been passing on the yacht. We took our time though, and the light was fading by the time Malcolm went in to order a round of brandies, again without asking if we wanted them or not.

Sipping brandy and watching the sun set behind the trees, I began to feel a little bolder and less apprehensive. I really wanted to talk to Tilly, and I was given the opportunity when Macolm and Pippa decided to take a walk along the towpath that led inland from the pub. Most of the other customers had left or gone inside, so it was safe to speak. Half of me wanted to ask how she could let him do it to her, but I knew the answer. The other half wanted to know what it felt like. I was still trying to decide what to say when she solved the problem for me.

'You were very good today. I thought you'd be naughty.'

I was blushing immediately and stammered out the first thing that came into my head.

'I . . . I don't really know how it works.'

'It's simple. There are rules, and there is the right way to do things. Break the rules or do things the wrong way, you get a spanking. It's ever so much fun.'

'But . . . I mean . . . I know you liked it, but . . . he didn't ask you or anything. He just spanked you!'

'That's the best way. It makes it so much stronger, knowing you have to go through with it, knowing he'll just do it no matter what I do or say. Do you like it less strict then?'

'I don't like it at all! I mean, I don't do it, I'm not into that sort of stuff.'

'Oh, I see! You'll love Malcolm then!'

'What do you mean?'

'If you like to pretend you don't like it. He loves that. So do I. Oh boy, am I looking forward to you getting it!'

'I'm serious, Tilly!'

'Yeah, sure, Chrissy. I believe you.'

'No, really! I mean it!'

'You're not joking, are you? I thought . . . I mean, Malcolm thought you were into it?'

'No! Not at all! Why should he think that?'

'Because you said so! At the club. That's what he told us, anyway, and there is no way he'd have invited you if he thought you weren't a spankee!'

'Why not?'

'Why not! Because of the way he runs the boat, that's why not! Didn't you realise?'

'No, why should ... Hang on, does Michael know?'

'Does Michael know? Of course Michael knows! Look, seriously, Chrissy, stop mucking about. Daddy ... um ... Malcolm said he'd sounded you out when he stood you dinner at his club?'

'Well, he didn't.'

'You are joking?'

'I am not joking. No, hang on ... Is that what swish is, another word for spanking?'

'Yes, of course.'

'I ... I thought it was something to do with sport.'

She didn't answer, but just sat there, staring at me as if I was an idiot, then suddenly broke into a huge smile.

'Oh, very funny, Chrissy! Do you know, I really believed you there.'

'I'm not joking, Tilly. I had no idea what he was talking about.'

'My God, you're not joking, are you?'

'No!'

'So you don't like being spanked, really?'

'No! Yes. I don't know. I've never been spanked!'

'You've never been spanked, not at all?'

'No!'

'But you like the idea, don't you?'

She was looking at me and smiling. I'd gone bright red, which was as good as admitting it. She laughed, a bright, cheerful sound, so full of mischief and happiness that it was impossible not to smile.

'Oh dear, what are we going to do with you?'

'Don't tell the others, please? I'd be so embarrassed.'

She giggled. Her face had lit up, so full of delight and naughtiness that I found myself blushing hotter still. I tried again, really begging.

'Please?'

'Well, OK, but if I'm not going to tell Malcolm, then he's going to expect to spank you.'

'No!'

'Then I had better tell him.'

'No!'

'Well, you're going to have to make your mind up, Chrissy. What's it to be, serious embarrassment or a smacked bottom?'

She was absolutely loving it, my embarrassment, my confusion, everything, her smile almost demented, like some sort of she-devil. I'd never seen a face at once so pretty and so wicked. She was right though, I had to make up my mind, and if I said to tell him and that I couldn't be spanked, then he was going to think I was a complete idiot. It would spoil the trip too, with two days spent in a bad atmosphere. I'd hate that. But I was terrified of having my bottom spanked.

I needed time to think; to get my head around the whole thing.

'He's ... he's not likely to want to spank me this evening, is he?'

'Not while we're tied up, no. Not that he really cares, and Pippa would love everybody to know, but he'll be well satisfied and we'll need an early start tomorrow, so it'll be straight into our bunks.'

'Satisfied? Because he spanked you?'

'No, silly. What do you think he and Pippa are up to right now?'

'They went ... He's going to spank her? In the woods?'

'If it's quiet, yes.'

She glanced towards the now gloomy bulk of the woods. I followed her eyes, thinking of them, Malcolm with Pippa across his knee, her round little bottom bare and pink, gasping out her emotions as he spanked her. Then it would presumably be down on his cock to thank him as she masturbated, or he might simply make her touch her toes and fuck her from behind, the way Michael had fucked me the first time.

I shook my head, trying to clear away the erotic images. I needed to come quite badly, and I was wishing more than ever that Michael was with us. Then it could be me who was taken into the woods, me who was given a good fucking, me who was spanked; as Pippa was, as Tilly had been. Her laughter broke into my daydream and something else occurred to me.

'I still don't understand, not entirely. I mean, doesn't Pippa mind him spanking other women? I mean, you're her sister!'

'Heavens! You are a little prude, aren't you? Why should Pippa resent me having a little fun? We're close. We've often shared boys, and it's not even as if Malcolm has sex with me. Well, only spanking sex.'

'Oh.'

'Don't tell me you've never had a threesome.'

'No! Yes ... sort of. I'm an only child anyway, but I'm sure I'd never share a man with my sister!'

She shrugged, showing complete indifference, as if the subject had begun to bore her, then went on.

'I'll tell you about Malcolm and Pippa, shall I, and the scandal?'

I nodded. She began.

'I said he was a governor at Mornington's, didn't I?'

'Yes.'

'She got a job there, straight out of university, teaching this and that, and they made her a sports mistress too. All fine, except for the fact that at university she had been a very, very naughty girl. In her first year she'd done a couple of photosets for a magazine, a spanking magazine.'

'Oh my! I suppose she needed to pay for . . .'

'The hell she did! We both had trust funds to see us through higher education. She did it because she was obsessed with spanking and wanted to show off her bare red bum to as many people as possible!'

'Wasn't that a bit risky, if she wanted to go into teaching?'

'She didn't, not as such. It was just the route her career officer advised her to take. She's not much of a one for making her own decisions, is Pippa. She goes with her emotions. So do I, but I'm not as bad as her.'

'That's me all through.'

'So you'll understand. She wanted to be in a spanking magazine, so she did it, and the hell with the consequences. I don't know who she thought would see the thing, but certainly not a governor at the school she went to.'

'Malcolm?'

'None other.'

'How embarrassing!'

'You bet, at first anyway. The magazine was called *Discipline in Uniform*, and he just dropped the title into conversation one day after a sports day. She picked up on it, of course, and yes, it embarrassed the hell out of her. I mean, just imagine it. The photos showed a sort of story, silly really, but fun, with her as a private in the army, being made to drill, and strip as she did it, down to her knicks, then spanked over a sergeant's knee. Of course having been in the army, it was right up Malcolm's street, and well, she is cute. It was her who went to him though, embarrassed or not, not the other way around. She got her first spanking from him in a hotel in Aylesbury.'

'And his first wife found out?'

'Yes, but not directly. It was really bad luck ... Well, no, it wasn't bad luck at all really, it was her fault. She always has to show off!'

'So what happened?'

'It went on for a year, always at weekends after important sporting events, in which Pippa would be involved and when Malcolm could turn up without exciting suspicion. Then came the big end of year sports day, with all the parents there, and after which all the girls were leaving. One family took their daughter out to dinner to celebrate her exam results, in Aylesbury. The father drank too much, the mother didn't drive. They stayed at the hotel. There were strange noises coming from the next room – smack, smack, smack, squeal, squeal, squeal. Pippa's like a pig when she gets going. He hears the door go, so he comes out to complain, and there's his daughter's history teacher, running down the passage in nothing but a towel, a towel that failed to completely cover a very red bottom.'

'Oh my!'

'Oh my is right. He was a miserable bastard, and complained. So out it all came.'

'So why was that Pippa's fault?'

'Because she went out into the passage in the hope that someone would see, silly! Come on, or do you make a habit of running around hotels at night with a towel so short your bum shows? She wanted to be seen, she just didn't expect it to be by one of her pupils' fathers.'

'So she got the sack?'

'Of course, and Malcolm had to resign his place on the board of governors. His marriage was already pretty shaky, or so Pippa says, and that went too. Then there was the libel case.'

'Libel case?'

'Yes. Haven't you heard of the Spanking Major?'

'No.'

'Well anyway, that was Malcolm. The bastard who'd caught Pippa went to the papers. It had all the ingredients, a pretty girl, a famous English public school and, well, you know how they love to see anyone even vaguely upper class fall on his arse, so they just lapped it up. One even called Malcolm a pervert, in print. He sued.'

'Sued? But he'd done it. There was a witness.'

'No, no, he didn't sue them for saying he'd been spanking Pippa; he sued them for calling him a pervert. That was his great line, when he stood up in the witness box, as calm as you please. What was it, let me get it right: "Of course it's not perverse. Any red-blooded Englishman would want to spank a young girl's bottom." He won, two million in damages.'

'Wow!'

'Hence the yacht, which is named after the foreman of the jury, Harold Jones, and Michael's flat, and a lot of other things, not that he was exactly poor in the first place. And, of course, he married Pippa.'

'And what about you?'

'I just tagged along.'

She swallowed the rest of her brandy. I was still taking it all in. They were so bold about it, about everything, as if what other people thought didn't matter at all, especially Malcolm. Thinking about it, Michael was the same, and I realised that his wonderful confidence went further than I had realised, to an absolute certainty that he was right, whatever other people thought. I sighed.

A call from the towpath signalled the return of Malcolm and Pippa. They were walking slowly, with her cuddled into his chest, looking utterly devoted. She was smiling too, a quiet, happy smile of absolute satisfaction. I wondered if I'd look that content after a trip across Michael's knee.

Malcolm was as firm as ever, stating that it was time for bed in a tone that brooked no argument. Tilly went without a murmur, even though it was barely ten o'clock, and I really had no choice but to follow. On board, the main cabin proved to be divided into two by a clever folding door, so that Pippa and Malcolm would be together in one compartment and Tilly and I in the other. They even shut the door to get ready for bed, which I was grateful for, but which still struck me as a bit odd when Malcolm had had Tilly bare across his lap in front of me.

It was odd, but it was also strangely typical, and gave me some much needed privacy. With the light out it was pitch black and silent too, after Malcolm had told Tilly to stop chattering. I lay there, feeling insecure and incredibly horny, so horny I wanted to masturbate then and there.

Before long Tilly's breathing had grown light and even. She was asleep. I had to do it, my need was just too strong to resist. My nightie came up. One hand went to my chest, cupping a breast. The other slid down the front of my panties. I was wet and ready, my clit eager for my touch. As I began to masturbate I fixed my imagination firmly on Michael.

There was no question that he had shown a lot of attention to my bottom, from the first. Twice I'd had sex with him, or rather, on two occasions, and nearly always on my knees with my bum in the air. He had patted me too, not smacks, but a hint if only I'd known. Now I did know, and why he liked me bum up. It was a prime position to spank me in. That was what he wanted to do, what he wanted to do most of all. He wanted to take me across his knee and pull down my knickers. He wanted to spank my bare bottom, to have me wriggling and kicking and squealing across his lap. I wished he'd done it. I wondered if he'd like to do it as Tilly had been done, openly.

The thought of it was almost too embarrassing to bear. Almost. I could understand what Tilly meant too, about it being better to give a man permission to do it and then take what was coming. That way I could enjoy the sweet apprehension of knowing it might happen at any time, but didn't have to suffer the hideous embarrassment of having to ask for it.

She was right. It was the best way. That way emotional ties didn't matter so much. So Malcolm could spank Tilly and Pippa wasn't jealous, and if she got turned on it was just one of those things – something that happened but which wasn't really talked about, like going to the loo. Somehow that made it seem deliciously rude, yet at the same time safe. My thoughts drifted down a yet ruder path, a naughtier one. Malcolm might spank Tilly, but he didn't fuck her. Malcolm might spank me, but he wouldn't fuck me, or make me suck his cock, just spank me. When he did, if I couldn't hold back my feelings and ran off to masturbate, I'd be treated with understanding, as if it was a slightly embarrassing accident.

I could do it, I really could, surrender myself to his discipline. Michael wouldn't be cross. He knew. It might even improve things between us. They might even share me, a father and son thing, sharing a girl to spank the same way an ordinary father and son might share a beer.

I giggled at the thought. I was having fun, playing with my pussy and laughing for the sheer pleasure of what I was doing and the rudeness of my thoughts. That would be the way it was, at the cottage, an ordinary domestic scene, with a grown-up family enjoying an after-dinner drink, and spanking the son's girlfriend.

It was a great fantasy. I'd do something wrong, something trivial, like fractionally overcooking the dinner. Nothing would be said, nothing at all, but they'd know. I'd know. Then, after dinner, perhaps after a brief pause for digestion, whoops, over I'd go!

They'd be so casual, lifting my skirt and pulling down my knickers as if it were the most natural thing in the world. Pippa and Tilly would be watching too, or half watching, perhaps still chatting or reading as I was stripped and punished in front of them, howling and kicking and thrashing around, just like Tilly had done. They'd take turns, both so firm, so strong, in complete control as I squirmed and writhed across their laps in my embarrassment and pain.

The fantasy broke. It wasn't right. I didn't know how it felt to be spanked, how much it hurt, or why that pain was so arousing, so it was impossible to imagine it. I had to come though, I was too close to orgasm to stop.

I might not have known how it felt to be spanked, but I knew all about the feelings that came with having my knickers pulled down in public. Valentina had done it to me, to embarrass me so that she could show off to some boy or other, after a game of tennis. I'd been bending to do up a lace on my trainers. My skirt had been whipped up and my knickers dropped before I could react, leaving them laughing at my red-faced humiliation as I frantically tried to cover my bum with her still holding my knickers down. They'd laughed so hard at the way I'd kicked and wriggled, but for all my hideous embarrassment I'd been turned on too, so turned on I'd masturbated over it later, just as I was doing now.

I could imagine it being much the same with the Callingtons. I'd be held firmly in place as my bottom was casually stripped, my wriggling and pleading ignored, except perhaps to draw a giggle from Tilly. Then my knickers would be down and I'd be showing everything from behind, rude and bare, ready for spanking.

It was going to happen at any moment. I bit my lip to stop myself crying out, still rubbing, still thinking of that awful moment when my knickers would come down ... pulled down by Michael, in front of Malcolm and the two girls, and it was going to happen, for real.

I was there, coming with a choking sob as I struggled to hold in what would have been a full-throated scream. My thighs were cocked as wide as they'd go, and at the very peak of my climax one knee began to drum on the bulkhead, in time to the spasms running through my muscles. I had no control over it whatever, and it broke my orgasm, which faded quickly. I lay still, my fingers still deep between my pussy lips, listening and feeling guilty.

For perhaps thirty seconds there was absolute silence, then Tilly's voice sounded from the darkness.

'Was that nice?'

9

I awoke to the rocking motion of the *Harold Jones* and the smell of bacon and eggs. Before I'd even put my feet on the floor I had begun to feel sick. The strange and lewd dream in which I'd been running naked down a hotel corridor chased by soldiers intent on spanking me faded, to be replaced by an urgent need for steady footing.

It was Tilly doing the cooking. She wasn't in her bikini, she was wrapped from head to toe in some sort of heavy-duty yellow coverall, with clips on her belt. Her hair was wet. She smiled happily.

'Get your weather gear on, Chrissy. It's a fast one today, and we'll be sailing closehauled most of the time, so no spanking for you today.'

I felt the same odd mixture of relief and disappointment I had before, until I peered out of the cockpit. The sky was overcast, with heavy grey clouds scudding past so close above I felt I could have touched them. Thin rain was lashing down on choppy water, while the leaves of the poplar trees were flickering from silver-grey to deep green as they turned in the gusts. Both Malcolm and Pippa were on deck, doing something complicated with rope. Both were wrapped head to toe in their waterproofs. Beyond them I could see the estuary, lead grey and set with whitecaps. The opposite shore was invisible. Tilly spoke again.

'Force five, gusting six, but it might pick up a little

once we're past Shoeburyness, with any luck. Come on, you know what happens to girls who dawdle.'

I wasn't looking, and squeaked in surprise as she planted a heavy smack on my bottom.

'Ow! Tilly!'

'That's nothing to what Malcolm'll give you if you don't get a move on, my girl. Unless you want to chicken out?'

'I . . . I don't know. I still need time to think.'

'What's to think about? Or were you diddling yourself over something other than what happened to me last night?'

I went abruptly red. She laughed and began to dish out breakfast. I went back to our cabin, feeling a little sick and a little scared, and wondering how she could be so jolly.

She wasn't the only one. When Pippa came down she was dripping water, with her hair plastered around her face in sodden rats' tails, as different from when I'd first seen her as it was possible to imagine. She was happy though, as happy as anything, talking excitedly in their incomprehensible jargon as she wolfed down bacon, eggs and bread. Tilly had fried everything in butter, and it must have been hideously fattening, but neither of them seemed to care.

By then I was dressed, although what I thought of as wet weather wear was enough to set them both laughing. Tilly lent me some of her own gear, including one of the belts with clips on it. She double-checked the fastenings on my lifejacket too, which left me more nervous than ever.

When Malcolm came down it was to declare us ready to set sail. He ate his breakfast in moments and the three of them went back on deck, leaving me to watch apprehensively from the cockpit as we slid slowly out into the creek. The moment we left the jetty the yacht began to rock faster, and less evenly too. I clung on tight, praying I wouldn't be sick, praying Michael would come, praying the wind would either die down or pick up so badly they'd have the sense to stay at the pub.

None of my prayers were answered. The rocking got worse as we came out into the estuary, and we began to pitch back and forth as well in a horrible rolling motion. I sat down, feeling utterly miserable and hoping fervently that they'd leave me to suffer in peace. A moment later Pippa's head appeared in the hatch.

'Come on up, Chrissy. We're going to teach you to sail.'

The first thing I saw when I opened my eyes was Michael. He was naked and staring out of the window with a faraway expression in his eyes. He turned as I pulled myself up on to one elbow.

He smiled, but there was a touch of resentment there too. I immediately felt worried that I'd done something wrong, but pushed the emotion down. If anybody ought to feel resentful it was me. OK, so we hadn't had sex, not since the disaster in the rowing boat, but if it bothered him he hadn't shown it. He'd been asleep before I was. He'd gone back to staring out of the window, but after a while he spoke.

'What a beautiful day. She'll be absolutely flying.'

I assumed he was talking about the wretched yacht. Outside the window low grey clouds were moving across the sky. It wasn't raining but there was a wet sheen to everything and it obviously had been. He was mad.

Mad but incredibly good-looking, and naked. Just

watching him as he bent to dig his mobile phone out of his case sent a jolt right through me, despite being still half asleep. I bit my lip. Somehow the feelings of the day before didn't seem so important. I'd forgotten what I was supposed to be doing too. He was frowning as he pushed at the buttons on his phone.

'Damn thing's broken. Infernal machines! Do you think I could borrow yours?'

'I didn't bring it. If I had the office would have been phoning me constantly. I'm the only one who really knows how anything works in my department.'

'Well, yes, I can see the sense in that. Still, I don't suppose Pippa's been allowed to bring hers anyway. Dad's frightfully strict on board.'

'He doesn't let her bring her mobile phone?'

'No. He hates the things.'

'And she puts up with it?'

He just shrugged and began to push at the buttons again. So for all Pippa's expensive tastes she wasn't the boss in her relationship. Somehow that didn't surprise me. After all, her husband was Michael's father. He threw the phone down and turned back to the window. I stretched, wondering about a morning fuck and why he made me quite so horny. Normally I'm not up for anything until at least noon. The sheet slipped down as I moved, exposing my breasts. He took no notice at all, but spoke, still admiring the rotten view.

'Are you really sure you can't manage the yacht? They'll be on the Deben this evening, and it's really not far at all. We could drive down, or better, take the train and stroll over from Felixstowe. It's ever so pretty along that piece of coast, and there's Sutton Hoo, where –'

'Today? Look at the weather, Michael!'

'That's just it, the weather's perfect. A fresh breeze coming up from the south-west. Ideal.'

'Not for me. Michael, I told you I get seasick. Now why don't you come back into bed?'

'Hmm ... it might get a bit choppy, I suppose. Still, I'm tempted. You could meet me in Great Yarmouth tomorrow evening.'

'You'd go on your own!'

'Well ...'

'Michael! Don't I mean anything to you? Doesn't what I've done for ... what we've done together matter?'

'Yes, of course, but you didn't seem interested last night. I thought you might have started your period or something. After all, you seemed a little moody yesterday.'

For a moment I couldn't find an answer at all. Was he really so insensitive that he hadn't realised why I was cross? Did he really think it was funny being utterly humiliated in front of some dried-up old farts? He did, obviously.

I was going to give him the answer he deserved, but held myself back. If the yacht reached Great Yarmouth tomorrow evening, we would presumably go to meet it. Chrissy would be on board. She was going to be upset, maybe upset enough to stand up to me. I'd known she was on the yacht and I hadn't told Michael, which was not going to look good. By then I'd expected him to be obsessed with me. He should have been, after buggering me!

Obviously he wasn't.

I wanted to scream at him, to tell him what an ungrateful bastard he was, to throw something at him, something hard. Then I'd dress, pack my things and call a cab. I'd be back in London within a few hours. No more Michael Callington, no more problem, no more exquisite sex, no more London flat and house in the country . . .

When I spoke it was in my most girlish voice.

'Sorry I was grumpy, Michael. Can I make it up to you?'

'You might very well be able to.'

He was smiling again. I'd rolled over, and the sheet had come right down, baring my bottom. He was looking right at it. I stuck it up.

As he came close my feelings were very mixed indeed. I was telling myself I was only doing what I had to. I was also thinking of the way he always made me come.

He took me around the waist, very gently, but with a strength I knew I could not possibly break. His fingers spread out over my tummy, lifting, to bring my bottom up higher and make my cheeks open, showing him my bottom hole. I fought down a sob, wondering how I could possibly let a man handle me that way even as my thighs came apart in acceptance of what he was doing. He would toy with me, explore my bottom and sex, put his fingers in me, rub at my clit, open me. When he was good and ready he would fuck me, maybe bring me off, then up it would go, up my bottom. I hid my face in the pillows, struggling to accept my own surrender as one large hand settled on my bottom. He spoke, his voice soft yet firm.

'You do have an adorable bottom, Valentina. Ripe for spanking.'

'No, Michael. We've talked about that. No spanking!'

'No? You don't know what you're missing, and I do think you rather deserve it, don't you?'

'Deserve it? What for?'

'For being a brat, of course.'

'A brat? What do you mean, a brat?'

He chuckled, then planted a firm swat on my bottom. It stung like anything and I twisted round.

'Ow! That hurt! Stop it, you pervert, and what do you mean by calling me a brat?'

He let go of my waist.

'Well ... a brat ... you know, the way you've been behaving, like a spoilt child ... a brat.'

'I have not!'

'No? I ... I thought you were doing it on purpose ... well, I hoped ...'

'What the fuck are you talking about? I do not behave like that, and why would I anyway?'

'To make me punish you.'

'What! Are you out of your mind? I've already told you, I don't do that sort of thing!'

'I know, but ... No ... I mean, don't you want that, deep down? I thought you liked plenty of attention to your bottom?'

'I do not want to be spanked! I can't think of anything more demeaning, or more ...'

I'd been going to say infantile, but I stopped. My anger had boiled back up, but I caught myself in time. It wasn't going to happen though, there are limits. Valentina's rule for dealing with men: attractive women don't have to put up with perverts. It was one I've never broken, and I've shamed a lot of men out of their nasty little habits. I knew Michael would not be one of them. Guilt didn't seem to mean anything to him.

I knew Chrissy would have let him do it, too. She has no self-respect. Once more I considered the idea of just leaving them to it, only to think of how smug she'd be when the whole story came out. It would too, including how I'd let Michael bugger me. That was unbearable.

Michael had gone back to the window. As I'd guessed, there wasn't so much as a hint of the shame he should have felt; far from it. For all his education and polish, he was a real Neanderthal underneath. Still, he was a rich Neanderthal, and his perverted habits had one major advantage. After a year, maybe two, I'd have strong grounds for a divorce with a settlement firmly in my favour. I forced down my feelings one more time.

'Sorry, Michael ... I ... I just don't, OK?'

What I wanted to do was demand how he could possibly ask such a thing of me, how he could even think of such a thing nowadays. I mean, he wasn't even thirty, and his attitudes belonged to the decade before he was born, two decades maybe, and they'd been wrong then. I mean, punishing girls by smacking their bottoms? Get real!

To my amazement he actually apologised.

'I'm sorry, Valentina, that was a bit of a misunderstanding, I'm afraid. As I said, I thought that was what you wanted, because ... because of the way you were behaving.'

I tried to hold the question back, but it came out anyway.

'Why? Why would you possibly think that?'

'Well ... well, it's what Pippa does with Dad all the time. It's a game, really, that's all, and you must admit, you do act up rather.'

'So Pippa and your father play spanking games?'

'Yes. Haven't you heard of the Spanking Major?'

'No. Hang on, there was a court case, wasn't there, last year some time?'

'Two years ago. That was Dad.'

'And you like it too?'

'Yes, of course.'

Of course! I wanted to tell him he was a pervert again, that it wasn't natural. I held back. The divorce was going to be a breeze. I'd get everything. I smiled.

'OK, misunderstanding. I suppose I have been a bit moody lately, and you're right too, wrong time of the month. Friends?'

'Friends.'

'No spanking though, just good old-fashioned sex.'

I lay back, opening my arms for him, and my thighs. For a moment he looked doubtful, but no man resists that offer, not from me. As he mounted me and the firm bulge of his cock pressed between my legs I thought of Chrissy, briefly. She didn't matter. For all her sluttish behaviour I was still better than her in every way. He'd stay with me, because whatever it meant sacrificing, I was worth it.

Salt spray splashed into my face as the *Harold Jones* dug her bows into the water. The sails snapped above me as I scurried across the deck and we were on a new tack, running directly into the mouth of the Deben. A grey flurry of rain whipped aside and I could see the land clearly, a bleak beach, a squat red tower, trees and reeds lashing back and forth in the wind. I shut my eyes as I swung myself into position, not daring to look at the foaming green sea beneath me, or anything else, only to open them abruptly as the yacht lurched down into another trough.

I had never been so scared in my life. All day we'd moved up the coast through ever worsening weather, sometimes out of sight of land completely. I was wet, soaked through with rain and spray and sweat. All I'd been able to do was cling on for dear life and try to do as I was told, certain that all three of them were mad and that we were all going to drown.

We hadn't, and as the water became abruptly calmer in the shelter of the estuary, I realised we'd made it. Relief flooded through me, along with the desire for a hot bath and a very, very large drink. Following Pippa's example I pulled myself in. She pushed her hood back, grinning at me.

'That was lively.'

I managed a weak smile. Her face was white, with strands of hair plastered to her forehead and drops of water running down her cheeks. I knew I looked much the same, and that she would feel the same: soggy, hot and aching. How she could be so cheerful was beyond me, and if I felt a little triumph, I was sure it was only because I'd survived.

'Get some coffee going while we tie up.'

It was an order, something I was getting used to. Mainly it had been Malcolm, but both the girls had given me a fair share of instructions. I tried to follow all of them, but for once I was actually keen to do it.

I went below, waiting until we had moved further into shelter before starting the coffee. By the time it was ready we were tied to a huge orange buoy at the centre of the channel and they already had the inflatable dinghy in the water. It was still choppy, but nothing after what we'd been through, and I found I could drink my coffee with just one hand clutching at a rail. Malcolm joined us, still managing to look authoritative despite being soaked. I thought he was going to comment on my ineptitude, and my stomach began to flutter at the thought of the possible consequences. What he said came as a complete surprise.

'Well done, Christina!'

Pippa and Tilly immediately echoed his praise, all three of them obviously trying to be nice to me because I looked so miserable. Malcolm went on.

'We'll make an able seaman of you yet, my girl. You weren't even sick in the end, were you?'

'Well . . . no . . . but I was hopeless.'

'Wet your knickers?'

'No!'

'Then you did better than Tilly her first time out in weather.'

'Daddy!'

Tilly had gone scarlet. Pippa laughed. Suddenly I felt a great deal better.

We went ashore, to a hut run by a club of which they were members. A hot shower and a change of clothes had me feeling human again, even a little proud of myself. After all, I had done it. I hadn't been sick and I hadn't wet myself, which would have been mortifying. Tilly obviously had once, so I wasn't so very useless after all, which was what she'd called me when I'd dropped a rope at a crucial moment.

There was plenty of time before dinner, so I tried Michael again, hoping he'd be on his way, or at least that he would answer. His phone was still off, so I accepted a large gin and tonic from Malcolm and went to sit with them in the club house, hoping he'd turn up.

The place was quite crowded, with a hum of background conversation, all of it about boats, the sea, the weather and so on, including ours. I was grateful, as while there hadn't been much time to think about the prospect of getting my bottom smacked, I still hadn't managed to come to terms with my feelings. Soon I'd forgotten all about it, and was listening to Pippa explaining what some of the flags and markers we'd seen meant. So when Malcolm rapped his knuckles on the table, I thought he just wanted to tell us what we'd be doing tomorrow. Both Tilly and Pippa immediately went silent. He spoke.

'Court then.'

Tilly gave an uneasy glance to the table nearest us. There was a mixed group, all young, all looking very serious as one demonstrated something with a set of complicated gestures and a salt pot. Nobody was paying any attention to us. From Tilly's expression it didn't take much working out what 'court' involved. Malcolm went on.

'Not a bad day on the whole. No technical errors to speak of. Still, you, Tilly, my girl, need to mind your language. One for you there, I'm afraid.'

She hung her head.

'Yes, Daddy.'

My stomach was beginning to flutter. If she could be punished for bad language, there had to be a dozen things he could pick me up on. It was coming, and I didn't know if I had the courage to refuse, or if I wanted to. He went on.

'A little insubordination on your part, Pippa, my dear...'

'No! That's not fair! I –'

She had blurted it out, then stopped suddenly, her expression changing to utter consternation. He laughed.

'But not enough to warrant any action, as I was about to say. Answering me back on the other hand, well...'

Her face had set in a sulky pout. He chuckled and took a swallow of his drink. I was having to squeeze my thighs together to prevent an accident as he turned to me.

'As I said before, Chrissy, you did well, damn well for a greenhorn. So nothing for you, unless you should do something foolish?'

It was a question, one posed to the sound of indignant gasps from both girls. Both of them were looking at me in outrage. I shrugged my shoulders, not at all sure what to do. Malcolm gave a small cluck of disappointment.

'Oh, well, fair enough then. If that's your game. So then, another stiffener, a leisurely dinner at the Ferryboat and back on board for the tailwork. Cheers.'

He raised his glass, to swallow the contents in one. So did Pippa. Tilly's glass was already empty. They were going to get spanked. I wasn't. I'd got away with it.

I still felt some of the apprehension that showed in their faces. They might both enjoy it, but they were certainly scared, for real, and I began to understand how it worked. It was a pleasure they could only achieve by surrender, to both pain and indignity, so for all that pleasure, their feelings were very real. I shared them too, for all that it wasn't going to happen to me immediately. I was still under threat, and the thought of watching, and knowing that I might well soon be getting the same treatment, was enough to have me squirming uncomfortably in my chair. My nipples were hard too, which was embarrassingly obvious. They were both the same, the bumps showing despite the thick woollen guernseys they were wearing.

Malcolm went to refresh our drinks, leaving the three of us in a nervous silence. Finally Pippa spoke, to me.

'You should have got it.'

'Why?'

'A hundred things, or a trick like the one he just pulled on me. Maybe he's saving you for Michael.'

Immediately there was a huge lump in my throat and my stomach was fluttering crazily.

'Saving me for Michael?'

I knew exactly what she meant, but I just wanted to hear the words again, and savour the delicious trepidation they had brought. Pippa went on.

'I'm surprised he's not here, as it goes, but he'll come, and then you'll suddenly find that there's a long list of errors to atone for.'

'Oh, God!'

Pippa laughed. Tilly just looked sulky.

'At least she won't be getting the rope's end. I'd forgotten it was my tenth.'

'Nonsense, you knew perfectly well! We get the rope's end every tenth offence, Chrissy.'

'Does that hurt more?'

Tilly shook her head as if in despair. Pippa glanced at the next table to check that nobody was listening in, then leaned across to me.

'Yes. It stings like anything, much worse than his hand. There's a handle too, and can you guess where that goes when he's finished?'

'No!'

She nodded. Tilly made a distressed face. I was already imagining how she'd look with the handle up her pussy and the piece of rope dangling down behind her. My own sex twitched in anticipation as I thought of how it would feel to have Michael do it to me, and in front of an audience. It was more than I could bear, but the urge to touch myself had suddenly become painfully strong.

Malcolm returned with the drinks and the conversation changed. He too was wondering where Michael had got to, but pointed out that by the next evening we'd reach Great Yarmouth. That was only a few miles from the cottage by land, although it needed the best part of a day to get there by water. Michael was sure to meet us there, or at the very least I could take a taxi over and find out what was wrong.

I was still hoping Michael would come as we walked across to the pub for dinner. I was feeling as horny as I ever had, and guilty, because it was in anticipation of watching the two girls get their spankings. I was going to need sex though, with a man, and it was both embarrassing and frustrating to think of giving in to the solitary pleasures of my finger after the punishment.

Dinner passed with the girls in a state of rising anticipation, silent and fidgeting most of the time, and drinking the strong red wine Malcolm had ordered as if they were in some sort of competition. I wasn't much better, and only Malcolm did any justice to his food.

Afterwards, we trooped down to the inflatable. Both Pippa and Tilly were more than a little drunk, and it was left to Malcolm to handle the dinghy. We had to help them aboard as well, with him pulling and me underneath to push. Normally touching other girls' bottoms like that wouldn't bother me at all. When I was about to see them spanked it was a very different matter, sending a shock right through me as my hands closed on the soft, rounded flesh.

That left me more guilty than ever as Malcolm

helped me aboard, and hornier too, to the extent that I was beginning to wonder about being able to control my own feelings. Again I wished Michael was there to take charge of me, more fervently than ever.

The three of us were sent below decks as Malcolm dealt with the inflatable. Pippa and Tilly went to sit on a bunk, so close their hips and shoulders were touching. Tilly was biting her lip, Pippa fidgeting with her fingers in her lap. Neither looked as if she was looking forward to what was coming to her. I felt more guilty than ever.

'Are you OK, really OK?'

Tilly nodded, a sudden movement of her chin, no more. Pippa looked at me in surprise.

'We're going to be spanked, Chrissy.'

'I know ... I thought ... it's just ... just that you seem so scared.'

She was looking at me as if I was an idiot. Tilly spoke, her voice quick and nervous.

'She doesn't understand. She wants it, but she hasn't had it.'

Pippa's mouth came open to speak, but shut quickly as her eyes flicked to the companionway. Malcolm's boots appeared, then the rest of him. Both girls hung their heads. He spoke, cheerfully.

'Better be about it, then, no sense in waiting. Now then, Tilly, tenth offence. That means the rope's end, as you know.'

Tilly nodded meekly. Malcolm went to a locker, to draw out an elaborate piece of ropework all too obviously designed for smacking girls' bottoms. It looked like a ping-pong bat in shape, with a wooden handle and a broad, flat business end made of plaited rope, only a little longer, and a lot thicker. It also looked like it would hurt like anything across my bottom. Pippa hadn't been joking either. The handle was polished smooth and just the right shape for poking into places it shouldn't go. Malcolm smacked it on his hand.

'Side by side, I think. Always makes for a pretty view, eh Chrissy?'

I could only nod dumbly. Pippa and Tilly stood slowly and turned around, taking each other's hands as they presented Malcolm and me with the seats of their jeans. Both had their heads hung down, and I could see the trembling in the hands where their fingers were locked tight together. Malcolm chuckled and reached down to stroke his wife's bottom, running a hand over the gentle curve of one cheek. I swallowed hard, unable to pull my eyes away from the twin denim-clad behinds. Malcolm gave an order.

'Buttons undone.'

Both of them responded immediately, their hands going to the front of their jeans to pop open the buttons.

'Flies down.'

I caught the faint purr as both girls eased their zips open.

'Half-mast!'

The girls' hands came back, in a unison that looked alarmingly practised. Thumbs went into waistbands, and pushed. Down came their jeans, revealing their knickers, Pippa's white with blue polka dots, Tilly's patterned with little red flowers. Both bent a little, easing their jeans to the level of their knees, and briefly hinting at the shape of their pussies beneath their gussets.

'Kneel.'

They went down – Pippa immediately, Tilly hesitating for a second before joining her sister on her knees. Both bent forward across the bunk, their hair hanging down around their faces, their hands clasped in front of them as if in prayer. Pippa was shaking hard, her neat little bottom quivering, while one of the muscles in Tilly's thighs had begun to twitch.

'Bottoms up, no crouching! Knees apart.'

They obeyed, both slowly lifting their bottoms and setting their knees open. Now I could see the shapes of their pussies clearly, while their cheeks were all too obviously open beneath their knickers. I imagined how they'd feel, wondering if those last, precious scraps of cloth would be removed to expose them completely. I knew the answer. Even I wasn't that naive.

Malcolm chuckled, and reached down for Pippa, only not for her knickers but for her guernsey sweater. It came up, her top with it, to show off her bra, then her bare tits as he tweaked the cups up. She let out a little sob, which I could well appreciate was at the unnecessary indignity of having her breasts exposed when it was her bottom that needed attending to.

Tilly had been watching from the corner of her eye, and stiffened as his hands went to the hem of her own guernsey. Up it went, and out came her tits, leaving her in the same humiliating semi-nudity as her sister. There was more to come, and Malcolm didn't delay, taking a firm grip on the waistband of Tilly's knickers and sliding them casually down off her bottom. Again he did it as much to expose her as to prepare her for punishment, inverting them around her thighs, low enough to make sure that she was left without a single scrap of modesty.

He gave her bottom a pat, just enough to make her cheeks quiver. I heard Pippa catch her breath as he moved to her. He took hold of her knickers and down they came, her bottom unceremoniously stripped bare, to leave her in the same rude pose as her sister. Malcolm stood up, rubbing his hands in satisfaction.

'As I said, damn pretty view.'

It wasn't ... it was ... I didn't know. What I did know was that it was an extraordinarily rude view. Everything showed, every square inch of their cheeks, every little pink fold of their pussies, every tiny crease of their bumholes. I hung my head, unable to look, and unable to stop thinking of how I'd be showing just as much in the same position. Malcolm spoke again as he picked up the rope's end.

'I always say you can tell they're sisters.'

He laughed. I blushed. I had to look again. I couldn't stop myself. It was true. From the rear they looked identical, with their trim little bottoms and neat pussies. The only real difference was that while Pippa had shaved her pubic hair into a neat triangle, Tilly's was thick and bushy. Both were quite obviously aroused. So was I.

Malcolm seemed in no hurry, admiring the two bare bottoms as he toyed with the rope's end. Pippa had begun to whimper in anticipation, while Tilly's bumhole was twitching as well as her leg. I didn't know whether to laugh at their discomfort or burst into tears of sympathy, but I was determined not to do what my body was telling me to – masturbate as I watched them being punished. Pippa broke the silence.

'Please, just do it!'

'With pleasure, my dear,' Malcolm answered, but it was Tilly's bottom he smacked, bringing the rope's end hard down across her cheeks.

She squealed and bucked, but returned quickly to the open, rude position as a wide red blotch rose up on her bottom. Malcolm turned to me.

'Would you care to do Pippa?'

'To do her? To ... to spank her?'

'Yes.'

'I ... I don't know ... if I could. I ... I thought the men did the spanking?'

'Oh, not necessarily. Pippa rather likes it from another girl. Don't you, my dear?'

Pippa gave a barely perceptible nod and hung her head lower still. Malcolm spoke again.

'Would you like to be spanked by Chrissy, dear? You needn't answer. Just shake you head if you don't want it.'

Pippa's answer was a broken sob. Her head stayed absolutely still. Malcolm gestured towards her bottom in clear invitation. I just sat there, open-mouthed. I was shaking, and so, so turned on, but I couldn't do it, I just didn't have it in me to smack her bottom. I shook my head. Malcolm answered immediately.

'A purist, eh? I understand.'

He turned back to the girls, swinging the rope's end up, backhand, and bringing it down across Tilly's bottom again. She cried out as the flesh of her neat little cheeks bounced to the impact, and once again bucked up. He moved closer, placing one big hand in the small of her back to hold her in place. Another smack came in. Again she squealed, louder. Again her bottom bounced.

She was already pretty red, and as he began to lay in she got quickly redder, her bottom flushing to the tune of her cries and the fleshy smacks as the rope came down, over and over. I'd soon lost count and she'd soon lost control, kicking her feet and wiggling her bottom in her distress, sobbing and gasping too, and clutching at the surface of the bunk.

For all her reaction she was responding, her pussy puffy and moist, blatantly ready for entry. I felt how she looked, and I was wishing more than ever that Michael was there, to put me beside the girls, spank me until my bum was the same rich red as Tilly's and take me into my sleeping cabin for a good hard fucking.

Her bottom was purple and blotchy by the time he finished with her, and I could see she'd have bruises in the morning. I knew what was coming, or thought I did, and sneaked a hand down between my thighs, just to touch myself lightly through my jeans as the handle went up. She was eager, her bottom lifted and her knees wide, and I could see every detail as he turned the rope's end in his hand, then pushed the handle to her moist hole and slid it well up.

I thought he'd leave her like that, to make her hold the utterly humiliating pose while Pippa was spanked. Instead he fed the handle in and out a few times, then pulled it free. It was sticky with her juice, and I found myself filled with a guilty hope that he would make her suck it. What he did was worse.

My mouth came wide in shock as the tip of the handle was put back to her body, only not to her pussy, but to her bumhole. She gave a muted sob and buried her face in her hands, but she stayed down, her bottom offered meekly for penetration. I actually saw her ring open, stretching wide around the thick wooden handle until she was open enough to take it. It slipped in, and all of it, right to the hilt.

Then he left her, with the rope's end hanging out of her well-smacked bottom like an obscene caricature of a beaver's tail, her bottom hole a taut ring of glistening flesh around the intruding handle. It was only then I realised that I'd been rubbing myself through my jeans. A great wash of guilt came over me at the idea of becoming aroused over her appalling humiliation, only to die as she lifted her head, smiled and waggled her bottom to make the rope paddle flap against her thighs. Malcolm chided her.

'Behave yourself.'

Tilly hid her face again. Malcolm had already come behind Pippa, and was feeling her bottom very intimately with his fingers – not just on her cheeks, but down between. For a moment he was actually touching her anus, tickling to make the little hole twitch and open, before he lifted his hand to plant a heavy smack across both her cheeks.

The spanking began, firm, heavy smacks laid across Pippa's bottom, to make her cheeks dance and set her gasping and squealing. It was still hard to control my feelings, to accept that her pain and apparent distress hid so much pleasure. I knew it did, but what finally conquered my inhibitions was sheer lust. It was all too rude, too deliciously improper, to resist. It was funny too, which made it easier. Just as Tilly had said, there was a pig-like quality to Pippa's squeals. It was hard not to laugh. So I let my hand slip back between my thighs and settled down to enjoy the sight of another woman given a bare bottom spanking.

Malcolm was so stern, so thorough, bringing the smacks down to make her bottom quiver and part, to show off the rudest details between her cheeks. He didn't need to show off her pussy, every single tiny fold was already on show, with her hole tensing and squeezing as her excitement rose. How Malcolm kept his cock in his trousers was beyond me, with his beautiful wife ripe and ready in front of him. He did, spanking and spanking, harder and harder, until at last she was responding fully, her red bottom lifted, her knees set wide in unashamed bliss.

I was rubbing myself, sure none of them were paying the slightest attention, and I was going to come too. My head was full of fantasies, of Michael arriving and making me get down beside them, of Malcolm demanding his cock be sucked before he fucked Pippa, even of the three of them, just taking me and using me ...

Suddenly it was too much. As Malcolm finished Pippa off with a crescendo of furious slaps to her crimson bottom, I was scrambling for my compartment. I was so confused, and I knew I was going to do something unspeakable if I didn't get out of there. I wanted to suck him, even to kiss the girls' burning bottoms or bury my face in Tilly's wet, ready sex as Pippa was fucked.

Malcolm just chuckled as I ran, but even as I pulled the dividing door to, I heard the rasp of his zip. His cock was out, he was going to fuck Pippa, and he would be just feet away. I sat on my bunk, shaking my head in my confusion and lust. Then I was doing it, pulling at the button of my jeans, desperate to get at myself. My fly came open, my jeans came down, my hand went into my panties. I shut my eyes as I found the warm, welcoming groove of my pussy and the hot, eager bud of my clitty.

I was masturbating, my head a whirl of rude images, of smacked female bottoms, of girlish cries, of cocks made erect by a woman's exposure and punishment. I wanted Michael desperately, to spank me until I howled and then fuck me on my knees. I wanted him to just take me, use me, with the others watching, with my pussy wide in front of them. I wanted the paddle too, and to know the awful sensation of having my bumhole stretched on the handle as it was pushed into me by the man who had punished me.

It barely registered when the door clicked. I knew

Tilly had come in, vaguely, but after what I'd seen, I didn't care how she saw me. It was better actually, adding to my fantasy of having all control taken away from me, so that I was in such a state I'd masturbate in front of another woman. Even when I felt her hands on my knickers there was just a final jolt of shame and then they were coming down. A moment more and they'd been eased off my legs, my thighs had come apart and she had buried her face in my pussy.

10

Michael was cooking bacon. It was barely eight o'clock in the morning, and Michael was cooking bacon. The man was inhuman. For the last twenty-four hours we had been having almost non-stop sex. We had fucked in every room of the house, just about. He'd even caught me on the loo and had me bent across the seat. We'd fucked in the garden too, despite the cool, damp weather, me with my skirt turned up and gripping my ankles as he pushed into me from behind. He'd buggered me too, only once, and that on my side on the bed to make it as easy as possible, but it had still been an incredibly strong experience. Never once had he lost his dirty, boyish enthusiasm for my body, or his desire to make me come. The last fuck had been sometime around four o'clock, maybe later, and he was already up, cooking bacon.

I lay staring at the ceiling, trying to untangle my emotions from what I knew I should be doing. Michael was so raw, so masculine, so animal. He made me come like no other man. He made me want sex like no other man. He also controlled me, took more than I really wanted to give without even a trace of guilt, and wanted more still. He hadn't mentioned spanking again, but I could tell he wanted it, from the way he always preferred me bottom up, or in positions that flaunted my rear view. I was sure that there would be other, dirtier things he wanted too. I prefer men to be just a little inhibited so that I can lead. Michael was more than just uninhibited, he was dirty.

His footsteps sounded on the stairs. I composed myself, sitting up with the sheet drawn a little way up to cover most of my breasts but not all. A long yawn dispelled a little of my sleepiness and I managed a smile as he pushed open the door with a foot. He was carrying a tray.

'Breakfast in bed.'

He wasn't joking. The tray contained a plate of bacon, eggs, mushrooms and fried tomatoes. There was toast too, a whole rack full, butter, marmalade, coffee and orange juice. Breakfast for me consists of a cup of black coffee, drunk slowly, maybe toast. He put it on my lap and strode across to the window. Brilliant sunshine streamed into the room as he threw open the curtains. I closed my eyes, my vision dancing in red, yellow and green blotches.

'What a glorious day! I was thinking we could put the sail up on the dinghy and take her down to Yarmouth to meet the *Harold Jones*. It's only twenty-three miles. Lunch on the way, maybe a quick stop among the reeds, eh?'

I managed to open my eyes. Outside the window fleecy clouds were moving across a bright blue sky. I thought of the discomfort of being fucked in the rowing boat, and imagined being caught again.

'It'll probably rain again.'

'Nonsense! I've been watching the forecast. The front we had yesterday is well past, and it looks like a good big area of high pressure will be settling down. Shame really, Daddy won't be too pleased if there's no decent sailing.'

'Won't we get stuck then? You'll have to row back.'

'Oh, I can manage. It'll be a good chance for you to learn too.'

I moved in the bed, picking up a fork to prod at the mound of food he'd made me. My body was stiff, every muscle aching, my sex sore, my bottom hole sore. I was not going rowing. I was not being fucked in the bottom of the dinghy, and I was not being fucked up the bottom in the dinghy.

'I'd rather the beach.'

'The beach? Well...'

'It is our last day properly on our own.'

'Ah, I see.'

'How about that place you said was really lonely?'

'Horsey? Well, yes, back in the dunes...'

He trailed off, smiling. I could see exactly what was going through his dirty little mind, me, naked among the sand dunes, bottom up, with his cock where nature had not intended it to be put. Well, it was better than in the boat. He went on.

'Sounds good. We'll take a picnic then, and drive down to Yarmouth afterwards. The *Harold Jones*'ll probably have her spinnaker up, so we'll spot her easily. I'll nip up to the village then, while you get ready.'

He went, leaving me slightly relieved, slightly disappointed that he hadn't wanted his cock attended to, at least sucked in return for the breakfast. As I listened to his boots on the gravel outside I turned my attention to the coffee and wondered if he'd notice if I simply tipped the rest into the kitchen bin.

I awoke to the memory of letting Tilly lick my pussy. It was not my first embarrassing morning after, not by a long chalk. Several times before I'd got drunk and horny and ended up in bed with someone I really hadn't wanted beforehand. There was a difference though; this time it was another girl.

My embarrassment rose as the memory flooded back with full force. I'd been masturbating. She'd come in, just pulled off my knickers and gone down on me before I'd had a chance to protest. Once she'd been licking it had been too good to resist. She made me come. Worse, she'd rolled me on to the bunk and gone head to tail, sticking her hot bottom in my face. I'd licked and so had she, and as she'd brought me up to a second orgasm, I'd felt her well-smacked bottom. I'd fingered her too. I'd even tickled her bumhole.

She'd been as drunk and as horny as me, so at least we had that as an excuse, and I wouldn't have to explain. There would be silence, though – that awful, guilt-ridden silence when your throat is so full of unspoken words that you feel you're going to choke . . .

'Morning, Chrissy, rise and shine. Get this down you.'

I looked up. She was standing by me, holding out a glass of orange juice. I took it, struggling for something to say, some way of excusing myself. She went talking on as she began to bustle about the cabin.

'The wind's dropped to three and swung round to the south. That makes for an easy run up the coast, and we're going to put the spinnaker up. Come on, girl, Malcolm and Pippa have already been ashore, and you don't want to be late on deck, do you?'

I was face down, and she fetched me a resounding and completely unexpected slap on my bottom, making me squeak and spill my juice. Then she just left.

It was not what I had expected, and I found myself wondering if she didn't remember, or simply didn't care. She'd been drunk, but not that drunk, so it seemed likely that she genuinely felt a bout of drunken lesbian sex was nothing to make a fuss over. Maybe it wasn't, for her. Maybe she did it all the time. I didn't, and if her attitude was going to make it easier to be with her all day, I was still feeling fragile and more than a little shocked, by her and by myself.

The smack, and the tingling sensation it left, also reminded me of what might happen if I didn't behave myself. I had wanted it the night before, desperately. Now the idea was scary. So I got ready as quickly as I could and joined the others on deck in time to help manoeuvre the *Harold Jones* out of the shelter of the Deben and to sea.

Michael was right. It was lonely. Standing on top of the dunes I could see for miles in every direction, sea to the east, flat land and trees to the west, dunes to north and south. Not a single other human being was visible, except Michael. We'd even had to leave the car in the village and walk the last half-mile or so.

I was feeling a lot better, and even looking forward to the prospect of sex among the dunes, so long as we could find somewhere absolutely safe and keep on the rug. Michael was obviously thinking along the same lines, some way ahead with all our gear as he searched. For a moment he disappeared from view. His arm appeared, beckoning.

It was perfect, a sandy hollow among the dunes, sheltered from the wind and completely hidden from view. It felt secure, like our glade in the woods. Michael obviously thought so, because as he began to undress he didn't even hesitate, but went all the way, nude. I watched, responding as always to his tightly muscled body and wishing he wasn't quite such a pig. He burrowed in one of the bags to pull out a tube of sun-tan cream.

'Do you want some?'

That was more like it. That was the way men should behave on the beach, offering to rub in sun-tan cream. The idea of him doing it naked was more appealing still.

'Sure, hang on.'

I began to undress, shrugging off my top and culottes. My bra followed, and I didn't even consider my bikini top. I was going to put the bottoms on and so keep a little dignity while he was nude, but I knew he'd just pull them off anyway. So off came my panties and I was bare in the sun, again.

As I lay down on the rug I was trying to tell myself once again that surrender was the sensible course of action, and that I could at least enjoy the illusion of being in charge while I was massaged. My body wanted to give in, my dignity abandoned as I was creamed in the nude, then soundly fucked with him on top of me and his cock wherever he chose to put it. That was what was going to happen, what I needed to happen, but it was very hard to deny that it was what I wanted to happen too.

He came to kneel beside me and I lay back, closing my eyes with my hands behind my head. Cool sun-tan cream touched between my breasts, then his fingers, spreading it out, but not over them, down on to my tummy and up across my shoulders. He began to massage, as I'd been sure he would, kneading gently with his fingertips as they moved up to my neck and down again.

On the next stroke he took my breasts in his hands,

smoothing the cream over them before going lower. My nipples had come out at that one touch, and I expected him to go back and begin to feel me for his own satisfaction. He didn't, but moved lower still, sliding his hands over my tummy, and lower still, to my upper thighs. For one moment he was touching the mound of my sex, but only that.

Fresh cream was applied to my legs and rubbed in with long firm strokes, covering every inch. Already the urge to open my thighs to him was rising, but I held back, not wanting to hurry the moment when for once he was doing things my way. He didn't hurry either, moving back up my body and massaging every inch of my flesh as he went, to slowly ease away the dull aches left by our exertions.

Had he wanted, he could have mounted me, and from the occasional brush against my skin I knew his cock was growing hard. He never touched it, just working on me until I was more than ready, with my nipples straining to attention and a trickle of warm fluid running down between the cheeks of my bottom. Even when he rolled me gently on to my front he didn't take advantage, despite my thighs coming a little open in instinctive welcome. He did go to kneel between my legs though, keeping me aware of his cock as he oiled my back with the same luxurious thoroughness.

By the time he got to my legs they were wide, and I no longer cared for anything except the pleasure he was bringing me. It was so nice, and when he finally reached my bottom I was desperate for his cock. He made me wait, stroking and squeezing my cheeks, letting his thumbs loiter between them and on the rear of my sex until I wanted to scream to be fucked. He went on, slow and even, his hands smoothing cream over my cheeks and between them, just brushing my bottom hole, just teasing my sex, until I had begun to lift myself up for entry, and beg. A moment later his rock-hard shaft had been laid between my cheeks.

I bit my lip, thinking he was going to bugger me, only for him to slide the head of his cock down between my cheeks, push, and ease himself up into me. He came on top of me, a fair bit of his weight settling on to my bottom, to press me down on to the rug, and we were fucking.

It felt glorious, and I knew he'd take his time, because he always did. So I relaxed, or as much as I could with his big cock sliding in and out of me, and let my mind drift. I imagined him as I wanted him, masculine yet obedient, virile yet able to take my lead, answering my every need at command. In a while he would take his cock out and rub me to ecstasy, to order, then sit back, big, hard cock in hand, waiting for my word. I'd make him suffer, humiliate him. I'd dress, and keep him naked all afternoon, serving me. I'd let him come, but it would be over the sight of me reclining in some elegant pose, in my bikini, not showing too much. When he came I'd make him eat the sperm and laugh to watch, just to punish the arrogant pig.

My fantasy snapped. I couldn't see it, not Michael. When he got close he'd come to me, to push his cock into my mouth, or to have me hold my breasts together to make a slide for it, or roll me over and poke it up my bottom. Whatever it was, it would be something dirty, something undignified, and I'd come, as I always did, as I would now if ...

He did it, as if reading my mind. Just as I was trying to turn my fantasy back to something with me in charge, he took his cock and pushed it right to my sex.

I heard my own cry as the firm, fleshy head pressed to my clitoris, halfway between despair and ecstasy, and I was doing it, thinking of his cock, up my bottom, that dirtiest, most utterly, unspeakably undignified of acts. He'd do it, too, I knew, in the open, in the bright sunlight, with me naked, my bottom stuck high for entry, behaving like a wanton, dirty little slut.

I was close to coming, and I was crying out for it, babbling obscenities into the rug as my hand pushed in under my tummy. Michael laughed, the sound so arrogant, so certain, that it drew sobs from my throat even as my fingers found my clitoris. Then I was masturbating, rubbing myself in dirty abandon as his cock found my oily bottom hole and pushed. I was wet with my own juice and with sun-tan cream, and eager too. Up he went, in slow, even pushes as I grunted and gasped beneath him, bringing myself closer and closer to orgasm as inch after inch of cock slid up my behind.

As his balls touched my fingers I knew he was all the way in, and that awful, desperately dirty piece of knowledge took me over the edge, making me scream as I came on his cock, my whole body focused on him, on what he was doing to me. He was pumping too, hard, then hard enough to hurt, even as the very peak of my climax hit me and I screamed out with all the power of my lungs.

He stopped suddenly, and I knew he had come in me even as I came myself. I sank down, sobbing and panting in reaction, feeling spent and guilty, but so, so gratified. I wanted a cuddle, to be soothed, held tight after my utter submission, to reassure me, all my bad thoughts gone. He obliged, kissing my neck as he squeezed me, only to stop abruptly and begin to ease his cock from inside me. I glanced around, half expecting to find some leering pervert staring at me from among the dune grasses. There was nobody there.

'What's the matter?'

'Well, you were a little noisy. Gay guys do cruise here sometimes, and . . .'

'What, for sex? Here? Ow!'

I'd squeaked because he'd pulled his cock out, and it had hurt a lot more than it had going in. I rolled, grabbed for my bag and began to dig for my bikini.

'You said it was lonely here. You might have warned me!'

'It is lonely, that's why they come here. It's not that they'd mind, more that you would, seeing how you are.'

I didn't answer him, as I was pulling up my bikini pants, still on my back. My top followed and I immediately felt a great deal more secure. Only then did it really sink in what he had said.

'How do you mean: how I am?'

He didn't answer for a long while. He looked content. He hadn't bothered to dress, or even cover himself. His cock was slowly deflating in his lap. Finally he spoke.

'Well, you know, a little repressed, maybe.'

'Repressed! I am not repressed! How can you say that, after what we've just done?'

'Don't be upset. When I say repressed, I don't mean repressed by the general standards of society. I mean repressed in broader terms.'

'What is that supposed to mean?'

'Oh, just that you always consider propriety, what other people will think. Now that's entirely fair, when it might influence your career or something, but you do it anyway, because you believe you should. That's what I mean by repressed. Like being seen naked, or caught having sex, even when people don't mind.'

'What are you talking about? Of course I mind if someone sees me naked, let alone having sex! That's just the way people behave! It's natural!'

'You don't mind people seeing you topless on a beach?'

'No, of course not, in the right place, with the right crowd...'

'But you won't go nude?'

'No! Well, not unless I'm sure I won't be seen, I suppose.'

'Did you know the first woman to wear a bikini in the UK was arrested? It was on Hampstead Heath.'

'That's outrageous!'

'And if she'd been in the nude?'

'It would have been her own silly fault, of course.'

He laughed.

'Oh, come on, Valentina, your choices aren't "natural" at all, they're just what's acceptable to modern society. You're not really telling me that there's any objective difference between showing your breasts and showing your bottom, are you?'

'Of course there is!'

He laughed again, closed his eyes and lay back. I knew he was wrong, but I was too cross to frame my argument properly. He was just so smug! After a while he spoke again.

'You'd wear a thong bikini, wouldn't you?'

'Of course, why not?'

'And you'd go nude, on a nudist beach.'

'Yes. I've got nothing to be ashamed of ... OK, fair enough, I like to fit in. Who doesn't?'

Again he didn't answer immediately, but lay back in the sand, his hands behind his head. He was watching me, his face set in a light smile just oozing condescension. I cursed him mentally, wishing he was just a bit less attractive and just a bit less full of himself. I took a deep breath, and spoke.

'No, maybe you're right. Maybe I do need to be brought out of my shell a little. I suppose I'm just too used to having to be in control all the time, having to be careful. After all, it's easy for you, but I have to be strong, at work especially. I just can't afford to let myself go. No man has ever made me feel protected enough either, until now.'

He reached out, to tousle my hair. I sighed and pushed against his hand. It had to be enough. If he wanted Chrissy, I would eat my hat.

The *Harold Jones* moved slowly towards the mouth of the Yare. Pippa and Tilly were stowing the great red spinnaker, which had driven us before the wind for hours. It had been a very different experience from the day before, a lot drier for one thing, and less terrifying. I'd actually enjoyed it most of the time, and I felt I'd done well, or at least as well as could be expected. Now I had been left to my own devices, standing near the bows to watch the shore.

My memories of Great Yarmouth came from one week's holiday as an eight year old, but I still recognised the pier and the block of amusement arcades and civic gardens where I'd taken my first ever pony ride. I'd never seen the docks though, and it was hard to pick details out of the line of buildings south of the bustling centre. Many seemed to be abandoned, grey concrete sheds and fading colours broken by the green of vegetation. There were plenty of cars visible, right up to within yards of the river mouth, but we were too far out to identify Michael's black Rover. I watched anyway, thinking how surprised he would be to see me, and how pleased. With luck we would be able to get away, for a night and a day of passion at the cottage while the others brought the yacht around to the Broad.

The motion of the yacht changed abruptly, a low vibration signalling the starting of the engine. Behind me the girls continued to work, stowing and furling the sails with brisk efficiency, until at last every one was done and we were moving under power alone. Both of them went back to join Malcolm and I followed at a gesture. In the cockpit, Tilly spoke, timid, yet expectant.

'What about court? The marina is sure to be crowded.'

'We shall see. I had considered taking a buoy on Breydon Water, which is lonely enough for your squeals not to matter. Still, as it goes, the three of you have been rather well behaved . . .'

Tilly's expression changed abruptly and her mouth came open, only to shut again at a single glance from Malcolm.

'Sorry.'

'I should think so too, young lady. Judge's decision is final.'

Pippa spoke, boldly, but with a distinct tremor in her voice.

'Might I just say, sir, that I think you're being a bit unfair. I know Chrissy's new, but she has made plenty of mistakes, and –'

Malcolm interrupted.

'And she is Michael's girlfriend, so we will put the matter to him, and one more word from you, young lady, and I'll have him do you in front of her. How would that be?'

Pippa went abruptly scarlet, but pursed her mouth

in a dissatisfied silence. Obviously they both wanted me spanked, and it was actually quite funny, when they'd clearly expected it to happen. Then again, it was going to happen, and if the implication that Michael had laid some sort of claim to me since our night of passion was wonderful news, then the idea of him spanking me in front of the others had my stomach fluttering.

Neither of them dared to protest any more, and the subject was dropped as we moved slowly into the river mouth and along a wide channel lined with ships. There were plenty of other craft around too, and we had to be careful, requiring everyone's attention until we had actually tied up. Malcolm went ashore to see the harbourmaster and I went back to scanning for Michael's car, until Tilly called me below. They were both there, and as I came in, Tilly closed the cabin door behind me. Pippa had a truly evil grin on her face, and my heart gave a little jump. Tilly spoke.

'Court time. Chrissy is sentenced to a spanking for being a sneaky brat.'

'You can't do that! Only Malcolm can do that!'

'Oh, yes we can.'

Pippa moved to a locker, to pull out two of the folding chairs we sat on for breakfast. I watched, my apprehension rising as she placed them facing each other, a foot or so apart. Tilly turned to me.

'Are you going to come over willingly, or do we have to make you?'

It was for real. They were going to spank me. I backed away, my hands out in front of me. Pippa's face broke into a wide grin. Tilly showed uncertainty, but not much. I started to babble.

'No, please, you two, don't! It's not fair! It's not funny! You can't!'

'Oh, yes we can.'

'No! Don't ... I beg ... think what Malcolm will do! He will ... he'll give you both the rope's end, bare ... he'll ... he'll ...'

'We know. It will be well worth it.'

They had closed in on me. I began to giggle. I couldn't stop myself, and I was lost. The slight uncertainty on Tilly's face vanished, to be replaced by a cruel grin. Pippa's hand darted out to catch me by my ear. It hurt, and I was squealing in protest as she dragged me forward. Tilly took my arm, helping guide me to them as they sat down on the chairs. I went over, still squeaking and still giggling, laid across their inter-locked knees, in spanking position for the first time in my life.

I couldn't have stopped them if I'd wanted to. My whole body seemed to have turned to jelly, and I just couldn't stop laughing, for all my very real apprehension. They took no notice, presumably used to girls who were about to be spanked getting into a state, and pushed me down so that I was forced to lift my bottom. They took my arms, one each, twisting my wrists tight up into the small of my back, and I was helpless.

It was all too easy to remember their pain as they'd been spanked, and as their hands groped under my tummy it really began to sink in. My trousers were coming down, my knickers too, probably, to leave me in the same rude, bare condition they'd been smacked in. I began to struggle, and to whimper, unable to find words for the huge lump in my throat. My button was popped, my zip opened. My jeans were down and my knickers were showing, making my bottom feel absolutely huge and utterly vulnerable. Tilly laughed and made a comment about the little yellow ducks on my knickers. Pippa gave me a smack across them and it had begun.

I felt a wave of relief as I realised I was to be allowed to keep at least a little of my modesty, presumably because it was girl spanking girl. Pippa gave me another smack, then Tilly, making my skin sting and tingle, then my relief turned to utter consternation as one of them hooked a thumb into the waistband of my knickers.

I heard my own forlorn squeal as the precious scrap of cotton was pulled away and I was bare, showing them everything, just as they had been made to show me. It was so strong, so rude, so arousing, and all I could do was sob as I was exposed completely, with my knickers taken right down to my knees. Tilly giggled. Pippa spoke.

'Here goes!'

Their hands landed on my bottom at the same instant, hard. I squealed in shock, taken aback by the sudden pain, far stronger than before. They just laughed and set to work, spanking me hard and fast. I went wild, squirming desperately on their laps, really fighting but only succeeding in making them laugh all the harder and spank me all the harder.

It hurt so much. I couldn't believe I'd wanted something so painful done to me, but I was completely unable to make myself say the words that would stop it. I struggled though, writhing under the slaps, kicking my legs out and tossing my head about, desperate to break free. It just went on, harder and harder, until at last I found my voice. I was begging immediately, the words spilling brokenly from my lips, incoherent pleas for mercy, for them to stop the awful punishment they were inflicting on me.

They held on tight, both of them, laughing wildly at me as they spanked my bottom, smack, smack, smack, totally indifferent to my frantic wriggling and ever more pathetic entreaties. It was awful, unbearable, but I had no choice, making my humiliation and self-pity rise up like a great bubble in my head, until I was sure I would burst into tears.

Then it began to change, the pain fading to warmth. Suddenly I didn't want to cry any more, and I did not want them to stop. It still hurt, but the pain had changed to a heavy, numb feeling, hot and tingling, rich and sensuous and so, so erotic. My pussy responded too, warm and ready. Tilly giggled and I realised they knew, and why they hadn't stopped, hadn't let me get up; cruel to be kind, but not the way Valentina understood it.

I began to stick my bottom up, and to purr, just soaking up what had been so unbearable just moments before. Still they spanked, in time, a cheek each, bringing me up and up, until I was begging again, not to end it, but for harder smacks. I got them, enough to have me gasping and pushing my arse higher still, eager for the lovely smacks, eager for entry too. As I realised I was going to come, Pippa spoke.

'Do her sweet spot, hard. I'll hold her.'

Immediately they had released my wrists. Pippa took me around the waist, firmly, but not to hold me down, to cuddle me. Tilly kept on spanking, right over my pussy, laying the smacks in with all her force. It just hit me, straight away, a great rush of pleasure, rising and bursting as she released a furious volley of spanks, setting my whole body quivering, each one seeming to go straight to my clit. I screamed out, coming, too far gone to care who heard or who saw, intent only on the glorious heat in my bottom and the ecstasy in my head.

Tilly went on spanking, keeping me there as I squirmed on their legs in my orgasm. Pippa took hold of my boobs, stroking them, even as the spanking stopped and Tilly's fingers burrowed into my sex. I just let them have me, exploring my body as I hovered on the very edge of orgasm, until Tilly's fingers found my clit and a second high hit me, long and tight.

At last I slumped across their knees, exhausted, dizzy, my bottom aflame. Tilly still had her fingers in me, Pippa was still fondling my breasts. I didn't care. I was theirs to do with as they pleased, in thanks for an experience more wonderful even than it had been in my imagination. Finally they stopped and Tilly spoke.

'You go, girl! What a dirty little bitch!'

There was no malice in it, none at all, only delight, and perhaps a little envy. I could only gasp out my true feelings in response.

'I ... I didn't realise ... I didn't know that could happen!'

Pippa answered.

'It doesn't, to most of us. You're lucky!'

I managed a weak smile as I stood up slowly. I was still on a high, and I wanted to be cuddled, and to talk about my wonderful experience, but most of all, to see my bottom. Both of them were giggling as I went to a mirror, to crane back and inspect my cheeks. I was very red, and my skin felt hot to the touch, also rough and strangely thick. It was a wonderful sensation, and it felt so good.

There was a bit of guilt because it was two women who'd done it to me and not a man, but that was minor. After all, it wasn't as if I'd had sex with them, not as such, it was just ... well, different. Still, I knew full well that if they'd demanded I lick their pussies I'd have been down on my knees in a moment. It was just how the spanking had made me feel, excited, rude yet uninhibited and eager to please.

Now I understood. Sex is always better with a rush of adrenalin; the thrill of a new partner, the fear of been seen outdoors. It was the same with spanking, only much, much stronger. It hurt, it hurt like anything, and the knowledge of the coming pain provided the adrenalin. Then the endorphins kicked in to bring on that warm, rosy glow that just made me want to spread my thighs for entry. There was the psychology too: the helplessness of being held down across a strong man's knees; the rudeness of having my bottom laid bare; the feeling of surrendering so absolutely. It all added up to an experience like no other. I was hooked.

It might have gone further, and I'd have certainly been willing, but they were worried Malcolm would come back and catch us, and urged me to pull my knickers and jeans up to hide the evidence. I did, even promising I wouldn't tell. At that moment I'd have promised anything, done anything. It was a great feeling, and made all the better because I knew that it would happen again soon, and that when it did, it would be Michael doing the spanking. My wonderful, firm, confident Michael.

I was so full of excitement I couldn't stop moving around, and after a while went up on deck for some fresh air. I saw it immediately, Michael's car, just backing into a space across the road from where we had moored. I could see him in it, and somebody else, which surprised me.

Then they got out. My jaw dropped. I saw blonde hair and realised he was with another woman. I saw her face and realised who it was – Valentina de Lacy. As they stepped around the car she took his hand, intimate, possessive, her face serene and smiling as they crossed the road. As I watched, my mind was trying to reject the evidence of what I was seeing, finding and rejecting excuses with frantic speed, but slowly it sank in.

She'd done it again.

11

There's always a bit of a sour period when Chrissy's coming down from one of her daydreams. It seldom lasts more than a day or two, but it was a tad awkward when we were supposed to be guests at the same cottage. I'd hoped she'd throw a tantrum so that I'd look calm and sensible to the others. Then I'd quickly be able to make a joke of it, and all would be well. After all, as Pippa was so attractive, she'd be sure to understand. Tens go out with tens, not fours. Pippa was maybe an eight, but that was enough.

What I didn't expect was for her to run away the moment she saw us. It was good though, because it was a really childish thing for her to do, and could only be to my advantage. Michael saw too, and watched her fat bottom wobble away along the street in surprise.

'That was Chrissy Green!'

'Yes. I suppose she must have blagged a trip on the yacht.'

'Yes, but why run off? Hey, Chrissy!'

She either didn't hear or wouldn't respond. Michael looked puzzled. I hastened to reassure him.

'Don't worry about it. She probably had some fantasy about coming up here in the hope of getting with you, and can't handle finding out we're together. The truth is, she's a bit of a gold-digger under that mushy exterior, and I think she was hoping to snare you. She lives in a dream world.'

'But . . . I mean, do you think she's OK?'

'She'll be fine. Give her a day or two and she'll have latched on to someone else.'

'I'd better talk to her, at least.'

'Why?'

He paused. I could see what he was thinking, that as he'd had sex with her he at least owed her an explanation. He didn't know that I knew, and it was not something he was going to admit to. As he hesitated she disappeared around a corner, fat little legs still pumping like anything.

'Leave her. We've got more important things to think about. For a start I need to speak to Pippa, after all. I got off to a bit of a rocky start with her. And you ought to introduce me to your dad and this Tilly.'

'Right.'

He was still looking for Chrissy, but turned back to the yacht as someone called his name. It was Pippa, standing on the deck waving. There was another girl beside her, younger, and equally attractive in a very similar way, evidently Tilly. I put on my brightest smile, ignoring Pippa's look of annoyance as I greeted them.

'Hi, Pippa! Hi, you must be Tilly. Good trip?'

'Yes, thank you. What happened to Chrissy?'

Michael answered.

'I don't know. She took one look at us and ran off.'

Pippa's face took on a look of serious exasperation.

'Oh, for goodness' sake, Michael! Don't you understand anything? She was coming up to see you! What do you expect?'

'How was I to know? She didn't say she was coming.'

'No, but . . .'

Pippa went quiet, her lips pursed tight. It was my turn to speak.

'I'm sorry, Pippa, there's been a bit of a misunderstanding. Michael and I are together, and if that has upset Chrissy, I really don't see that we should let it create a bad atmosphere between us.'

She turned to me in astonishment. I went on.

'I owe you an apology too. I was a real bitch at that club, and I'm truly sorry. You see, I didn't know you were Michael's stepmum. I thought you were a rival, and I was jealous because ... well, because you look like you just stepped off the cover of *Vogue* or something, you really do. Isn't that funny?'

At the moment she looked more like she'd just stepped off the cover of *Yachts and Yachting*, or maybe a sewage workers convention, with her shapeless yellow waterproofs and bedraggled hair. I laughed and held out my hand.

'Friends?'

She hesitated, then took my hand. I moved forward to kiss her on the cheek, to which she responded grudgingly. I'd guessed right. She knew the score. She wasn't the sort to stand on principle either. Nor was her sister, who accepted a peck on her cheek with ill grace but said nothing. That just left the father.

I heard Michael call out to me as I ran. I didn't stop. The tears were streaming from my eyes and I couldn't bear the thought of him, or anyone else for that matter, seeing me. So I kept running blindly until I had to stop because I couldn't see through my tears.

There was a fence and I flung myself down against it, to sit sobbing my heart out on the grass. It was unbearable. So many times she'd done the same thing to me, so many times, and every time I'd told myself it was for the best; that if he preferred her he obviously wasn't right for me. It had always hurt, but this was worse, far worse. I'd worshipped Michael. I'd thought we had something special together, something that would keep him interested in me.

Now it wasn't going to happen. He'd obviously fancied her the moment they met, and I could bet she'd given in quickly enough, despite knowing he was with me. I even knew what she'd say – cruel to be kind – as she explained how it would never have worked between Michael and me. It wasn't going to happen, not this time. I'd go miles away, somewhere I wouldn't have to watch the two of them together; somewhere I'd never have to see either of them again.

Even as I said it to myself I knew I was lying. I knew what I'd do, what I always did. I'd hang around them, Valentina's little lost puppy, like I always did, until it was time for that horrible phrase – 'private time, Chrissy'. Then I'd go off, miserable as they made love together, only to take up the puppy-dog routine immediately afterwards. It was so pathetic and I knew it was, but I'd never had the willpower to stop myself, and this time would be no different. Most of my stuff was on the yacht anyway, so I had to go back.

People were starting to stare and I didn't want to speak to anybody, so I got up. I had to go back to the yacht, but I couldn't, not yet. I could just picture it, Michael with his arm around Valentina and me sitting there like an idiot with everyone knowing I'd thought he was with me. She'd be nice about it, which would just make me feel worse, as if my needs could be set aside with a consoling smile. Then she'd have her little talk with me.

The trouble was, she was right. I'd been stupid to

think he would be interested in me when he could have her. She was what every man wanted, what every man needed, both as a partner and as a status symbol. She was right to take him away quickly too, because otherwise it would only hurt me more when it happened later, with some other woman, as it inevitably would. He was just too good for me.

I knew it but I didn't want to accept it. Certainly I didn't want to be faced with it or to come back to the *Harold Jones* after my stupid little show of emotion with my face tear-streaked and my eyes all red and puffy. So I began to walk along the side of the waterway, knowing that they'd catch up with me eventually. I was also hoping that by then Michael and Valentina would have gone back to the cottage by car, so that her lecture would at least be postponed.

Everything was going round and round in my head, and it was all I could think about. So when the path veered away from the water I followed it, assuming it would join again.

An hour later I was completely lost.

It was an uphill struggle but I was winning. Somehow Malcolm Callington seemed to have got it into his head that Chrissy was Michael's girlfriend, and that I was some sort of home wrecker. Fortunately Michael had the guts to stand up for himself and explain that a casual fling with Chrissy didn't give her any claim to him. After that it was just a question of me charming the old fool.

He was pretty cold at first, but after I'd insisted on buying supper for everybody and he'd got the best part of a bottle of wine inside him, he began to thaw. I was beginning to wish Chrissy would come back too, so I could get the awkward little conversation I'd inevitably have to put up with over as well.

We finished supper and she still hadn't put in an appearance, and I began to wonder if she hadn't lost it completely and gone back to London. All her things were on the yacht, but she apparently had her cards, and it was just the sort of stupid and overdramatic gesture she liked to make.

As the station was just a few hundred yards away it began to seem more and more likely that she really had gone. That was going to make life a lot easier. The others were worried, but I knew all I had to do was ring her in the evening and she would be forgotten, while a few sympathetic but carefully chosen comments would make her behaviour look both inconsiderate and child-ish. I bided my time, until Malcolm had begun to glance at his watch, then put in my penny's worth.

They swallowed it, slightly reluctantly, and off we went, Michael and I by car to the cottage with most of the luggage, the others to a mooring Malcolm had booked for them. It was going to take a day to get the yacht up to Hickling Broad, and Michael was deter-mined to do it. I agreed, not wanting to make an issue of it so long as I didn't have to sleep on the wretched thing. The thought of his river trip cheered his simple male mind up considerably, and I helped soothe his conscience by trying to ring Chrissy from the village. There was no answer, as I'd expected, and he accepted my explanation that she was sulking.

By the time we were back at the cottage with a bottle of wine open he had forgotten about Chrissy. I gave him a treat anyway, just to be sure, stripping for him and going down on his cock to suck him to orgasm while he sipped on his wine. It was one more breach of my own rules, but I figured it was worth it.

It certainly got him going, because instead of letting me finish him off, he bent me across the settee for a long, leisurely fuck. As always, he was so fast he made me dizzy, and he brought me off twice on his cock before he came himself, all over my upturned bottom.

That was only the start. By the end I'd had my dress and panties pulled off, to leave me naked. He stripped too and picked me up to carry me up the stairs, over his shoulder. I was flung on the bed and he immediately buried his face in my sex, licking me while he tugged himself slowly back to erection. We fucked again, going through a dozen different positions on the bed before he came. The next was in the bathroom, his familiar trick of catching me on the loo and simply lifting me on to his cock, once I'd finished, of course. That took ages, and left me sore, tired and ready for bed. Not Michael, who was ready again after a quick coffee, and buggered me over the bed with the assistance of my cold cream.

Once he'd finished, I really was up to my limit, sore in both holes and too tired to keep my eyes open. It was well worth it though. He hadn't so much as mentioned Chrissy all evening.

It was getting dark when I found the pub. I'd been wandering along footpaths for over two hours, pretty much in a daydream at first, and then worried. I'd tried to get back to Yarmouth and the yacht and found myself at a dead end where the path reached an aban-doned windpump. I'd made for where I could see sails above distant reed beds and found myself on the wrong side of a fifty-foot-wide dyke from the road. There had been a road sign showing that it was only two miles to Acle, and I decided to follow the dyke, only to find myself trying to cross farmland with wide ditches between every field. At last I'd turned back to the north and found a track leading to a village, and a pub, the Wheatsheaf.

I was hungry and desperately thirsty. So I ordered a plate of fish and chips and a lemonade and went to sit in the beer garden, as far away from the occupied tables as I could. I felt small and stupid and very alone, miserable and unwanted. Everybody else seemed to be so happy as well, which made me feel worse. There were a few tourists, a pair of elderly men, and a group of local boys, all absorbed in their own business, talking or laughing, all drinking.

Drinking was what I needed to do myself if I was ever going to pluck up the courage to face the others. I was sure they'd be worrying about me, Tilly and Pippa at least. I also knew that the sensible thing to do was ring for a cab and go to the cottage as I had no way of finding the yacht. Valentina would be at the cottage, and Michael.

I ordered a double brandy and drank it, all the while thinking bitter thoughts about my life. By the bottom of the glass I wasn't feeling any braver, just sadder, so I ordered another. It didn't work either, leaving me watching the light fade in the west through a veil of tears. The third left me in a well of self-pity so deep I didn't feel I could even move to stand up.

The tourists were gone, the old men too. A retired couple had been and gone. They'd been at least seventy, and they'd held hands as they sipped their drinks, making me feel more maudlin than ever. I was feeling ever more stupid too, for daring to think I might interest Michael. As Valentina had so often pointed out, chasing attractive men only ended in tears. She was right, it had.

The local lads had gone, or so I thought, until one came back out into the beer garden to pick up something he'd left on the table. He was huge, well over six foot and fat, with a great red lump of a nose and a tangle of yellow hair. I immediately felt sorry for him, imagining how unpopular he would be with the local girls. Valentina wouldn't have given him a second glance. Or she would, to set him up on a date with me.

The thought put a weak, self-deprecating smile on my face for a moment. It was true, he was just the sort she always seemed to pick out for me. Next to Michael he would look very poor indeed, yet from the way he moved, the way he carried himself, I suspected he wouldn't see it that way. Men never seem to be aware of how they stand among themselves from the woman's viewpoint, but then, that was exactly my problem only the other way around.

He had sat down to tie his boot, and I watched as his thick red fingers twisted the lace into a clumsy knot. His hands were huge, bigger even than Michael's, and rough, calluses showing in the multicoloured light from the garden decorations. I imagined the strength in them, and a little nasty fantasy began to run in my head, of how good it would feel to chat him up and make him punch Michael. If anyone could do it, he could, and I let the idea run, only for it to change, to a vision of him with Valentina across his knee as he spanked her bare bottom.

It made me giggle despite myself. I knew he wouldn't dare anything of the sort. Even if he hadn't been worried about the consequences he'd have been putty in her hands, like all men, but it was still a nice idea. She would be outraged, a spitting hell-cat, all claws and teeth and spite. He was so big though, such a lump, he probably wouldn't care. He'd do it anyway, calmly, slowly, the way he moved, unhurried as he dragged her screaming and kicking across his knee. Her dress would come up, her designer knickers would be pulled down ... no, torn off, and stuffed in her mouth to shut her up. Then he'd spank her, really spank her, until she howled ...

My fantasy broke abruptly as I realised he was talking to me.

'What're you drinking, love?'

I tried to answer, to turn down his offer, but nothing came out, only a choking gurgle.

'You all right?'

I wanted to say yes, that I was fine, that I wanted to be left alone. He was being nice to me. I just burst into tears. A moment later he was beside me, his enormous arm around my shoulders, saying soothing things in a deep, thick voice. I tried to stop myself crying, choking back the tears and feeling a complete idiot, but it didn't really work. I couldn't even make myself understood properly, and if I wanted him to go away, I felt a bitch for it, rejecting him when he was only being kind.

So I let him hold me until I finally managed to get myself under control. As soon as I'd stopped crying he got up, saying he was going to fetch a drink. He came back with a lager, which I gulped down, then a second as we talked. I could feel my head spinning, and I was barely taking in what I was saying, but I didn't care. I just felt numb. After a while I figured out that he was called Jack.

By the time the landlord came out to tell us to drink

up I was giggling at his stupid jokes. I got up, vaguely thinking about taxis, only to discover I couldn't walk properly. That was just funny, and it was funnier still when I tripped over the table leg and fell on my bum. Jack gave me a hand, pulling me up and helping me as we left.

There was a big pool of golden light outside the pub, but it was dark in the lanes, pitch dark. Jack didn't seem to mind, and he did seem to know what he was doing, supporting me and occasionally pausing to fondle my bottom and snog me. That was nice, and when I asked he got his cock out, a huge, thick one that tasted of man and went stiff in my mouth in no time.

I sucked him until a car came past, sending me into a fit of giggles as the headlights swept by, briefly showing me the thick pink trunk of the cock I was sucking and the tawny bush of his pubic hair. He didn't seem to think it was so funny, and took his cock away. I wanted it back and wanted a fuck, but I couldn't get up again, and fell in the ditch. He picked me up then, and I think he said he'd give me a fuck if I was a good girl, so I asked him if he was going to spank my bottom. He laughed then, and I knew he was going to do it, so I pulled down my jeans and knickers for him as soon as we were in his house, and took out my tits, and he spanked my bottom and he let me suck on his cock and fucked me, and fucked me again, and let me suck on his balls and spanked me some more when I asked, and fucked me again, and did it between my tits and in my mouth ...

12

My head hurt. So did my bottom and my pussy. I was in the nude, lying on a grubby mattress with the sheet twisted around my body. Slowly it came back to me – Valentina and Michael, walking, getting drunk, Jack.

There was no sign of him, and I was in what looked like the roof space of a barn, a single room with huge wooden beams and planks for a floor. I couldn't remember climbing up there, or being carried, but I obviously had. I couldn't remember undressing either, and I was sure that when we'd been fucking I'd had my top and bra up and my jeans and knickers down, quickie style. I could remember fucking though, and giggling stupidly as he spanked my bottom, and a lot of other rude details.

I badly needed a wash, and to brush my teeth, and some aspirin. There wasn't even a basin, let alone a medicine cabinet, although there was a new and expensive-looking computer. Typical male! There was a mirror, and I was ruefully inspecting the bruises on my bottom when I heard the creak of a door from below me. I made a dash for my discarded knickers, only to discover that they were torn and covered in mud. I couldn't remember letting my trousers down before we'd got indoors either, but I pulled them on anyway, just in time for Jack's head to emerge in the trap door. He looked at me, grinning. I managed a smile.

'Get some of this down you.'

He was holding out a big earthenware mug, full of milk. I took it, gratefully swallowing about half of it before I realised that the reason it was warm was that it had come straight out of a cow. It was delicious anyway, and I finished it, lowering the mug to find him staring openly at my bare tits.

'Fuck me, but you are gorgeous.'

I covered myself instinctively, blushing, only to take my hands away again. It was just silly, after what we'd done, and besides, it wasn't as if I could cover everything anyway. He was still grinning.

'You posh birds really go, don't you? More milk?'

'Yes, please.'

His head disappeared again. I heard a voice, not Jack's, making a joke, then him, laughing. Not wanting to get caught naked, never mind with an all too obviously spanked bottom, I began to dress. My bra was OK, but my top was torn so badly it left one tit hanging out. My jeans weren't torn, but they were covered in mud, as were my shoes and socks. Fortunately my cards were still in the jeans pocket.

Dressed, I looked a bigger mess than I had naked, a complete ragamuffin. My hair was a bird's nest, my face dirty with mud and worse, my clothes filthy. I looked as if I'd been dragged through a hedge backwards, which as far as I could remember was more or less what had happened.

I could just imagine how Valentina would react. She was going to love it. If she found out about Jack, she was really going to love it. It would suit her perfectly for me to get pissed stupid and let the first man who showed an interest fuck me, the first man I met. She'd suggest I have a fling with him to help me get over

Michael, as if I could change my feelings so easily. She was not going to find out.

I would go back to London and pretend I'd gone straight there. That would save a lot of embarrassment. It would save me doing my puppy dog at heel bit too, which I just knew I'd end up doing if I stayed on in Norfolk. All I had to do was smarten up, get into Yarmouth, and go.

Jack was good about it, even though he found the state I was in funny, and offered me a lift into Acle, which was the nearest station. He let me wash in what turned out to be his parents' farmhouse, which was highly embarrassing with his mother, father and sister all there and knowing full well what had happened. He lent me a shirt too, which came down to my knees.

By then it was getting late, and my resolve was beginning to weaken. I kept thinking of how passionate Michael had been with me, and how complimentary. Jack had been the same, if rather cruder, but I knew deep down that both of them had only done it to get into my knickers. Given the choice between me and Valentina, they'd choose her every single time.

What Jack hadn't said was that the lift was by tractor. That left me perched next to him, high enough to see over the hedges across the flat Norfolk countryside. That hurt, with the sails showing above the fields and the scattered windpumps, just as I'd been picturing it when thinking of Michael and the time we'd spend together. Jack's happy, teasing chatter barely registered.

The traffic was solid, and not because of us, giving me plenty of time to reflect and grow slowly more and more morose. Soon I was telling myself that it would be sensible just to stay long enough to retrieve my things from the yacht, then go. I knew I wouldn't, but as we reached the bridge over the river I was close to snapping. There were moorings, and cruisers and yachts, bringing back all my memories and hopes. I watched, chin in hand, close to tears as we moved slowly past. Somebody on the bank was waving, jumping up and down and shouting my name. It was Tilly.

If Chrissy had had any tact or feeling, she'd have gone home. Of course she hadn't. Instead she'd done her drama queen bit, getting everybody worried by disappearing for the night, and then just happening to be crossing a bridge on her way to the station as the yacht was moored nearby. It was the bridge Michael and I had agreed to meet the yacht at the day before, where she'd been dropped off by some hayseed. Obviously she had known all along the yacht would be there. The whole thing was just designed to draw attention to herself and to gain sympathy. I was beginning to get fed up with her.

Not that I could really say anything – or at least not what needed to be said. The only thing I could do was to behave like a grown-up and hope she had the sense to do the same. If she didn't, what should have been a gentle and relaxing cruise along the river was going to turn into an absolute nightmare. So I gave her a friendly greeting as I got on the yacht.

'Hi, Chrissy. Are you OK now?'

All I got was a look of reproach. She was going to be childish about it.

Michael and the others had immediately gone into some complicated nautical discussion, which gave me a chance to set things straight.

'Chrissy, listen to me. We're on holiday. We're guests of the Callingtons. The least you can do is try and behave sensibly.'

This time she answered me.

'How ... how can you do this to me, Valentina?'

She was still being childish, babyish in fact, because she looked as if she was going to burst into tears.

'Chrissy, you're being silly. Just calm down. I'm not going into this right now, but I'd have thought you would have had more sense this time.'

Her mouth opened, making her look like a goldfish. She turned and stormed off to the pointy end of the boat, to stand at the rail. I knew she was crying. I'd tried, but if she didn't even have the common decency to behave in front of other people, what could I do? Michael approached.

'We're going to take her straight up to Hickling. You'll like it, it must be one of the most beautiful pieces of river in the Broads. A bit crowded, mark you, but everywhere is these days. Did you know that when Dad was young you could come up here and you'd see as many working boats as pleasure cruisers?'

'Well, that's the Stone Age for you.'

'Very funny. I'll be taking the helm. Would you like to help?'

'Not really, thanks. In fact, wouldn't it be better if we drove back to the cottage?'

'Drove back?'

'Yes. We could have all afternoon together, just the two of us. It would be our last chance.'

'Yes ... I'd love to, of course, but ... well, I've already missed out on the trip up, and ... oh, come on, Valentina, you'll come to appreciate the river, you'll see. Just stick with it.'

It was typical. He was so thick-skinned, so insensitive, that he didn't even realise there was a problem with being on the yacht at the same time as Chrissy. I could have played up, I could have made a more overt offer of sex. I didn't. This was Michael Callington. I couldn't very well leave him with Chrissy, either. It was a nightmare.

I wasn't playing sailor girls though. Instead I climbed up on top of the cabin to sunbathe so I wouldn't have to put up with her accusing silence and the awkwardness among the others. A few minutes later they'd managed to splice the mainbrace, doff the mast and shank the sheeplines, or something equally silly, and we were off.

There was nothing to be seen, with flat fields in every direction, except the occasional boat passing in the opposite direction. I was quickly bored, and wishing Michael and I were alone again. Things were a bit frosty between him and the two girls, also his father. That was another black mark against Chrissy, but it did mean I was likely to have more time alone with him, at least once he'd got his fix of boating.

Michael was steering, and Chrissy was at the front, sulking. I could hear the others talking in the cabin below me, not very clearly, but enough to catch the occasional word. Things seemed to be quite heated, with Malcolm Callington even mentioning court, although I didn't catch the context. It was clear that he had some sort of gripe with them, and I began to wonder if it wasn't to do with me. It made sense. After all, he was a man like any other, and sure to want me around so he could have a good ogle. So it made sense that he'd want Pippa and Tilly to show me a bit of respect, which they were sure to resent.

They both seemed to be pretty weak-willed, and I was sure he would win out in the end. So I took off my bikini top, just to give him an extra reason for wanting me around, and to remind Michael what he was missing by being so obstinate. There were plenty of other people to see too, and it was quite satisfying to be causing a stir, especially when so many of the riverboats seemed to have been hired by groups of young men.

It was a particularly loud wolf-whistle from a pleasure cruiser that drew Malcolm Callington on deck. I lay still, my eyes closed, apparently indifferent, but I knew he'd seen, and when he didn't say anything I also knew that my little show was effective.

I went on sunbathing anyway, content to lie there and daydream while the rest of them got themselves in a state over the situation. After all, I knew how it would work out, and if the two girls ended up a bit jealous and resentful of me, then it would be nothing new.

After a while the sound of an unusually loud engine made me turn my head, to find a really big river cruiser coming towards us. Like so many of the others, the people on board were all young men, and mostly drunk or well on their way. There were the usual whistles and crude comments, which I ignored, only to find myself still thinking about them after they passed.

One man, a beefy kid maybe not even out of his teens, had called out an invitation, to come on board and 'see what real men can do'. It was amusing, a typical piece of laddish bravado, when he knew full well that no woman would do anything of the sort, and also that he and his mates wouldn't have known what to do if I had taken up their most generous offer.

They'd have just been embarrassed, and no more able to carry out their dirty suggestions than fly. I'd have been completely in control, the centre of attention, and if I'd stayed topless, they would have been besotted, treating me like royalty. That is how I like men to behave, how men ought to behave, and it was a nice thought, and a consoling one after the amount of pleasure I'd taken in being under Michael's control.

There's something I read once about alpha and beta males, the alphas being the ones who do the fucking, the betas the ones who just talk about it. There was some truth in it, I'd thought, and Michael was definitely an alpha, the boys on the boat definitely betas.

I love it when there's a whole gang of men, all desperately eager to please. That was how it would be on the boat. Maybe I'd even choose one, if there was somewhere private we could go. I'd ride him to ecstasy, after having him lick me, and all the while knowing the others could hear, maybe were even trying to peek. They'd get so horny, so desperately, helplessly horny they'd end up masturbating over the thought of me and their friend, even masturbating each other. That really was funny, to think of two men so driven to distraction by my unavailability that they ended up having sex with each other.

My nipples were getting harder, which was something I didn't want to show, so I rolled over, still smiling over my fantasy. It was only when I opened my eyes to adjust the towel I was lying on that I realised Chrissy was watching me. She turned away immediately, but I knew she'd seen me smiling.

It was unbearable. Valentina was being so smug, sunbathing topless on the cabin roof without a care in the world while I was close to tears. I could read her thoughts, satisfaction at another easy victory over stupid little Chrissy; rude thoughts about what she'd be doing with Michael that evening, and ideas for what she would say to me when I'd calmed down.

That was the worst thing. She was treating me as if I were a child in a tantrum, waiting until I'd got over it before explaining to me why she'd done it. I wasn't going to take it though, not this time. I'd stay cold, refusing to speak to her, maybe I'd even slap her stupid, grinning face.

I wouldn't, and I knew I wouldn't. If I didn't make up when she chose to I would eventually, and it would just make me look weaker than ever, more pathetic. It had been the same with Simon Straw, and afterwards I'd followed them around constantly, without even enough pride left to stay away – my puppy-dog act. I'd do it too, I knew I would.

There were options. I could stick with Tilly, only I knew that I'd constantly be thinking about Michael and Valentina. That would sour the growing friendship between Tilly and me. I liked Tilly. She was fun and playful, with a personality quite like my own, only with more confidence – far more confidence. She was uninhibited too, rather more uninhibited than I could really handle. It might go too far. We'd made love, sort of, and she might want to do it again, only I knew that if she did I would feel I was doing it not because I wanted to, but because I couldn't have Michael. Then there was Valentina, who was sure to realise. Valentina thought that lesbians were women who got together because they couldn't get men. That was what she'd think of me.

I could even make something of my one night stand with Jack. He knew where the cottage was and would be coming to get his shirt. It would be easy to play up to him, and if it would be just what Valentina expected of me, then it wouldn't be the first time. The bad thing was that once he saw her even he would prefer her, so he'd be thinking of her as he made love to me, which wouldn't be the first time either.

It was better to be her puppy dog.

We lunched at Thurne, with Valentina doing her best to ingratiate herself with everyone, especially Malcolm. It was baking hot, and she was in a miniscule bikini and a wrap, drawing plenty of attention. Nobody paid much attention to me, still in my dirty clothes and oversized shirt, except to give me funny looks. We didn't linger, for which I was grateful, but moved on along the River Thurne, with Valentina back on the cabin roof.

They'd left me alone all morning, but Tilly came to talk to me, trying to cheer me up by describing what Malcolm was going to do to her and Pippa for spanking me. They were going to be caned, bare-bottomed and touching their toes, a ritual she described to me with the now familiar mixture of apprehension and enthusiasm. First she needed to know something. Her voice dropped to a whisper.

'What's the bitch likely to make of our little games?'

'Valentina? She'll freak!'

'Bother. You're sure?'

'I'm sure. She thinks it's perverted. She's got these rules she worked out as a teenager. She reckons it's only men who like that sort of thing, and the more attractive a girl is the less she has to put up with.'

'What? I've never heard such a load of rubbish!'

I shrugged. She went on.

'Hell! I was hoping Michael had put her over by now. After all, she's a total brat, and I don't know why else he'd bother with her.'

'Because she's gorgeous.'

'Nah, she hasn't got enough flesh for him. You're more his style.'

'Thanks, Tilly! You really know how to cheer a girl up. I'm not that fat!'

'Fat? Who said anything about fat? A nice spankable bottom is what Michael likes best, and boy do you have one, as we know.'

She winked. I blushed and smiled, feeling good about myself just for an instant until I remembered what Valentina's reaction would be to the discovery that Tilly and I had made love. She glanced back to Valentina, who was on her back, her firm, perfectly formed tits sticking up against the skyline. A motor cruiser was passing, the old boy on the foredeck letting his eyes wander, to Tilly, looking cute in her green bikini, to Valentina and staying there. I shook my head.

'She won't have let him, and she certainly wouldn't submit to court.'

'We'll just have to do it when she's off with Michael then, I'm not going without spanking just because she's here!'

'I'm not sure if I feel like it, actually, not any more.'

'Oh, come on! Chrissy! You cannot mean that! What, you're going to mope the whole time just because stupid Michael hasn't got the sense to see which side his bread's buttered!'

I forced a smile past the lump in my throat. She was trying to be nice, but I knew the truth – Valentina's truth. Tilly look at me and spoke again.

'So no spanking and no . . .'

I knew what she meant. I shook my head, the lump in my throat bigger than ever.

'Sorry.'

'Great!'

She stood and walked away, back down the boat. I looked after her, wishing I'd been able to explain and feeling more sorry for myself than ever. It was all my fault too, as Valentina would undoubtedly tell me, as if I'd had the sense not to set my sights too high in the first place, nothing would have happened.

It was late afternoon by the time we got back to the cottage. Although we could see it as we went past, it turned out the lake was too shallow to take the yacht to the mooring where the rowing boat was. So we had to go right to the end and find a space in a little marina. There was a pub, and we stopped for a drink before Malcolm and Michael got their inflatable dinghy ready to take us back.

I wanted to make it very clear that we were in two groups: Michael and me, and the rest. So I suggested walking back to the cottage and offered to pick up something for dinner on the way. They accepted, Michael a bit grudgingly, as being a little boy at heart he wanted to go on the water.

Providing dinner proved less than easy, as the village only had a couple of miserable little shops. I managed as best I could and gave the bags to Michael to carry as we set off down the lane to the cottage. He had seemed a bit distant, and I was sure it was since he'd spoken to Tilly alone while we were on the yacht. That had been immediately after Tilly had spoken to Chrissy. Obviously Chrissy was being a bad loser as usual and had tried to put a spoke in the wheels. I couldn't let that happen. As soon as we were out of the village I took Michael's hand.

'Is there another way back to the cottage, a more private way?'

He looked at me, and grinned. It was done, as simple as that. Men are so primitive. I'd seen the footpath sign before, and guessed it went the way we wanted, as it couldn't very well go into the lake. Before, I'd preferred the comfort of the cottage. Now I was prepared to put up with grass, just as long as it reaffirmed Michael's feelings for me, and took long enough to make sure the others could guess what we'd been up to.

The path was overgrown, and Michael had to use a stick to clear the way. I didn't mind as it slowed us down and meant nobody was likely to catch us. Not that I intended to do it in the middle of the path anyway. Once we reached the trees at the edge of the lake I pulled him in among them and down on to a patch of soft grass.

He was eager, not surprisingly, after watching me sunbathe all day, and he had me naked in no time, my wrap peeled off and my bikini stripped away to leave me in just shoes. He seemed to like that, not bothering to undress himself, but just slipping his shirt off. I let him lead, content to be stroked and kissed until I was ready for his tongue. He went down on me of his own accord, licking me to the very edge of orgasm before turning to his own needs.

His cock came out and into my mouth, his hands still on my breasts as I sucked him to full erection. I took his balls in my mouth too, rolling them over my tongue and mouthing on the big sac as I tugged gently on his erection. Then it was on my back in the grass, his cock sliding smoothly up into me, and we had begun to fuck.

He was as good as ever, fast and hard and even, making me breathless with pleasure and eager to come. I got what I wanted, Michael performing his cock trick as I lay rolled up on the ground, rubbing right on my clit until I came and immediately pushing back into me.

It felt great as I lay back for what I knew would be a good, long fuck, not just because I was full of cock, but because he was mine. Even when he pulled out to put me on my knees and fuck me with my bottom spread wide to his gaze there was no resentment. It was me he had like that, me he wanted, and, however dirty he was with me, ultimately I was in control.

He was dirty too, finishing himself off by rubbing his erection up and down in the crease of my bottom, with his hot come spattering over my back. I took it, grateful he hadn't decided to put his cock up my bottom, and even sucked him clean when he offered himself to my mouth.

Afterwards all his coldness was gone. We lay together in the grass for a while, my head on his chest, me still naked, Michael stroking my bottom in a wonderfully intimate way. As I'd hoped, we arrived back at the cottage long after the others. I'd made sure there was a little grass in my hair and on my wrap, and sure enough, I got a knowing glance from Pippa and a jealous one from Chrissy. I knew at some point soon we'd have to talk about it, but I wanted to delay that moment for as long as possible in case it turned into an ugly scene and Michael saw. Along with bodily functions, something else you shouldn't let your man see is you arguing with another woman in an unseemly way, like some awful feuding council-estate martriarchs.

I set about making dinner, chicken pieces in a

vaguely Mediterranean sauce with pasta, the only thing I'd been able to get the ingredients for. It went down well enough anyway, and I even insisted on helping Pippa wash up. By the time we'd finished, she was pretty well thawed out, and even Tilly was being reasonably friendly. Chrissy wasn't helping her cause either, with her long face and lack of conversation, and by the time people began to drift off towards bed I was sure that with a few more days I'd be able to make them realise that in choosing me Michael had been led by more than just his cock.

For all his bizarre sexual habits, Malcolm Callington struck me as pretty old-fashioned, or maybe it was his bizarre sexual habits that were old-fashioned. In any case, he was definitely head of the family. I was worried he might object to Michael and me sleeping together, but when we went up he barely glanced around, save to say goodnight. Chrissy had already gone to bed, *still* sulking, for goodness' sake, and with Malcolm and Pippa in the main bedroom, she'd had no choice but to share what was obviously intended as the children's room beside ours with Tilly. That left her on the opposite side of a partition wall to our bed, and it was more than I could resist not to tease Michael into mounting me for a good, noisy fuck before sleep.

13

It didn't seem so bad in the morning. It never does. I'd slept like a log, physically and emotionally exhausted.

Now I just wanted to forget the whole thing, and try not to think about it too much, either Michael or how silly I'd been. I didn't want Valentina's inevitable lecture either, and got up early to take a walk by the broad. It was beautiful. I love water, at least to look at, and the combination of reeds and sky and boats was immensely soothing in a way I'd completely missed the day before, let alone when I'd been really furious.

Slowly I began to see my actions for what they were, a tantrum, and a completely unreasonable one at that. Michael was with Valentina, and obviously had been since the day they'd driven up together, maybe before. That made my own dreams on the yacht nothing but empty fantasies, and guilty ones at that, for wanting my friend's boyfriend. I was just being silly, and I was fervently wishing I'd made a bit less of a display of myself by running off when they had turned up in Yarmouth. It had been stupid to get drunk and let Jack pick me up as well. As it had turned out, he'd been nice, but there was no denying he'd taken advantage of me, and it could just as easily have been some complete psycho.

The only sensible thing to do was to behave myself, to follow Valentina's rules. That was the way to be happy and not to get hurt. I wouldn't tell her about the spanking, or what Tilly and I had done, but I wouldn't do it any more either. It showed a lack of self-respect, as she said.

I'd reached an old windpump, which I knew we were entitled to use, for birdwatching or just admiring the view across the broad. I wanted to go in and climb to the top, which the landlord had made into a sort of observation room, but I found the door locked. I knew the key would be at the cottage, but the others were likely to be up and I still wanted to be alone for a while. So I walked on along a footpath between high, tangled hedges, and back in a long loop to the track on which the cottage stood.

There was a tractor parked outside, Jack's tractor. My heart gave an unexpected jump at the sight, as much from the thought of Valentina meeting him as from the prospect of seeing a man I'd let fuck me so comprehensively. I was hoping he'd just come to the door, and that she wasn't up, but I was out of luck. He was seated at the kitchen table, mug of coffee in hand, talking to Michael. Valentina was to the side, in a short robe that left the full length of her beautiful long legs showing. He wasn't looking at her, but he would have been, I knew.

I managed a smile, reminding myself that it was inevitable he would prefer her, and only natural. Pippa and Tilly were there too, dressed, but both looking cute even in just jeans and tops. I was very much the ugly duckling, and I was the one he'd had. That was the way it went.

Not that he seemed particularly bothered, greeting me with a big grin and then going back to his conversation with Michael. They were talking about a dyke that ran across Jack's land, and which apparently hadn't been navigable since before the war. They were trying to clear it, in the hope of making the farm a popular tourist spot, and had come across the hulk of a wherry. Michael was fascinated, and Malcolm too when he returned from the village with the papers. Before long they had volunteered to help, and we had been volunteered in turn. So we were going to be seeing more of Jack.

I could see it coming, every detail.

The things I have to put up with. It was straight out of the sort of boy's own adventures my dad used to read when he was a kid, and still kept in boxes in the attic.

Still, things were going my way. There was no question I was with Michael, and it couldn't be difficult to get Chrissy off with Hayseed Jack. He was her type, big and gormless and overweight, like a bull. I could see he fancied her too, a primitive reaction to her fat bottom and oversize breasts, like a baboon getting horny over a mate's bright blue arse. She is such a slut she was bound to go for it, and I wasn't at all sure they hadn't already been up to it.

The idea was to hack some great rotting barge out of about a hundred years' worth of undergrowth. It sounded dirty, sweaty and dull, but at least they couldn't very well expect me to help. I took a rug, planning to sunbathe while they played their games, and perhaps get to know Pippa and Tilly better.

We went to the farm after retrieving the car from Acle. The ditch they were clearing ran right past the farm, then into what they said had once been a lake, but was now a sort of soggy wood. I nearly rebelled at that, Michael or no Michael, but they had made a path through it for the digger, and there was a grassy area beyond.

That was ideal, and I spread my rug out to watch. By the time I'd put my sun-tan cream on, both Michael and Jack were actually in the ditch, up to their knees in water, while Malcolm was working on the bank. They were all stripped to the waist, which was a sight worth watching. Michael I'd seen, but it was still good to watch his lean, muscular body with the muscles working on his back and arms, and a sheen of sweat quickly building up. Jack was also worth a glance, to my surprise, because while he was fat by any standards, he was even bigger than Michael and enormously powerful, not just a bull, but a prize bull. Even the old man was good for his age, lean and wiry.

Chrissy always was a bit of a tomboy at heart, and doesn't care how she looks, so I wasn't surprised when she took off her jeans and waded in with the men, getting in their way as they tried to clear the tangle of brambles and stuff from around the barge thingy. What did surprise me was when Pippa and Tilly, who I'd thought would have had more self-respect, joined in and were soon looking a fine mess.

That left me to doze in the sun and enjoy the view. They'd brought a book, *Norfolk Craft on Dyke, Broad and Sea*, which I pretended to read, all the while wondering about the possibilities of the next few days. I really needed to get Michael to myself a bit more, which meant getting rid of Chrissy or she'd be constantly at heel. Jack seemed ideal for the purpose and he was certainly interested in her, sticking close and pointing out dragonflies and other dull nature things. She was making a fine show of herself too, wet from the waist down, with her top plastered to her skin and half of her wobbly bottom hanging out of a pair of sodden panties. He would know a slut when he saw one, I was sure.

Then there were the other three, who seemed to stick together like glue, so much so in fact that I'd begun to wonder if there wasn't some sort of perverted ménage à trois going on. It seemed pretty weird when they were sisters, but then I knew old Callington was a perve, and considering the age gap between him and Pippa they obviously didn't care what other people thought anyway. From what Michael said, the old man spanked his wife and she liked it. I was surprised at Pippa, when she could have had anyone she wanted, but she was pretty posh, and posh girls often seem to be weird. The same went for Tilly.

The fact that the entire family were a bunch of perverts was going to be good ammunition in court. I could really play it up, contrasting my innocence and humble but honest origins with their upper-class depravity. The jury was bound to be on my side. Not that I was planning to go too fast. Michael had been better behaved over the last few days, really from the time I'd put my foot down over the spanking. Obviously being firm worked, for all his machismo, and I was beginning to wonder if I couldn't mould him after all. Once properly trained, he'd be worth sticking with, at least for a few years.

It was hot, sweaty work, but fun. We'd cleared the bow of the old wherry and it was really quite exciting watching the wreck emerge, like being an archaeologist or something. It was in better condition than we'd expected, and Jack was beginning to talk about restoring it. He was also paying a lot of attention to me.

Considering what we'd done, and that Valentina had been making it very obvious she was with Michael, I wasn't surprised.

My feelings were mixed. A big part of me still felt too hurt to respond, for all that I'd accepted that trying for Michael had been foolish. I also knew that it was what Valentina would want me to do, and expect me to do, and that made it more acceptable but also triggered resentment. Finally there was the fact that he had fucked me, and it had been good, so it didn't feel right to give him the cold shoulder.

Not that it made much difference with everyone else around, but he kept looking at me, and all the more after I'd slipped in the water and soaked my top. That left the material plastered to my tits, with my nipples showing through my bra, and there was nothing I could do about it, save strip off and show the lot anyway. I didn't quite have the guts, with my huge balloons and the others with their perfectly formed chests.

So I stayed that way and kept working, and he kept stealing glances. If I was showing a bit, so was he, bare from the waist up and with his jeans wet through. His cock looked huge, even though it was at rest, and as far as I could remember it was maybe bigger even than Michael's. That added to his appeal, for the sake of it, and because Valentina likes large cocks as well, so I'd have something better than her, or at least as good.

As usual, when it came to it, I went with the flow. He suggested cider and pork pies for lunch, and asked if I'd help him fetch them from the farm. So off I went, knowing full well that he was likely to make a pass at me. Sure enough, he did, and not exactly a subtle one either. Both his parents were off somewhere else, and the house was deserted. They made their own pies, and he simply took a tray from the coldstore at the back of the house, then marched into the cider barn, put the tray down, selected a pie and took out his cock, grinning. Valentina's rules for dealing with men – never accept a dirty pass, make them wait. She'd have slapped his face. I went down on him.

He was big, very big, thick and long and meaty. He tasted good too, strong, but very male, especially as he began to grow in my mouth. I took his balls out for him, stroking them as I sucked. They felt furry and warm, and I paused to kiss them and suck each briefly into my mouth, making him gasp. He was still eating the pie, and showering my head with crumbs, which I tried to ignore as I went back to sucking his cock. It seemed safe, so I pulled out my boobs, cupping them in my hands to tease my nipples and show off to him. He gave an appreciative grunt, stuffed the last of the pie in his mouth and reached for a bottle of cider.

It was a bit much, having his lunch while I gave him a blow-job, but I was getting too horny to care. He was erect, and it was going to be very easy indeed to pop down my knickers and let him have me on the floor, doggy-style. Down they came, making myself available to him, and sure enough, he took me by the hair and eased me off his cock. It sprang free, wet and hard and ready, the sight making me want to be pushed down on all fours and to stick my bottom up for entry. He didn't, but put the bottle to my lips, tilting it so that I was forced to let my mouth fill.

I guessed what he wanted, and took him back in my mouth, sucking on him with my mouth full of cool cider. Some spilt from around my lips and splashed down over my bare breasts, the cold liquid bringing my nipples out to full erection. He sighed with pleasure and tilted the bottle again, pouring its contents out over my face and his cock and balls. I sucked it up, and once more the taste of apples mingled with that of cock. He was going to come like that, I was sure, in my mouth, but I wanted fucking, and my own orgasm.

Pulling away, I got down to present him with my bum, my knickers at half-mast to leave everything showing. He gave a grunt and got down behind me, pressing his erection between my cheeks. As he started to rub in my bum crease he tilted the bottle once more, to splash cold cider out across my bottom and let it run down over my pussy. It felt wonderfully chilly on my hot flesh, and as his cock slid down I lifted myself higher still for entry. I was still bruised from the marks of the spanking he'd given me, and it felt great knowing he could see, knowing he would be thinking of how he'd handled me as he fucked me.

His fingers found my pussy, to stretch my lips apart. I moaned, revelling in the intimate inspection of my fanny, then gasped as cold cider filled my hole. It was such a shock, but then his cock was going in and I didn't care any more, panting out my ecstasy as he began to fuck me. One huge hand found my bottom, pulling one cheek aside to show off my bumhole and the junction of cock and pussy. More cider cascaded down as he emptied the rest of the bottle over my bum, all the while working himself in and out as it trickled down our bodies.

I had to come before he did, before his lovely cock left my body. He took me by both hips, slamming himself in, faster and faster. I reached back under my belly, to find my pussy, stroking, taking hold of the taut sac of his balls, to feel them as I was fucked, stroking again. My pussy was wet with cider, my tummy too, with more dripping from my tits. It felt wonderful, to be soaked like that and fucked on my knees with my knickers down and my top well up, showing everything, rude and bare, his to take pleasure in, his to fill to the brim with big fat solid cock...

I was coming before I really knew it. He was absolutely hammering into me, shaking my whole body like a toy in his huge hands, so strong, so powerful. I felt my body go tight and I was crying out my ecstasy into the tiles of the floor, then writhing on him, desperate for all the cock he could give me as I came and came. I got plenty, pushed deep in, over and over again, with a fresh burst of ecstasy hitting me each time. It was so good, and right at the peak I could feel myself tightening on his cock, before I went limp in his hands.

He just kept on fucking, grunting and puffing, his fingers locked on my hips, rendering me utterly helpless. I took it as I panted into the pool of cider on the floor. My boobs were splashing in it too, as they bounced to the rhythm of my fucking, and my knees slipping, my whole body out of my control.

I couldn't have stopped him doing it in me, and my body wanted it. He didn't, but pulled out after a last deep shove. I was turned, by main force, just spun around, slipping in the cider pool. His cock was pushed at my mouth and I took it in, sucking in eager expectation of an immediate mouthful, only to have him it jerk it free, grab my tits and fold them around his erection, pushing hard up.

I saw his cock emerge from between the big pink pillows of my breasts, and I saw the come erupt from the tip. I shut my eyes just in time, and he did it, over my face and into my open mouth, a gesture so wonder-fully rude that I was masturbating again even as the second spurt splashed across my cheek.

He watched as I did it, still holding his cock as I brought myself off in front of him. I was squatting down, my sodden panties taut between my knees, my mouth agape, both eyes shut, with his hot come run-ning down over my face and breasts. As I came I was thinking not of him, but of how rude I was being, how dirty, just the way I'm supposed to be.

Chrissy and Jack had been gone a long time, and that could only mean one thing. She really is such a slut. I mean, all that fuss over Michael, and she's shagging some farm boy in five minutes.

When they eventually did come back, my suspicions were confirmed. She'd gone off in her wet panties and top, regardless of who might see her, and she came back the same, only her hair was wet too. So she'd showered, and it hadn't been to cool down or get the mud off her legs. They were behaving differently as well, trying not to be obvious, but failing miserably.

Lunch was all I'd expected, great big crusty pork pies and rough cider straight from the bottle. They obviously hadn't discovered plates, or glasses, or cutlery, or servi-ettes, as there weren't any. The cider was at least cold. It was also strong, leaving me feeling pleasantly drowsy after lunch, horny too, after a whole morning watching half-naked men at work.

It would have been nice to have some fun with Michael but it was hardly practical without everybody knowing exactly what we were doing. Unlike Chrissy, I prefer not to have my sexual encounters made public knowledge. So I told myself it could wait for the evening, put some more sun-tan cream on and settled down to doze in the sun. The others went back to their game.

They had exposed quite a bit of the barge, and were pulling up reeds where the side was in the water, Chrissy included. She was making a show of herself, with her wet panties riding up into the crease of her bottom as she bent to pull at the roots, with more and more cheek spilling out each time. She was just feet away from Michael, but I wasn't worried, as she didn't look sexy at all, just ridiculous.

It was only when she bent right down, showing just about everything, that I realised her bottom was bruised. There was no question about it, dull bluish blotches showing on both her cheeks. I didn't imagine for a moment that she'd fallen on her arse. She'd been spanked, and quite recently.

It was just the sort of perverted behaviour she would let herself get talked into, or simply have done to her, so it didn't entirely surprise me. The question was: who had done it? Michael was into it, but he'd never been alone with her, not since London, so that option was out. I couldn't see Jack doing it either. He was a typical country lad, without the brains to think of sex as anything other than sticking his cock in the nearest convenient hole. That left Malcolm Callington, the Spanking Major himself, a known pervert who had had Chrissy to himself for several days.

So he'd spanked her. That left several questions. Had she been willing? Had he taken her panties down? Had he fucked her afterwards? What did Michael make of it? Did Pippa know?

Some of the questions I could answer. If Michael couldn't see the state her bottom was in, he was blind.

He hadn't reacted in any way at all, which suggested he knew, or just didn't care. More likely he knew, and as Chrissy had been sulking, she could hardly have told him. His father might have done, but that struck me as weird, too weird even for them. I mean, how many fathers and sons discuss their sex lives?

So it was more likely to have been Pippa or Tilly, who were both pretty close to Michael. If they'd told him, they knew. Not just that, but it was hard to imagine Malcolm Callington getting enough privacy on the yacht to dish out spankings without everyone else aboard knowing about it. Even if he'd done it while the others were on deck, they'd have surely heard. It was bound to be noisy, both the slaps and the girl's cries, and I knew Chrissy – she'd have absolutely howled.

That meant they had some sort of cosy little spanking club going, just the sort of perverted thing I'd have expected, and which Chrissy would have joined in. Not that she's particularly perverted herself, just a slut, too weak-willed to resist, and always desperate for acceptance. The only thing I didn't know was how dirty it got.

Gold star for deduction, Miss de Lacy.

It was all very intriguing, but what could I get out of it?

14

Michael was taking Valentina out to dinner. That meant court.

I was still feeling very ambivalent about joining in. Since having sex with Jack again I felt less crushed, and spanking was a new thrill I very much wanted to explore. I didn't feel I should be letting Malcolm do it to me though, or even Pippa and Tilly. That didn't mean I couldn't watch.

The idea of seeing the two of them caned was enough to set my stomach fluttering. Valentina had suggested the dinner to Michael, implying that he hadn't been paying her enough attention during the afternoon. He'd accepted, and suggested a well-respected fish restaurant in Norwich. That left us the whole evening, or would have done had not Jack picked up on the dinner idea and asked me out to Great Yarmouth for fish and chips.

I'd accepted, and after a quick conference with Malcolm and the girls had asked him to pick me up at seven, which left at least a clear hour in which I could watch the caning. It was perfect, as it not only left me safe from Malcolm, but from my own dirty feelings towards Tilly or any further revenge the girls might have in mind.

We'd cleared a good half of the wherry by teatime, and called it a day. Back at the cottage we showered and changed, Valentina into a beautiful evening gown,

Michael into smart casuals, and myself into rather less smart casuals. Pippa and Tilly went to shower last, sharing, and came down in skimpy shorts and bikini tops, supposedly so that they could catch the last of the day's sun in the garden. I knew better: that was where they had chosen to be caned.

Their apprehension must have been dreadful if mine was anything to go by. Valentina dawdled over her make-up, and in the end didn't leave until gone six. I watched them go from an upstairs window, still jealous but far more excited by the prospect of what was about to happen. When the car was finally out of sight I ran downstairs, to report to Malcolm that they really had gone and that it was safe to give the girls their punishment.

We came out together, to find both Pippa and Tilly lying face down on the lawn, watching us. Both got up as we approached and turned to stand to attention, like soldiers. It was as if they were in uniform too, tight white shorts and bright green bikinis, making them look more identical than ever, almost as if they were twins.

Never one to neglect a detail, Malcolm had a cane on the *Harold Jones*. It was a real old-fashioned school cane, with a crook handle and knobbles. Just looking at it sent a shiver right down my spine, and the prospect of being whacked with it was absolutely terrifying. The girls couldn't keep their eyes off it either, and I was very, very glad Jack was taking me out.

Malcolm came to stand in front of them, fingering the cane as he let his eyes linger on their near-naked bodies. He reached out suddenly, to twitch Pippa's bikini top up and spill out her breasts. She reacted with not more than a tremor, setting the flesh of her breasts quivering. Her nipples were hard, her skin prickled with sweat, and I don't think it was from the heat. Tilly's bikini top followed, the cups casually flipped up to expose her breasts. Like her sister, her nipples were erect and, like her sister, she barely reacted to the exposure. Malcolm gave a satisfied nod.

'About turn.'

Both moved together, turning smartly and stamping their feet in unison, to present him with the backs of their shorts, the material taut across the twin bulges of their bottom cheeks. There was a little cruel smile on his face, and he was obviously enjoying himself immensely. I could see the pleasure in it too, after so many years in the army, of making his wife and sister-in-law drill topless.

He stuck the cane under his arm like a swagger stick and began to walk around them, very slowly. When he reached the front, his hand came out, to snip open the button on Pippa's shorts and ease down her zip. Tilly was given the same treatment, and both girls' shorts were left loose on their hips. He came behind again, took hold of Pippa's shorts and pulled. Down they came, to her knees, leaving her covered only by the green bikini bottoms. Those followed, tugged smartly down as if it was nothing to expose her bottom and pussy outdoors. A twitch in one thigh muscle betrayed her emotions as she came bare, no more.

I was trembling and biting my lips, unable to hold my own feelings back. They were so much braver than me, Tilly not even flinching as she was stripped, shorts and bikini bottoms pulled down into a tangle around her knees before Malcolm stood to admire the two bare bottoms at his disposal. He glanced at his watch, nodded and looked away. They were left standing, bare and vulnerable, Malcolm not checking his watch again until at least five minutes had passed. He then snapped out an order.

'Assume position.'

Both girls went down immediately, bending to touch their toes and part their pert apple-shaped bottoms, showing off pussies and bumholes. It is such a rude position for a girl to be in, so open, so yielding ... so humiliating when it's because she's about to be whacked with a cane and by a man thirty years or so older than her. I wanted it myself, just the same.

I could see their faces, upside down and framed in curtains of silky hair, Pippa with her eyes shut, Tilly watching Malcolm with an expression of serious trepidation. He took a step to the side, flexed the cane and put it to Pippa's bottom, pressing to make her flesh swell out above and below.

'Six strokes, as agreed.'

The cane came up and down, hissing through the air to land plumb across Pippa's naked bottom. She cried out in pain, shaking her head to make her breasts and bottom quiver even as a thin white line sprang up across her cheeks. The line turned quickly red as Malcolm pulled back the cane once more. I could only stare, my feelings of sympathy and arousal both strong, guilty, yet already badly in need of a hand to my pussy.

Six times the cane lashed down across Pippa's bottom to leave six red lines across her beautiful pale skin. Each was double, with a thin line of richer red to either side. He had done it just so too, laying five perfectly parallel and the sixth across the others, like a five-bar gate. That really got to me, as if it was not enough to give his wife the cane, he had to amuse himself by making patterns on her bottom. It had got to her too, her pussy flesh puffy and moist, all too obviously ready to take a cock.

'Up.'

Pippa responded immediately, pulling up her shorts and bikini bottoms even as she stood. She was flushed, her fingers trembling as she pulled her cups back down over her breasts, her mouth a little open, and eyes wide and moist. She came to me, squatting down on the lawn to watch her sister's punishment.

Tilly had begun to shake, the flesh of her bottom quivering slightly. Her cheeks tensed as the cane was laid gently across them, and she shut her eyes. It came up and down. She screamed as it hit, clutching at her ankles, but stayed down, her breath coming in sharp, ragged pants. The second stroke lashed down. Again she screamed, and her bumhole began to wink, a sight so rude I found myself closing my eyes in sympathy for her.

I opened them again at the thwack of her third stroke, because instead of screaming, she gasped, and there was no mistaking the pleasure in the sound. Pippa gave a little sigh and put her hand on my leg. The fourth stroke came down. Tilly gasped and twitched. Already her pussy was running juice. She was going to want it attended to, I was sure, and I knew who by. I wouldn't resist. Maybe I would do Pippa too, down on my knees, taking both to ecstasy under my tongue; maybe I'd suck Malcolm too, maybe they'd strip me, spank me, cane me . . .

The ring of the doorbell broke my fantasy. Tilly jumped up and fled into the house, giggling, her lowered clothes clutched in one hand. Malcolm quickly tucked the cane into a bush, not a moment too soon, as

Jack's head appeared around the end of a hedge. I smiled.

I was blushing, I couldn't help myself, and he must have realised we'd been up to something. He didn't say anything though, except to greet us and shake Malcolm's offered hand. Pippa went indoors to fetch drinks and Tilly came out again, now decent, and for the next ten minutes we were discussing the wherry and the old dyke as if nothing had happened.

My feelings hadn't changed. I needed sex so, so badly, and I needed spanking sex. Jack would be game, I knew, but only after dinner and a few drinks. I couldn't wait that long. Fortunately he was in a four-wheel-drive and not the tractor, which is not the best vehicle when it comes to spanking and fucking sessions.

He was keen to get moving, but I wasn't having any of that. Even as we set off I was burrowing for his cock, and his lust had taken over before I even got it out. He pulled over to the side of the lane and I was down on him, taking his lovely big cock in my mouth even as it sprang free of his fly.

'My, you are urgent!' he said.

I pulled off his cock just long enough to pant out a response.

'Spank my bottom. Fuck me,' I implored.

He laughed and stuck my head back on his cock, holding me down as he came to erection. I moved, kneeling up on the seat, my bottom high, the way I wanted it. His hand came around my body to ease up my skirt. Thick, rough fingers slipped into my panties, then into my body, pushing deep up my pussy.

'You're soaking! What have you been up to?'

I shook my head on my mouthful of cock. It was not

time to talk. He laughed and began to finger-fuck me, until I was squirming my bottom on his hand as I sucked on his cock. He was ready, and as he eased my head off his cock I thought for one awful moment he was just going to fuck me. He didn't, but manoeuvred me, still holding me by my pussy, across his lap.

My head bumped on the door. He opened it. I squeaked in alarm as I fell forward, half out of the car, my bum stuck up in the air over his lap. Anyone who came past was going to see me, see me getting my spanking. I began to struggle, giggling stupidly even as I tried to escape.

I might as well have tried to escape a gorilla. He held me tight, one arm around my waist, lifted my skirt, pulled down my knickers and began to spank my bottom. Immediately I was completely out of control, laughing and squealing as he laid into me, slapping away so hard it knocked the breath from my body. It hurt, but it was nice from the start, hot and stinging, to put me on the most wonderful sexual high. I didn't care that I might be seen, or how rude and undignified my position was, I just wanted to be spanked and spanked and spanked.

He obliged, laughing as he slapped away at my bottom, with his huge hand cupping most of my flesh. I could feel his cock against my tummy too, and I knew where it was going once he'd finished with me.

It was when we heard a car in the distance that he stopped, pulling me in and slamming the door just in time to stop them getting an eyeful of my upturned, rosy bottom. It was an elderly couple, and once they'd passed, we just dissolved into laughter.

Not for long. I was getting into position even as the sound of their engine died, over the seat with the headrest pulled off. My bum came up and he was behind me, mounted on my back, his cock pushing up between my cheeks, then to my pussy and in. I cried out as I was filled, jerking at my top at the same time. My boobs spilled out and he was fucking me, pumping away frantically on my back with my red-hot bottom pressed against him. Even when we caught the sound of another car he didn't stop, and I couldn't.

We must have been halfway to Norwich before Michael realised that all his cards were in another pair of trousers. He only had thirty pounds in cash and I hadn't brought any, so there was nothing for it but to go back.

As we drove, I'd been thinking of what I could gain from my knowledge of their dirty little games. I needed to know a little more, but there was no hurry in any case. The answer was to wait, and to build up my ammunition, perhaps even lead Michael into thinking he could carry on while he was with me. Valentina's rules for dealing with men – know thy enemy.

I could make a deal, telling him he could spank Tilly, which I was sure he did, even Pippa. If Chrissy was still around I could include her too, then when the time came I would be in a very strong position indeed. In fact, it was best to include Chrissy, and while the others might try to deny it, she was so soft that she was sure to tell the truth, the whole truth and nothing but the whole dirty truth.

It was perfect. As soon as we were engaged I'd give up my wretched job. I'd still play dirty for Michael, at least until we got married, maybe longer. Possibly it might even be worth waiting until the old man pegged it, depending on how much he was going to settle on

Michael. Then when I got bored, or fancied something younger and more pliable, pow!

Michael was concentrating on his driving, which was maniacal, and hardly said a word until we were nearly home, and then it was to swear.

'Good God!'

Good God was about right. There was a four-wheel-drive parked by the roadside and we had a clear view through the windscreen of a huge, hairy backside. It wasn't still either, but pumping up and down, its owner clearly well up his girlfriend, who had to be the last word in sluts.

She was. It was Chrissy. As we passed I got one good look at her, or at least at her bottom, which was stuck up over the seat, with the tarty black skirt she'd put on turned up on to her back and a pair of bright pink panties down around her thighs. It was Jack on top of her, although it wouldn't have surprised me if it had been someone completely different. What did surprise me was his cock. I saw it for just an instant, as he pulled back. He never left her body, but most men would have had it waving in the air so far back. He was huge!

Then we were past. Michael laughed, but I was left staring back, the image of that gigantic cock pushing into Chrissy's body burnt indelibly into my mind. I'd known he was a decent size, from the afternoon, but I had never suspected the full truth of it. He wasn't just long either, but thick, really thick. It's the thickness that counts, and just the thought had my skin prickling all over.

The house smelt of sex, and I was sure Malcolm and Pippa had been up to something, maybe even Tilly as well. Both girls were in nothing but skimpy shorts and bikini tops, the way they'd been sunbathing earlier, but they were indoors and both of them seemed more than a little agitated when we turned up.

We took the cards and left immediately. Jack and Chrissy had finished, but we caught up with his car in Hickling village. For a while we were behind, until Michael managed to overtake. I waved cheerfully as we sped past, and again caught a glimpse of his broad red face. He looked as bovine as ever, but if he looked like a bull, he was hung like one too. He was also Chrissy's new boyfriend.

It had turned out according to Valentina's rules, as I suppose it was always going to. She had the best. I had the rest.

As she was sure to point out when she got the chance to give me my lecture, I would have been much better off if I'd accepted my place from the start. I'd have enjoyed my sail up the coast and had a happy time with someone suited to me during the holiday. Of course I wouldn't have met Jack if it hadn't been for my little tantrum, but if not him it would doubtless have been someone similar.

I did at least have one major consolation. I'd discovered the joys of a well-spanked bottom, and if it was something Valentina was sure to disapprove of, then she'd probably also see it as further evidence of my lack of style. Meanwhile, I could make the best of what I'd got.

Cock-wise, I'd got plenty, and Jack was eager to supply. It was a great evening, scampi and chips on the front, mucking about in the amusement arcades, then down under the pier for a long, slow suck of his cock. I did it squatting down in front of him, and at least two other couples were nearby, up to much the same in the darkness, to judge by the rude, wet noises they made. By the time he came in my mouth I was well ready myself, and finished off with my fingers down my knickers as I licked and sucked at his cock and balls. Afterwards he said he'd never been with such a dirty girl, which was obviously meant as a compliment, but which I jokingly pretended to be offended by, hitting him with my bag. His response was to hoist me up over his shoulder and carry me to a bench, where he spanked me, just on the seat of my skirt, but with quite a few people watching.

That had me in fits of giggles, and after a couple of drinks at one of the seafront bars I was ready for more. He wasn't, quite, and it took a lot of teasing, including flashing my boobs for him in a back street, before he gave in. I ran, and let myself get caught in a quiet alley, where he fucked me up against a wall with my knickers off and his hands under my bare bum.

By then I'd forgotten all about Michael and Valentina. I was drunk, horny and having fun, in my element. I managed to lose my knickers, and had to go bare under my skirt as we walked back along the front, which felt deliciously naughty. Jack even pulled my skirt up at the back a couple of times to flash my bare bum, which just made me dissolve in giggles.

I felt naughtier still in the warm darkness inside his car, and pulled up my skirt to masturbate as soon as we were clear of the houses. He kept his concentration on the road for about a minute, before pulling over to have me suck on him as I brought myself to my third orgasm of the evening. By then he was erect, and I got fucked over the seat again, bum up, and given a couple of swats for being so rude once he finished.

It seemed pointless to make him drive to Hickling and back just so he could drop me off, so it was back to his parents' farm and the converted space above the attic, to drink cider while we played macho computer games very badly, and for one final fuck before I fell asleep in his arms.

Michael's fish restaurant was everything I'd expected: sophisticated, exclusive and expensive, definitely expensive. It was the least I deserved after putting up with the bucolic amusements he seemed to mistake for leisure, and I made a point of choosing the most expensive dishes. That meant starting with a plate of langoustine and a salad drizzled with red-wine vinegar and moving on to freshly caught lobster. Michael didn't notice, but it was still satisfying. He chose a delicious wine too, one of the best on the list, explaining at length that it was from some vineyard in which the grape perfectly complemented the soil or something.

I didn't really want dessert, but ordered some fancy confection of chocolate and liqueur anyway, with which Michael insisted on ordering another bottle of wine. I imagined some hideous sticky thing, but it was actually delicious, and even more expensive than the first.

When the time came to pay the bill he did it without a murmur. I prefer my men to blanch a little when they pay a dinner bill. It makes it absolutely clear I'm not a cheap date. But this was Michael, and he was still talking about some rowing event he'd won in Cambridge as he handed over his card. I don't think he even read the total.

He had barely touched the wine, as he had to drive back, so I had most of both bottles, with an Irish coffee to follow, which left me pleasantly tipsy, and pleasantly horny.

I knew he'd want sex on the way back in the car. I was prepared to give it, but it wasn't really him I was thinking of, but Jack, with his huge cock pushing into Chrissy's body. People who say size doesn't matter don't know what they're talking about. OK, so it may not feel all that different inside, unless the guy's either a complete needle dick or deformed, but it makes all the difference to look at, to hold, to suck. I like big cocks, and I like beautiful cocks, and by the look of it, his was both. So was Michael's, a little less impressive perhaps, but that wasn't what really mattered. I had Michael's. I didn't have Jack's. I was working myself up into a fine state as we drove back towards Hickling. It was easy to imagine how it would be. All I'd have to do was flirt a little and Jack's attention would move from Chrissy to me. He'd do as he was told too, grateful for my attention, letting me ride his wonderful big cock all the way to orgasm. It wouldn't even present a problem afterwards, as I could explain that it was our little secret and return him to Chrissy, at least until the next time.

I wasn't at all surprised when Michael pulled off the main road and drew into the parking area of a picnic spot. I was horny enough to put up with sex in the car, and we were soon kissing with the seats down and his cock growing rapidly to erection in my hand. Not wanting to crumple my dress, I peeled down to bra and panties, along with my stay-ups. He liked that, getting very passionate indeed as he took me in his arms again.

As always, he just took over. We were kissing and I was stroking at his cock, then he had rolled me up to pull off my panties and slip a finger into my ready sex. My bra followed the panties and I was next to nude, with him still fully dressed and just his cock bare. I began to tug his clothes, eager to have him naked, but he wasn't having any of it. He turned me face down, as if I were just a doll. His mouth went to the nape of my neck, nibbling gently as he swung his leg over my body, and he was on top of me, his cock pressing between my bottom cheeks.

There was the familiar stab of resentment as he slid into me from the rear, but it soon went, with him moving faster and faster inside me and his mouth at my neck, bringing me to helpless ecstasy within moments. I thought he'd make me come like that, and I began to push my bottom up against him in the hope of getting my clitoris attended to. Sure enough, he pulled out, only to take me firmly by the hips and lift me into a kneeling position, mount me and slide his cock back in.

It was how Jack had been fucking Chrissy, more or less, and that was just fine by me. I let my fantasy run, thinking of Jack's great, ox-like body and huge, rough hands. To control a man like that would be wonderful, and I'd make sure he did just what he was told. I'd teach him to make me come the way Michael did, the way Michael was about to, as he took his cock in hand and began to rub it on me.

I made myself as comfortable as I could, my legs braced well apart and my bottom lifted to the pressure of his cock. I was going to come, in moments. My fantasy was growing, to take in the thought of sitting astride Jack, using his huge cock to pleasure myself, using him as Michael used me, in front of Chrissy.

He stopped. His cock went up, to my bottom hole. I

gasped in protest as he pushed, but I was loose and he went a little way in immediately, a sensation just too good to resist. My cheeks were wide, completely open to him, and a lot of his weight was on me. There was nothing I could do anyway but just take it and try not to grunt too much as it was pushed up, inch by inch, until the full, fat length was inside me.

He buggered me again, as dirty and disrespectful as ever, but for all that it felt glorious. It felt more glorious still as his hand reached round under my tummy to find my clit, and even more disrespectful. He really did treat me like his sex toy, sticking his cock up my bottom and masturbating me to make me come while he was in me. Not that I tried to stop him, wriggling on his cock in utter ecstasy as sheer physical pleasure took over, my fantasy forgotten as my climax rose up and exploded in my head.

Even as I came, he came too, deep inside me, our cries of pleasure merging for a moment before trailing off, his to a satisfied sigh, mine to a sob. It really was too much, and I found myself scowling as he pulled slowly out. I'd let him do it, and he knew how I responded, so he expected it all the time, and took it when he wanted it. That's not the way I work. I give when I want to give, and while I can't deny liking it, my bottom is a big privilege.

There was no use explaining. I knew he wouldn't understand, men never do. Yes, I'd enjoyed it, but if he was going to carry on treating me like that I needed something to restore my own sense of worth, of being an object of adoration. I would definitely have to have Jack.

15

It was just a question of time and place. Once I'd got rid of Michael and Chrissy, preferably separately, and found an excuse to be alone with Jack, the rest would be easy. It turned out to be even easier than I'd expected.

There was a fresh breeze in the morning, and they were keen to take the yacht out. Chrissy wasn't there, which meant she had spent the night with Jack. So I volunteered to wait for her and said that we'd meet them in the pub at Hickling once the yacht was ready, or to go without us and meet up at Potter Heigham for lunch if they were late. They disappeared off across the lake in the inflatable dinghy and I was alone.

Chrissy and Jack turned up an hour later in his four-wheel-drive. She was looking thoroughly pleased with herself, and was friendly to me, even admitting that she'd been wrong to chase Michael and apologising for making an exhibition of herself. He was keen to get back, presumably to get on with whatever it was they did at the farm. I soon put a stop to that.

I was in my bikini and wrap, which I didn't think he'd resist for long. Sure enough, he agreed to come over to Hickling for lunch. I suggested taking the rowing boat in case the yacht left while we were driving round. Chrissy jumped at the idea. So it was down to the boathouse, at which point I managed to twist my ankle, quite badly.

Profuse apologies, a little show of pain, a little masculine protectiveness for the weak and helpless female, and Jack was helping me back to the cottage, and the car, while Chrissy rowed off across the lake. Neat work, Valentina.

The rest was easier still. I asked him to carry me across a rough bit of track. He picked me up. He was holding me, near-naked, his cock pushing against my hip as we moved. Back at the cottage I asked him to carry me up to my bed, made a teasing remark about him getting hard and that was it. I mean, for all the sophistication of his response, he might as well have been a real bull.

He asked if I wanted it. I nodded and out came his cock. It was huge, really impressive, thick and smooth and meaty. I took it in my mouth, sucking as he began to paw me. He was clumsy, and a bit rough, pulling off my wrap and flipping my bikini top up with eager fingers. I opened his trousers as he grew in my mouth, determined that if I was going to go bare, so was he. Coarse fingers took hold of my bikini pants, pulling them down over my bottom. I came off his cock.

'You first. I want you to strip naked, and I mean naked.'

I'd been right. Once I took charge, he was as soft as anything. His clothes came off, all of them. Nude, he looked more ox-like than ever, with his great slabs of muscle and flesh, and the huge cock sticking up from under his belly. Deciding nude was better than dishevelled, I quickly peeled off my bikini. He watched, grinning and tugging at his cock. I knelt up on the bed, my knees wide, my breasts in my hands.

'Do you like what you see, Jack?'

'Sure.'

'Well, you can have it, if you're a good boy. Now lie down on the bed.'

He nodded and went down, holding his cock in his hand, his eyes never once leaving my body. I straddled him, my knees barely touching the bedcover across his massive thighs. As he pressed his cock to my sex, I lifted a little then sank down, sighing as I filled. He felt great inside me, and as I began to fuck him I was telling myself that seducing him had been a very good move indeed.

He really was like an ox, a great, passive beast, lying beneath me as I pleasured myself on his erection. It was perfect, so different from Michael's smugness and control-freakery. Even when he took me by the hips and began to push into me from beneath that was fine, his grip so strong that I could play with my breasts as I rode him and still feel stable.

I wanted to come, eventually. Not soon though, and nor did he, making me glad he'd had Chrissy to take the edge off his appetite before he got down to the serious stuff – pleasuring me. It was quite funny to think about actually, Chrissy getting a quick, rough porking, probably down on all fours, with her pig-like body quivering to the hard, urgent motions of his ox-like one. Real barnyard stuff.

I laughed at the thought. Jack grinned in response, doubtless thinking it was just from the sheer pleasure of being on his cock. I wriggled, feeling his balls squirm against my bottom, and his grin became broader still. I rode on, sliding him in and out, rising to take the head of his cock into the mouth of my sex, wiggling myself on to him again, stroking my breasts, really enjoying myself.

Jack's hands moved to take a firmer hold on me, by

my bottom. He stretched my cheeks, opening my bottom hole fully to the air. I thought of Michael and the delight he took in buggering me. That triggered a fantasy. My eyes closed and my hand went to my clit.

Michael would come in, catching us. He wouldn't be cross, though. He'd realise what I needed, that ultimately it was my satisfaction that counted. I'd tell him he could have me, as I was, if he learned a little respect, if he learned that I came first. He'd nod, his cock already free of his trousers, and erect. I'd tell him to strip. He'd obey.

Naked, with his hard cock in his hand, he'd come up behind me. His big cock-head would press to my bottom hole. I'd let myself open, taking him, slowly, easily, until his fully glorious length was up my bottom, even as Jack pumped into me from below. I'd still be in control, rubbing myself to ecstasy as they moved inside me with an even, firm rhythm, giving me their cocks for my pleasure.

My clitoris was burning under my finger. Jack was pushing harder, bouncing me to make my breasts jump and my hair fly. I was going to come, thinking of what I'd got, what I'd have – two fine young men, two men to pleasure me. Maybe they could really be persuaded to share me, one in each hole, my body so wonderfully full, Jack in my sex, Michael up my bottom, taking me, taking me all the way . . .

I came, crying out as I tightened on Jack's penis and my legs clamped on to his body. He just kept on pumping, my big, patient ox, all cock and muscle, all for me. It lasted well, and he kept a steady rhythm up until at last I was satisfied. He hadn't come, but that wasn't really my problem. I climbed off, expecting him to demand a suck and that I'd have to read him a rule or two. He didn't, just taking hold of himself as he left my body, to tug on the shaft, his eyes fixed on me.

He may have been hoping for something more, but I needed a shower.

I paused in mid-oarstroke. Jack had disappeared from sight, holding Valentina in his arms. She'd come down with a nasty bump, but ...

No, it was just me being suspicious. She really had fallen, and it had been decent of him to help her. It was just my suspicious mind that was wondering if she hadn't been acting up. After all, why would she bother with Jack? He was overweight, not nearly as good-looking as Michael, and had a lot less money to spend. He just wasn't her type.

The bow had come round in the wind, leaving me looking down the length of the broad, towards Hickling. The surface of the water was ruffled, with windsurfers and people in dinghies making the best of the weather. I could see the *Harold Jones* too, in the distance, and someone on deck, either Pippa or Tilly. They had her covers off, which meant that if I didn't get there quickly I'd miss them.

I swung the boat around and began to pull towards the village. The cottage came into view once more, or at least the upper windows, and the roof of Jack's car. They hadn't left. Again a nasty suspicion came into my head, and a memory. There had been a boy I'd been with briefly when Valentina was going out with Andy Dawtry. His name had been Dan something-or-other. I'd dumped him because he wanted me to suck his dick in front of his mates, just to show what a big man he was. He'd boasted he'd had Val while he was with me, that she'd come on to him. It had seemed ridiculous, when she was with Andy, and I'd put it down to spite because I'd finished with him. It had been odd though, because he'd said she went on top. Most boys wouldn't admit to letting a girl go on top.

Again I stopped rowing. The car hadn't moved. There was something else wrong too. The bathroom window was steamed up. Her ankle was so bad she needed to be carried and she was taking a shower?

Seducing Jack hadn't just been a good move. It had been a great move. It had made me feel much better about Michael and, more importantly, about myself. There was more. Michael liked Norfolk. He could be counted on to go frequently, more frequently still with a little encouragement. With luck he might even be persuaded to buy one of the little riverside holiday homes I'd seen as we made our way up to Hickling. That way I'd have him and Jack on tap, maybe others. I'd have to be careful, of course, so as not to give him any ammunition when the divorce came, but I'd still be in a strong position, with the notorious Spanking Major as my father-in-law.

Jack had gone downstairs to try and find a beer. I was in the bathroom, thinking as I showered of a life of ease and wealth. Possibly I'd be able to secure the London flat, even the flat and the Norfolk house. It would need a lot, maybe photos of Michael spanking Tilly, Pippa even. With those I could really go to town, playing the innocent, aggrieved wife with a husband who was not only an adulterer but a pervert. I'd get everything, the flat, the car. Of course I really needed a kid to put the final touch to it, but there are limits. Valentina's rule for dealing with men – no brats, ever.

My happy daydream was interrupted by Jack. He

was holding his cock, still erect. For a moment I considered telling him to get out, but abandoned the idea. A good, worshipful attitude was what I wanted from him, and if letting him ogle my body was going to add to that, then fine. Body worship is good – my body, their worship. Besides, I didn't want him resentful.

So I put up with it, letting him masturbate as he watched me shower. I thought he'd come, but he didn't, just preening his cock, obviously proud of his dimensions. It was getting to me a bit, and by the time I'd finished I was even wondering if I had the time to fuck him again, or maybe have him go down on me.

I stepped from the shower, reaching for a towel to wrap around my body. As I bent for a second to do my hair I knew he would have a view of my bottom sticking out from under the edge, a good teasing view. Yes, I was going to do it, sit on the stool and have him lick me, and if he wanted to come in his hand, then fair enough...

His hands took my hips, suddenly, lifting me as if I weighed nothing. I cried out in alarm, only for the sound to turn to a gasp as I was simply sat down on his cock, the full length pushing up into my body in two firm shoves. I was going to protest, but he was already bouncing me up and down on his cock like a doll, and the words died in my mouth. It was too good. My hands went to my breasts, and I'd given in, saying it would be just the once even as he eased me forward. I went down, over the bath, and I was being fucked doggystyle.

My resentment of the rough treatment faded to the feel of his cock. It was good, undeniably good, undignified or not. A voice in the back of my head was telling me that Michael had changed something in me, even as Jack put his hands to my bottom. It was true, he had, but I couldn't cope with it, not just now, not with my cheeks spread by his big thumbs, my bottom hole on view, available . . .

'What a gorgeous arse, I'd like –'

'Oh, God, do it then . . .'

His hands left my bottom. His cock slid from me. I hung my head down into the bath, shivering at the prospect of anal entry, and his hand came down, full across my bottom. I squealed in shock, trying to turn even as he took me hard around the waist and a second smack landed, harder still, knocking the breath from my body. A third landed, a fourth, and I was being spanked, really being spanked, furious indignation flaring in my head as I finally found my voice.

'No! Stop it!'

He stopped.

'What's the matter?'

'What the fuck do you think you're doing?'

'Spanking your arse, like you said.'

'I did not!'

'You did.'

'No, I . . .'

I trailed off. Suddenly I didn't want to tell him what I actually had wanted any more. It was just too embarrassing. He went on.

'Sorry. I thought that's what you girls were into.'

'Just because Chrissy Green is a pervert doesn't mean I am!'

I stood up, to pull the towel around me once more. I was feeling confused and a little ashamed of my own reactions. It had never been that quick before, or so hard to fight the urge to get down on all fours and take a man's cock up my bottom. I knew who to blame too:

Michael Callington. I wasn't too happy with Chrissy either, for filling Jack's head with perverted ideas.

Jack just stood there looking stupid and holding his cock. I wasn't interested, or I was trying to tell myself I wasn't, because I knew what would happen if I gave in again. I'd ask him to bugger me, because it was what I really needed. I also needed coffee, or at least I managed to tell myself I did. I went downstairs to get it, saving myself. Jack followed, ambling after me. He spoke as we reached the kitchen.

'Sorry, Val. I'm just not used to this kinky stuff, that's all. I know what you wanted, all right? I'll do it, yeah? Like I said, you've got a great arse.'

I turned on him, intending to give him a piece of my mind. No words came out of my mouth. He was standing there, his cock in one hand, the butter dish in the other, grinning. I moved back against the table, trying to fight my need. He came close. An arm came around me, under my bottom, to lift me on to the table. I heard my own resigned moan as I went back.

His cock pushed to my sex and in, bliss mingling with regret as we began to fuck. My legs came up, rolled high to let him get in deep. He obliged, pushing hard in. I closed my eyes. One big hand took hold of both my ankles, pushing my knees up against my chest. Something touched between my well-parted bottom cheeks, something greasy. I moaned again as a well-buttered finger pushed up into my bottom. He was going to bugger me, and I couldn't even find the will to pretend I didn't want it.

I was shaking as his cock pulled slowly from my sex. He was still fingering my bottom, and even as he pulled out, his cock moved down. I let myself go loose, accepting him as he pushed, and it was in, his lovely penis easing slowly up my bottom, filling me, until I felt I would burst.

As he began to move inside me I was clutching the table in ecstasy. He still had my ankles, holding me still as he buggered me, as if he needed to. I was willing, more than willing, really eager, but still wondering why I was so dirty.

There was no answer, only pleasure, as I pushed my hand down to masturbate as he had me right in front of him, in full view. I didn't want to do it, but I had to, and come before he did. His pushes got harder even as I began to rub, and harder still. I heard myself as I began to grunt in response, unable to hold back the rude, animal noises drawn from my throat. I was going to come and began to think dirty, really dirty, as the image of them both having me rose up, only different.

They'd find out about each other. They wouldn't fight or argue, they'd come to me, tell me I was a dirty bitch, strip me, put me on all fours, and take me up my bottom, each in turn, in my mouth first, then up my bottom . . .

I screamed, coming on Jack's cock in burning, blinding ecstasy. It was so good, better even than the last, and left me weak and limp as a rag doll as he took a firm grip on my legs and began to pump hard into me for his own orgasm.

I knew what I wanted to see as I walked towards the cottage: Valentina laid out on the settee with a mug of coffee in her hands. I knew what I was expecting to see too, nothing, because the two of them would be upstairs, shagging, or in the shower together.

What I did not expect to see was Valentina rolled up on the kitchen table in the nude with Jack inside her, and up her bottom at that. I just stared, all my bad feelings rushing in, betrayal and self-pity and anger and sorrow, until I thought my head would burst. I couldn't face them. I couldn't face an argument. I couldn't face the awful mealy-mouthed explanation Valentina would trot out.

So I ran again, the way I always do, tears streaming as I dashed back to the rowing boat. I was choking with emotion, so overcome that I was halfway across the broad before I even had the sense to think what I was doing. I couldn't go to the yacht, not in the state I was in, and I couldn't go to the cottage, not with them there. So I pulled in the oars, letting myself drift in among the reeds of an island, where I put my face in my hands and let my misery flow over me.

She had taken Michael away from me, and now Jack. Not that there was anything to stop me going on with Jack, except my own pride, what was left of it. In fact, even with the cold pain of the betrayal still fresh, I knew I probably would. If I made a big performance of it, Valentina would just have one more satisfying detail to add to her conquest, Jack and I alone. Besides, I'd known he preferred her to me anyway, I'd known he would even before they met.

What I wasn't going to do was forgive her, not this time. She had Michael, and the only reason she could possibly want Jack was because he was mine, to show that she could take him. Well, she had done it too often. I might stay with Jack, if he still wanted me, but I would not forgive Valentina de Lacy. I would get my revenge.

I could tell Michael . . .

Only I couldn't. I knew exactly what would happen. They'd deny it.

They'd deny it, and Valentina would make me look like a spiteful little bitch in front of everybody. Not that she'd be nasty. No, she'd be kind about it, defending me on the grounds that I was only saying it because I was upset over Michael. That would make it worse.

In fact, more or less everything I could do would only make it worse. I'd end up looking spiteful, pathetic, and a jealous loser. Everyone would understand why both Michael and Jack had preferred her, and nod wisely, and make little knowing remarks behind my back. The best I could hope for was pity.

I knew vaguely that boats were passing between the channel markers just a few yards away. They could see me but I didn't care, until I heard Tilly's voice hailing me. I wiped my eyes quickly and looked around to find the *Harold Jones* gliding past. Tilly waved in greeting and called out again.

'Pull alongside and throw me the painter.'

I managed a weak nod, determined she shouldn't see the state I was in as I pulled out from the reeds. A few swift strokes took me up to the yacht and she was helping me aboard, and speaking in a rush as she did so.

'... and no Valentina. Perfect. We'll have court and then the punishments below decks as we ... Chrissy? What's the matter? You've been crying?'

It came out, all of it, in a broken tumble of words, starting just as Michael's head appeared at the top of the companionway.

There were no words to express my feelings, so I kept them to myself. Jack wouldn't have understood anyway. Men are so simple. To them, pleasure is pleasure.

To me, pleasure, or at least some pleasure, comes at a cost.

I was cross with myself for enjoying something so dirty so much, but even more cross with Michael for bringing my carefully suppressed love of anal sex back into my life after so many years. I was determined to make him pay, too, and Jack. So I showered again and dressed, this time with a summer frock on over my bikini rather than just a wrap. By the time I'd finished Jack was waiting in the car, and we were at the waterside in Hickling a few minutes later.

They weren't there. Obviously Chrissy hadn't had the sense to make them wait, even though I'd said we would drive around so that Jack could drop me off. We hadn't been much over an hour in total, so I went to look out across the lake in the hope they'd still be among the cluster of yachts within sight. They weren't, or at least I couldn't see them, but then one yacht looks much like another to me.

That meant driving around to Potter Heigham and meeting them for lunch. Fortunately it was on Jack's way. Unfortunately it also meant I had about three hours to kill. I was in no mood for sex in the woods, or any more sex at all really. My bottom was sore and I was feeling fragile. He wanted to get back to work too, so made no fuss about dropping me at the pub where we'd arranged to meet.

I ordered myself a double G and T and went to sit by the window, where I could see the river. It was busy, with boats of all sorts coming and going, and people doing all sorts of boring nautical things. I could remember that the Callingtons' yacht was white, and that it had a man's name, but that was all. Not that it mattered, because it wasn't the yacht I needed to recognise, but the crew. That was easy.

Whatever else had come of the morning spent with Jack, it was interesting to know that Chrissy wasn't just the passive partner in their little spanking games. She actively encouraged it, or at least she had actively encouraged Jack to do it. So she really was a pervert rather than just weak-willed and desperate for attention as I'd imagined. That surprised me a bit, as she had always seemed to agree with me about that sort of thing. Then again, she would agree with anybody about anything, she's so feeble. Possibly she had just used it to attract Jack, to make herself seem more interesting. That made sense.

I sank a second G and T, and a third, before going out to the waterside to see if there was any sign of them. There wasn't, which was irritating because it was nearly noon. I couldn't remember how long it had taken to get from Potter Heigham to Hickling but I was sure it hadn't been all that long.

I went inside for another drink, then ordered a salad for lunch. I was thinking of what I was going to say to Michael about taking so long, which would have been more satisfying if I hadn't known he would be so infuriatingly calm about it. I wanted to say it anyway, and a good deal more.

My patience had just about reached its limit when I happened to glance at the car park. A big black Rover was pulling in. Michael's, I was sure. The yacht must have sprung a leak or something. I waited. Malcolm Callington got out to hold the back door for Pippa, then Tilly. He shut the doors. There was no Michael, no Chrissy.

They were talking, heatedly, as they came towards the pub. Malcolm entered first, his expression serious, and growing more serious still as he came towards me. It was Pippa who spoke.

'Valentina, hello. I . . . I'm afraid we have some rather bad news for you.'

'Yes?'

'Michael and Chrissy have taken the yacht.'

'Taken the yacht? What do you . . . Where?'

'Holland.'

It was Tilly who had spoken, and her tone was very different. Both Malcolm and Pippa were placatory. Tilly was angry. I looked between them as what she had said sank in.

'Holland?'

Malcolm Callington spread his hands in a gesture of resignation. Pippa spoke.

'All's fair in love and war, Valentina.'

Tilly turned her a burning look.

'No, it is not. We have rules nowadays, or at least decent people do. Look, I'm really sorry, Valentina. They just upped and took the yacht, from Hickling. We were in the pub, and Michael said he needed to talk to her, and they went outside, and the next thing we knew they were halfway across Hickling Broad!'

Malcolm was holding out a piece of paper.

'They left this note. Look, Valentina, I'm terribly sorry and all that, but as Pippa says, all's fair in love and war. Now I think the best –'

Tilly cut in.

'No, it is not fair! Michael made a choice, to be with Valentina. Chrissy had made it plain she had something going with Jack. They can't just change their minds every five minutes!'

I wasn't really listening. I'd taken the note. It was brief – 'Dear All, Gone to Amsterdam for some peace and quiet. Sorry about the boat. Michael.'

That was it, not even a mention of me. A picture of her bent down across his knee with her fat, wobbly backside stuck up in the air for spanking rose up with my anger. I could see exactly what the little bitch had done, and why she'd made so little fuss about leaving me with Jack. The moment my back was turned she'd made a play for Michael, undoubtedly promising him a chance to spank her fat backside. After all, she had to know he was into it, and if she'd offered Jack, why not Michael? He'd gone for it, which was typical of the arrogant, self-centred bastard!

It didn't matter about Michael. He just thought with his cock, like all men. It did matter about Chrissy. If she thought she was going to get away with it, she had another thought coming. Nobody does that to me, least of all Chrissy Green.

The *Harold Jones* moved gently through the water. Michael was at the helm, steering us carefully between the banks of reeds and past the boats coming the other way. It was tricky, and needed all of his concentration. I was glad, as that gave me time to think.

We'd been put together, more or less, by Malcolm and Pippa, and that should have been what I wanted more than anything else in the world. It was, at heart, but I had a lot of pride to swallow before I could really accept the situation. After all, he had chosen Valentina over me. Valentina's rules for dealing with men – never accept a man back.

She was right. Or, at least, she was right if you wanted to be a successful modern woman, with a full complement of dignity. All the magazines and TV shows said the same, one way or another, which wasn't surprising. That was where she took her rules from. I knew it was right, but I didn't feel it was right. I wanted Michael back.

He was his normal self, calm and confident and patient; above all patient. He wasn't going to speak, so I had to. I still managed to put the moment off a dozen times, and with a dozen increasingly pathetic excuses. When I did, it was hardly a dazzling piece of oration.

'So?'

He gave me his big, confident smile and put an arm around my shoulder, but said nothing. Nor did I, for a while, just soaking up the feeling of being held by him, but my tattered pride finally got the better of me. The least I deserved was an apology. An explanation would have been nice.

'Why, Michael?'

'Why what?'

'Why Valentina, silly!'

'Oh . . . just because . . .'

'Just because, nothing. Why, when you had me? No, don't answer that, I know, she . . .'

'She was there, that's all. Nothing more. How was I to know you were so keen . . . and so much fun.'

'We'd been to bed!'

'Yes, but we didn't say anything.'

'No commitment?'

'No.'

Valentina's rules for dealing with men – if a man takes you to bed he's committed himself to you. Obviously nobody had told Michael. I'd touched a nerve though.

'I'm sorry, Chrissy. Call it a lack of communication.'

didn't know I was special to you, and I didn't know you were coming up on the yacht. Be fair, once I was with Valentina, I couldn't just switch to you, could I, not when you just turned up out of the blue. At the least I needed an excuse, and after she went with Jack, well, there it was. I always preferred you, believe me. You're much prettier, your figure is far nicer. You're sweeter too, and more my type of girl.'

'Meaning I enjoy having my bottom smacked?'

'Yes.'

I couldn't fault him for honesty, at least. His little speech had been nice to hear too, even if it was obviously just flattery about preferring my figure to Valentina's. It was still nice.

I'd got my apology too, and an explanation of sorts. It was an exasperatingly male one, true, but then, what was I to expect? If there was one thing you could say for certain about Michael, he was a man.

The same was true of someone else – Jack. In fact, he was more like one of the animals on his farm, with a direct link from eye to cock, missing out the brain. He'd have been an easy target for Valentina, so easy it was hard to blame him.

He'd be all right though, and I'd been wrong about his lack of appeal. Valentina and I were probably just the latest in a long line of tourists who had succumbed to his earthy charms. It was easy with him, holiday sex, and I didn't suppose he'd mind. At least if he did mind it would be in much the same way as he'd mind when he finished a pie or reached the bottom of a bottle of cider. It might be gone, but there'd be more soon enough.

So I was going to take Michael back. Not immediately, but I would. First I needed to let my emotions calm, and to talk and relax. That was what the rest of the day was for, that and to make sure Valentina was a very long way away indeed. For that I had to rely on Malcolm Callington and Pippa and, most of all, on Tilly. I trusted them, but as the *Harold Jones* nosed into Horsey Mere I was still looking anxiously around.

The conversation was getting heated. Malcolm and Pippa were suggesting that I should simply go back to London, which was outrageous. They even ordered lunch, as if nothing important had happened. I couldn't bear to be with them, they were being so smug and condescending about the whole thing, so I went outside. Tilly seemed to have some idea of what I was going through and came out after me, with a map, speaking as she sat down.

'You're not going to let her get away with this, are you?'

I was going to tell her that I was perfectly capable of looking after myself, but I held back. Obviously I needed to find Michael and Chrissy, and I knew they'd still be somewhere around, as it had taken the best part of a day to get from Hickling Broad to Great Yarmouth before. I needed an ally, someone who knew the area. She did. She also drove. Without her I was stuck. With her I had a chance. She understood too, I guessed, because, like me, she was a single, attractive female, and, also like me, she couldn't stand to see a fat little bitch like Chrissy getting above herself. I shook my head, too angry to speak. She went on.

'Has the yacht gone past?'

'How would I know? They all look the bloody same to me. Sorry, Tilly, I don't mean to be angry with you. It's just . . . just . . .'

'I know. He's a bastard.'

'No, he's a man, all dick and no brain. She's the one I want to get my hands on.'

'He's a bastard, believe me. I found out quickly enough.'

'You were with him?'

'For a bit, yes. He reckons because he's good-looking he can just sleep around as he pleases, and whoever he's with will just take him back. Not me.'

'Not me either.'

I took a drink to hide my rage. She was right. I couldn't take him back, not now. It was impossible after what he'd done, because I'd never be able to have sex with him again, that was for sure. That meant my whole plan was out of the window, after I'd sacrificed so much, and all because that fat, greedy little bitch Christina wanted her arse smacked! When I caught her I'd teach her what smacking really meant, I'd slap her stupid face right into next week, and Michael's too.

Tilly had opened the map and was pointing to it.

'They must have passed already, and there are only two places where the road meets the river downstream of here: Acle Bridge and actually in Yarmouth.'

'Drive me down to Acle Bridge then.'

'They might have passed there already. Besides, what if they just sail on past? No, we need to drive down to Yarmouth, where they'll have to stop, and we should pick up the inflatable first just in case.'

'Whatever. Just help me find them.'

'Count on it. Come on, we can take the car while Malcolm and Pippa are eating.'

I nodded and downed my drink as she made for the car park. She'd pinched the key and we were gone before the others noticed.

We talked as we drove, and she told me how he had asked her out when they'd met, shortly before Malcolm and Pippa got married. Four months they'd been together before she found out about his constant cheating. Now she put on a brave face for her sister's sake, but underneath she had never forgiven him.

I'd been wrong about the spanking. It wasn't just a cosy little clique of perverts. It was worse. Malcolm was notorious for it, and Pippa accepted it because she more or less had to, and because he was a good catch. Tilly hated it, but was loyal to her sister and liked the lifestyle. Malcolm Callington was a real bastard about it too, getting off on spanking his wife in front of other people, including Chrissy. On the yacht, Malcolm had threatened to spank Chrissy and she'd gone for it, like the perverted little slut she was.

It all made perfect sense, and as we drove I grew more and more angry. I could see now that Malcolm and Michael were nothing more than a pair of perverts, abusing their wealth to lure girls into their dirty games. Chrissy was no better and thoroughly deserved Michael, but that was not going to stop me. By the time we got to Yarmouth I was so angry I felt like killing both of them.

We were going to go to the marina, but as we crossed the river Tilly saw the yacht. They were making for the open sea, obviously scared that we'd catch up with them. They were right, but they'd made a big mistake thinking they could get away so easily. We'd picked up the inflatable in Hickling, and Tilly knew exactly what to do.

She didn't try to wave them down or anything stupid; she drove right out to the point and parked. There was a pebble beach, and we got the inflatable ready just as the yacht came out of the river mouth. They were going flat out, but we were faster, and had caught up in no time.

They weren't even on deck, doubtless because they were up to their dirty tricks in the cabin. As Tilly brought the inflatable alongside the yacht I caught the rail, pulling myself on board. Tilly lost her nerve and pulled away, but I didn't care. I didn't need her. I didn't want her either. Michael and Chrissy were in for a shock, from me.

It had been a long afternoon, a lovely afternoon. There had been no sex, just talk and laughter, and holding hands under the wide blue sky. We hadn't mentioned Valentina, not once. She was still there though, in the back of my mind. They thought they could get rid of her, but they didn't know her, not like I did. They didn't know how angry she could get. They didn't know how vicious she could be.

Whatever happened, I had had one perfect afternoon. We had moored at Horsey Mere and walked down to the village pub. Michael had bought me lunch and we'd walked on, down a long track to the dunes that fringed the sea. It was a beautiful place, beautiful and lonely. We'd walked for miles, along the top of the dunes. There had been a seal, playing in the waves, and we'd watched for ages, hidden among the grass so she wouldn't be scared. We had only turned back when we reached the fence of a naturist camp. Some people were actually playing volleyball, which made us both laugh.

We had arranged to meet Tilly back at the pub, and I grew more apprehensive as we approached, sure that something would have gone wrong, even that I would find a furious Valentina waiting for me. Michael was more worried about his car, making scathing remarks about Tilly's driving, and going to inspect it for scratches as soon as we reached the pub.

I wasn't going into the pub alone. I didn't need to. Tilly came out, smiling and holding a tray of drinks.

'Hi, Chrissy. These are on you, I think.'

'Where's Valentina? Did she ... did she fall for it?'

'No.'

'No? Shit!'

'She was cross. She wouldn't go.'

'So, so where is she?'

'I took her into Yarmouth.'

'Why? To the station?'

'No, to the beach.'

'The beach?'

'Yes, and a little further. Didn't I tell you she wouldn't be able to recognise the *Harold Jones*? She was cross, and pissed ...'

Michael cut in.

'Talk sense, Tilly, or you're going across my knee here and now.'

Tilly pouted.

'I was talking sense, beast, but ... you can spank me if you really want to.'

'Shut up and get on with it!'

'Oh, all right. As I said, Valentina was pissed, and cross, and I knew she couldn't tell one yacht from another, so I drove her to the point at Yarmouth, waited until a similar yacht came out and put her on it.'

'You put her on the wrong yacht?'

'But she'll just get off at the next port and come right back!'

'Oh, not for a while. The yacht was Norwegian.'

16

I would never, ever have had the nerve. Tilly had, obviously, and both Michael and Pippa thought it was hilarious. Malcolm was less pleased, pointing out that Tilly's actions were irresponsible and even dangerous. He also pointed out that the chances were high Valentina would have been put ashore.

We didn't particularly want to run into Jack either. So we took the *Harold Jones* down to the staithe at West Somerton, a dead end well apart from other waterways, which seemed pretty safe. Everyone was in high spirits and if I was still a bit nervous, their mood was infectious, and I was soon laughing with the rest of them as we sipped punch on the deck. What Tilly had done was wonderfully naughty, and even Malcolm found it impossible not to be amused. She had done it for me too, and while she said it was only because Valentina had been spoiling the holiday, I knew better.

I also knew what was going to happen. Tilly had been naughty, very naughty. She was certain to have to face the consequences, not because of how Malcolm felt, but because she wanted to. Sure enough, as the light began to fade her happy smile faded to a hang-dog expression. She looked up at Malcolm.

'I suppose it's time for court then?'

'Court? Yes, there are one or two matters that need attending to, as it goes. Here and now would be as good a time and place as any, I suppose.'

There was an immediate knot in my stomach. The nearest other boat was some way away, the nearest house further still. I stood up as Malcolm went into his military routine.

'Below decks! At the double!'

They went, at the double. I followed, a little less smartly, and earned a pat on the bum from Malcolm. That startled me, making me wonder if he had designs on my bum for something more and setting the butterflies fluttering in my stomach.

By the time I got down the companionway, Pippa and Tilly were already standing to attention to one side. I joined them, uncertain, nervous, but above all, not wanting to be left out. The men came down. Malcolm seated himself on one of the folding chairs.

'Michael, wine, if you would be so kind. A Barolo, I think, the evening is becoming a little chilly.'

Michael went forward, returning with a dark bottle. The three of us were left standing to attention as he opened it, chose glasses, sampled it and poured for his father and himself. Only when he had taken a sip and made a few appreciative noises did Malcolm speak.

'Very well, let us begin. This is the first three-girl sitting we've had in quite a time, eh, Michael? What it won't be is even. Pippa, my dear, you seem to have been remarkably well behaved. It's astonishing what six-of-the-best can do.'

Pippa shrugged, smiled and very casually stuck out her tongue. Tilly dissolved into giggles. Malcolm chuckled.

'As you seem determined to be wayward, that will earn you a spanking, on the bare, OTK.'

'Yes, sir.'

'So, to Tilly. Well now, here we seem to have plenty to deal with: reckless behaviour, insubordination, unwarranted pride and more, I'm sure, but if I gave you what you deserve, we'd be here all night, wouldn't we?'

'Yes, sir.'

'A spanking, then, to warm you up, and then a dozen of the cane, bare, of course.'

Tilly made a little noise in her throat, nothing more. Malcolm went on.

'Now, as to you, young lady ...'

He was addressing me. I swallowed the huge lump in my throat to speak.

'Yes, sir.'

'Well, for one thing you have, or rather you *had*, execrable taste in friends. That in itself is a spanking offence, considering the trouble you have put us to. Then there's failing to make the intensity of your affection clear to Michael before ...'

'But ... but ... that's not fair, sir!'

'... and talking back. I think a good long session over my knee is called for, that is, if you have no objections, Michael?'

I turned to Michael, hoping he would turn down the awful request and hoping even more strongly that he wouldn't. He lifted his glass, to spend an agonisingly long moment taking a single sip before he spoke.

'Not at all. I'll do the same, I think.'

'Both of you!'

'Silence in the ranks! Unless you'd like to join Tilly in finding out how a round dozen cane strokes feel?'

'No, sir.'

'No? What a shame, and such a delightful bottom

too. Still, we must make the best of spanking you, eh? Now then, Pippa first. Tilly, top up, hands on head! Chrissy, do sit down. Have some wine?'

'Thank you.'

I sat down, glancing towards Tilly as I took a glass. She took hold of her top to lift it, revealing a sports bra. Another quick tug and that was up too, her firm breasts quivering but barely dropping at all, her nipples standing stiff and proud. With her chest completely exposed, her hands went up, to rest on top of her head.

Michael held out the bottle, offering to fill my glass. I accepted, watching the rich red wine flow even as Pippa stepped close to Malcolm and draped herself elegantly across his lap. He took her around the waist and casually flicked up her skirt, revealing lacy white knickers, obviously expensive. Michael stepped around me to give himself a better view of Pippa's bottom. He was still holding the bottle. Malcolm had paused, waiting until we all had full glasses before pulling down his wife's knickers.

She gave a little sob as her bottom came bare, but lifted it for punishment just the same, making her cheeks part to show off the rear of her already moist pussy. The marks of her caning still showed, the neat five-bar gate showing as dull bruises on the pale, smooth skin of her beautiful bottom.

He put his hand to her bum, making the flesh quiver, raised it and began to spank. I swallowed hard and squeezed my thighs together as her bottom cheeks began to bounce to the smacks. I still didn't understand why it should be so arousing to watch another woman punished, unless it was at the prospect of getting the same treatment myself. It worked anyway, enough to have me squirming in my seat as Pippa's bottom grew slowly pinker.

She was good about it at first, just kicking her legs a little and gasping as each slap fell. Only when Malcolm aimed a couple of smacks at the back of her thighs did she start to lose control, giving her little piggy noises, which made me giggle. Her thighs came open too, stretching her knickers taut and making her rear view ruder still, with the tight dimple of her bumhole showing between her cheeks.

I found myself blushing at the sight, and thinking of how I would shortly be in the same rude, open position. It was affecting Michael too, his cock all too obviously hard in his trousers. Catching my eye, he came close, his hand coming to rest on my shoulder. I took it in mine as my eyes went back to Pippa's bouncing bottom.

She was soaking wet and I could smell the scent of her pussy, adding to my embarrassment and my arousal. Soon I'd be in the same position, my pussy flaunted for all to see as my bare bottom was spanked pink, and I was sure that I was already as wet as she was. It would be OK, I knew. Even if I lost control and masturbated in front of them it would be OK.

It was still a shock when Pippa suddenly cocked up her leg across Malcolm's knee, to spread her pussy on to his leg. My mouth came wide open at the sheer rudeness of it. He kept on spanking, harder, as she began to rub herself on his leg, bucking her bottom up and down with frantic, wanton energy, her bum cheeks spreading and tightening, her anus stretched wide each time she lifted.

I just stared, gaping as she was spanked towards her orgasm, hardly able to believe how lewd, how abandoned, she was being. It was just so intimate, to rub herself off in front of us as her bottom bounced and quivered to the slaps. My hand went between my thighs, to feel the soft bulge of my own sex as my eyes feasted on Pippa's. Every little pink fold showed, opening and closing as she rubbed, her pussy hole an open passage into her body.

She came, Malcolm delivering a final torrent of hard spanks as she cried out in her ecstasy. Her body went into spasm, her pussy contracting hard, her bumhole winking, both her legs shaking uncontrollably. My eyes were fixed on her, my fingers locked on Michael's hand. I needed him, desperately, his hand applied firmly to my bare bottom, then his cock inside me.

When Pippa's cries and the smacks of Malcolm's hand on her flesh stopped, there was absolute silence. He let go of her waist. She stood, slowly. Her knickers fell down. She was flushed pink, perhaps as much with embarrassment as in the aftermath of her climax, but she was smiling too. Malcolm drew her in as she bent to kiss him, and for a long moment they held each other, Pippa trembling visibly in his arms. I looked down, the moment somehow more intimate than her orgasm. Only when Malcolm spoke did I lift my eyes.

'Right, into the corner with you, my dear. Keep it showing.'

'Yes, sir.'

She went, her head hung, her skirt held up in both hands, to stand by the companionway, her rosy bottom turned to the cabin. She was still shaking a little, with one red bottom cheek twitching occasionally. Malcolm chuckled and rubbed his hands. His eyes went to Tilly, to me, and back before he spoke.

'Tilly's warm-up, I think, should come next, then

Chrissy while Tilly waits for the cane. So, who'd care to do it? Michael? It's been a while.'

Tilly looked at me, her eyes full of longing.

'No. I will.'

My voice was shaking as I said it. I knew she was into girls, maybe even preferred girls, and I didn't mind, not that one time, not after what she had done for me. I'd never spanked anyone before either, but I knew how, and not just in a physical sense.

One word from either of the men and I'd have backed down. Neither spoke. Michael took a step to the side, leaving my lap clear. I moved the chair a little, to make sure they both had a good view of her bottom as I spanked her, and looked up into her eyes, trying to sound firm as I spoke.

'Come on, let's have those jeans down. Not your knickers, I'll be doing those.'

She gave me the most wonderful look as her hands went to the button of her jeans, gratitude and shame and excitement all rolled into one. I nodded, accepting her submission. Her button came open. Her thumbs went into her waistband and her jeans slid down, revealing the soft bulge of her pussy within little blue polka-dot knickers.

'Very pretty, now down over my lap.'

She stepped forward, to lay herself carefully down across my knees. I felt her weight, and the soft flesh of her tummy. My arm went around her waist, holding her. Her bottom came up, stretching the spotty knickers taut across her trim cheeks. I was really going to do it, to spank another woman, and I was fighting down my guilt even as I hooked my thumb into the waistband of her knickers, and telling myself it was only because she wanted it. It was true. It seemed a strange way of thanking somebody, to spank her on her bare bottom, but I was sure it was the best thank-you I could give.

Well, it was partially true, because the thrills running through me as I peeled her little spotty knickers down off her bottom were not to be denied. She stuck it up as she came bare, her cheeks spreading to show off her bumhole and pussy in open, rude display. I caught her scent, and the memory of licking each other came back, the taste of her sex and the feel of her newly spanked bottom.

I laid in, clutching her to me and letting go with a salvo of hard spanks to her bottom. I had to, it was that or go down on the floor and bury my face between her legs in front of everybody. She had squeaked in surprise as the spanking began, and went on squeaking, kicking her legs and giggling too, delighted by what I was doing, for all the pain. I kept at it, spanking and spanking and spanking, until her bottom was a hot red ball under my hand.

In no time she had begun to get urgent, pushing her bottom up and sighing between slaps. My palm was stinging, but still I spanked her, determined to do it properly, and not to look feeble in front of them. Only when Michael gave a gentle cough did I stop. I was panting and grinning, thoroughly pleased with myself, and more so as they began to clap. Tilly got up, clutching her bottom and craning back to see what I'd done to her cheeks.

'Ow! You bitch, Chrissy, that was hard!'

I shrugged. Malcolm looked up at her.

'Bad language. Thirteen strokes. Into the corner with your sister.'

Tilly pouted, but went to stand close to Pippa, her trousers and knickers well down to show her bottom.

Like Pippa, her cane marks still showed, rich red against the overall pink glow I'd given her. She was going to get more, filling me with the same mixture of sympathy and cruel pleasure I'd had before.

That would come. For now I needed my own bottom spanked. I took up my wine glass and drained it. Michael had gone to sit on a locker during Tilly's spanking. Malcolm was waiting for me too. I rose, wondering who I should go to first as my fingers went automatically to the button of my jeans. Both looked calm, casual. My jeans popped open, the zip pulling apart to the pressure of my tummy. Malcolm spoke.

'Good girl, Chrissy. You're learning.'

'Yes, sir.'

I looked at him, hesitant, then at Michael. As our eyes met he patted his lap, that tiny gesture that meant so much. As I stepped forward I let my jeans down, showing my knickers, a gesture that felt far, far more yielding than baring myself for sex. He moved forward a little, giving me plenty of room on his lap as I wondered which way to go. One way and they'd see the silly expression I was bound to make as I was smacked, the other and they'd see my bottom, full moon, nothing hidden at all.

I went bottom out, telling myself I was a slut even as I bent across Michael's knee. It was right though, to show off the way the others showed off, to hide nothing, because I'd been naughty, and because I wanted them to see. Then he had taken hold of me, his big, powerful arm circling my waist, and I just melted. It felt so good to be held by him again, to be held bare, to be held for punishment.

He took a firm hold of my knickers and it was better still. My tummy jumped as they were peeled down, pulled casually off my bum to leave me bare and ready and left tangled with my jeans at the level of my thighs. He'd taken them well down, far enough to show my pussy, giving the same rude rear view I'd seen of Pippa and Tilly. Now it was me, and I knew they were watching.

Michael's hand settled on my bottom, feeling my cheeks, squeezing and patting, to see how big I am, how soft I am. I felt my cheeks part a little as I was fondled, and I knew he was inspecting my bumhole. Malcolm chuckled and a fresh blush suffused my cheeks. Michael's hand lifted from my bottom and my cheeks went tight in anticipation.

I cried out as the first slap fell, a sob of raw emotion. It was what I'd wanted, so badly, what I'd thought I would never get when he was with Valentina, and now it was happening. I was being spanked by Michael Callington.

There was no pain barrier to get over. I was too high. From the first I was sticking my bottom up, eager for the slaps, my pussy responding, warm and ready. I wanted fucking, then and there, while my bottom was being smacked. I wanted my boobs out and my bottom spread, utterly exposed as I was fucked and spanked. I wanted my face in Tilly's sex too, or Pippa's, both if I could. I wanted everything, everything rude, everything wanton, and all focused on my body.

He kept on spanking, slow and steady, each firm smack bringing me that little bit higher, that bit closer to orgasm, until I was squirming on his lap and trying to cock my leg up over his as Pippa had done, so I could rub myself off. I couldn't, not with my jeans the way they were, leaving me writhing stupidly on his lap in my desperation to get my pussy to his leg, utterly wanton, but too far gone to care.

Pippa laughed. Tilly giggled. I just kept on writhing and Michael just kept on spanking. Suddenly I was there. The girls' laughter had tripped something in my head, some need to be thought lewd, silly even, and I was coming. Michael realised and put his full force into the slaps, bringing his hand hard down over my pussy, again and again as I screamed and writhed against his body.

It was perfect, so wonderful, and even when I'd finished and lay slumped in exhaustion across his knees he kept on spanking, just pats. I could have lain there for ever, completely content, and I think it would have gone on a lot longer if a voice hadn't broken the spell.

'Hey! At least pass her around, Michael!'

It was Tilly. Malcolm answered her.

'You are supposed to be doing corner time, young lady.'

I stood up, feeling rather sheepish at how far I'd allowed myself to get carried away. They'd all seen me come, and I had quite simply never done anything so rude before. I was smiling though, and I could see they didn't mind one bit. Both girls were looking at me, their faces flushed with excitement, Tilly's especially. Malcolm was waiting, as patient as ever, but I could see the outline of a big hard cock in his trousers. As I came to him it was impossible not to wonder if he would want his erection looked after, and what the others would think if I offered to suck his cock.

To my surprise he stood. I took a step back, expecting him to take his cock out and suddenly unsure what to do. He didn't, but took me firmly by the ear. I squeaked in alarm even as I found myself being pulled slowly down across the table. My jeans and knickers fell down as I let go of them, and I was over, my face pressed to the table. Malcolm let go of my ear and began to fondle my bottom as he spoke.

'There we are, something for everybody. Come along, girls.'

They came, eagerly, Pippa to my rear, Tilly to my head, both giggling in delight. The spanking started immediately, Malcolm and Pippa holding me down as they shared my bottom, a cheek each, slapping and fondling. At my front end, Tilly took me by the chin and turned my head to kiss me, even as her spare hand slipped beneath my chest.

I just let them have me, dizzy with pleasure as I was spanked and stroked. My nipples came hard in an instant, and even when Pippa slid one long finger into my pussy I gave no resistance. They could have done anything, caned me, had me suck Malcolm's cock, let him fuck me, anything. I'd just have lapped it up, purring in pleasure.

Soon I was dizzy and getting wanton again, wiggling my hot bottom and sticking it up to the slaps, as much in the hope of a helpful finger as more spanking. I was kissing open-mouthed with Tilly, and thoroughly enjoying it as she rubbed my breasts through my top. I didn't care if she was a girl, it was nice. Pippa's fingers invaded my pussy again, her thumbnail began to tickle my bumhole, and I realised they were going to bring me off, when Michael spoke.

'Excuse us a moment.'

The others gave way. He took hold of my arm and I was being lifted, stood up on my feet. For a moment I wasn't sure what he was doing, then he had taken my hand and was leading me exactly where I wanted to go, into the other cabin. I followed him, shuffling in my lowered knickers and jeans. Michael ushered me through with a pat to my bottom and closed the partition behind us. I stood waiting meekly with my lowered garments clutched in my hands. Now it was private, and it was going to get rude, or rather, ruder still.

He made a motion, signalling that I should lift my top. My hands went straight there, willing, but more than that, wanting to be ordered, enjoying the sensation of being told to expose myself. I watched his face as I lifted my top, exposing my bra before taking hold of the cups and pulling them up to leave my boobs showing, bare and round, in my hands. His eyes betrayed his feelings, despite his best efforts to stay looking stern, and I found myself giggling, delighted in his reaction. He raised one eyebrow and patted his lap.

I closed my eyes in pure bliss as he eased me down, revelling in every sensation, every emotion, as I was prepared for spanking once more. I went right down, supporting myself by my hands and with my legs braced apart until my knickers were stretched taut between my knees. Michael took me around the waist, my bottom came up and the spanking began again, firm slaps right under my cheeks, every one sending a jolt straight to my pussy.

Solid smacking noises were ringing out as he dealt with me, making it quite obvious what was going on. I heard Tilly's laughter from beyond the partition, and fresh blood suffused my face. She could hear. They could hear. They'd hear me spanked. That didn't matter, after what they'd done. They'd hear me fucked too, because I was going to be.

It wasn't long. He spanked me until my whole bottom was one big throbbing ball of heat. He went on spanking as he tugged off my shoes and socks, my jeans and knickers. My top and bra followed and I was nude – nude and hot-bottomed, ready for his lovely cock. He eased me upright to sit me on his lap, facing him, spread wide, my pussy aching to be filled. His hand went to his fly.

Out came his cock, into his hand, then mine. I began to tug, enjoying the hard hot shaft, so male, so virile, so ready to be pushed deep into my body. He pulled me in, cradling me to his body, one hand at the nape of my neck, the other tucked beneath my burning bottom. His cock pushed to my belly. I wanted it inside me, urgently, more desperately than at any time in my life. He obliged, simply lifting me by my bottom and popping me on, so strong and so in control. I clung on to his neck, sighing as my pussy filled with lovely, thick cock, my face buried in his shoulder.

My fucking began immediately, Michael moving me up and down on his erection and pushing into me at the same time. A finger had found my bumhole, tickling me, to send little extra shivers of pleasure up my spine and remind me how rude I would look mounted on his cock. I was wishing Tilly was there, even the others, to watch the big cock go in and out of my pussy, so I could make a real exhibition of myself, even to lick me from behind, her tongue moving up from his balls to my bumhole and back, over and over.

His actions were as rude as my thoughts, or nearly. The finger at my bumhole was going deeper, opening me with my own juices. I could do nothing but sigh into his neck, delighted by the sensation, however rude.

He pushed deeper, burrowing in, stretching my little hole as he fucked me, never so much as pausing, until I had begun to wonder if he was going to bugger me. If he wanted to, he could. I didn't want to stop him. He could have me any way he liked, and after all, what better thing to do to a spanked girl?

He did. He lifted me off his cock and around, sitting me down with my bum the way he wanted it. I reached for the bunk opposite, my eyes closed as my bottom was raised and spread, opening the hole to his erection. I felt it, round and firm against my slippery flesh. I relaxed, moaning as I accepted it.

So up he went, with me panting and trying not to grunt and giggling because I couldn't help myself. It went deep into me until I was sitting on his lap again, only fully penetrated up my bottom. He began to move on his cock, and to slap at my cheeks as he buggered me. I clung on to the bunk, sure I'd fall if I let go, but wanting to play with my tits as they swung under my chest, to touch where his cock was in my body, and rub at my pussy until I came.

Michael obliged, as considerate of my needs as ever, his hand curling around to find my clit. He kept on spanking too, and moving in my bottom, bouncing me on his erection even as he masturbated me. It was perfect, spanked and buggered and rubbed off, all at once, and by him, by the man who'd dumped Valentina de Lacy for me.

I was going to come, at any moment, all I needed was the perfect rhythm. I got it. The thwack of a cane being applied to soft female flesh sounded from beyond the partition, and Tilly's cry. Michael shoved hard, deep up me, and my own cry rang out in time to her second.

He began to pump, slow, steady and hard, rubbing and slapping all the while, each pump in perfect time to the cane strokes and Tilly's cries.

My legs braced, one hand went to my boobs. His cock jammed in again, so deep I felt I was going to burst. Again and I felt my bumhole tighten on his erection. Again and my muscles locked. Again and I was coming, all control gone as I thrashed and squirmed on him, with every one of Tilly's cries burning into my thoughts as I focused on what was happening – me spanked and buggered, her spanked and caned.

It was the best, so long, so intense, so rude. If it hadn't been for Michael I would have collapsed, and it wasn't until I finally found the strength to rise that I realised he had come up me at the very peak of my ecstasy. That was better still, knowing it had been mutual, and that he had kept control of my body's responses even as he came himself.

I gave him a long, deep kiss before we began to tidy up, or rather, before I tidied Michael and myself up and dressed. He wanted to walk, and to talk, and so did I. We couldn't hear anything beyond the partition, but he knocked anyway, which seemed a bit silly, especially when he immediately pushed the door open.

What we saw was quite a shock, even then. Tilly was down on her knees, her bottom still bare, her hand back between her thighs, masturbating completely shamelessly while she sucked on Malcolm's cock. Pippa was beside them, stroking her sister's hair.

Michael nodded politely to his father and led me past, up the companionway and into the night. As we stepped off the *Harold Jones* and on to the staithe I could still hear the sounds of Tilly sucking Malcolm's cock. They faded as we began to walk along the riverbank, hand in hand, but my head was still full of rude images, of Pippa being spanked, of spanking Tilly, of Michael's cock in my pussy and up my bottom, of Malcolm's cock in Tilly's mouth as her sister stroked her hair. It was rude, deliciously, wonderfully rude, all of it, but especially her. It was against all the rules, to go down on your knees and take a much older man's cock in your mouth, worse when he was your brother-in-law, worse still with your bottom spanked to a hot, red ball by another woman, worst of all when your sister was stroking your hair as you did it. It was awful, and it was wonderful.

It wasn't perverted though. Malcolm was right too. Spanking wasn't perverse, any more than oral sex ... or belly-button piercings ... or high heels. It wasn't perverse, it just wasn't in fashion. Valentina was wrong. Her rules were wrong. She wasn't living as she should. She was living as society thought she should. Maybe it worked for her, but not for me, not any more. I want to be like Tilly, and Pippa, and Malcolm, and Michael.

Finally I managed to speak.

'Do ... do they always do that?'

'Oh, only now and then. Tilly prefers girls usually.'

It was so casual, so easy. It was for me the way to really enjoy sex, to revel in things because they were nice, not avoid them because some magazine or some friend said they were dirty or demeaning. If the way I felt was wrong, either mentally, just floating on a cloud of pure pleasure, or physically, with my bottom glowing with warmth, if it was against the rules, then the rules were crap.

I squeezed Michael's hand, absolutely happy for the first time in a very, very long while. It didn't matter about Valentina or what she did. I didn't need her. With

luck she'd be a good part of the way to Norway, but
even if she wasn't I didn't care. For now I certainly
didn't care. I was with Michael. I'd been spanked. I'd
been fucked, and there would be more to come, plenty
more. I cuddled into him. He responded, his arm sliding
around my waist. For a while we walked in silence
then he spoke, gently.

'I'm sorry about Valentina, Chrissy. It was a mistake
but she was there, and, well, you know how men are. If
an attractive woman throws herself at you, it takes a
saint to resist that kind of temptation.'

'I know.'

'I'm glad things worked out, very glad.'

'So am I.'

'Chrissy, I think I need to say that you are the
sweetest, and the most beautiful woman I've ever met.'

'Oh, nonsense! I'm short and freckly and I've got a
snout for a nose and a fat bum and big wobbly tits . . .'

'Exactly.'

'Hey!'

He laughed, then went silent. When he did reply, he
sounded different, earnest.

'Chrissy . . . do you think . . . it might be an idea to
get married?'

I stopped dead.

'Marry? You really want to marry me, Michael?'

'Well . . . yes!'

'You have to be joking. You're a complete bastard!
But I'll play with you.'

LOOK OUT FOR THE ALL-NEW BLACK LACE BOOKS – AVAILABLE NOW!

All books priced £6.99 in the UK. Please note publication dates apply to the UK only. For other territories, please contact your retailer.

WICKED WORDS 8
Edited by Kerri Sharp
ISBN 0 352 33787 7

Hugely popular and immensely entertaining, the *Wicked Words* collections are the freshest and most cutting-edge volumes of women's erotic stories to be found anywhere in the world. The diversity of themes and styles reflects the multi-faceted nature of the female sexual imagination. Combining humour, warmth and attitude with fun, imaginative writing, these stories sizzle with horny action. Only the most arousing fiction makes it into a *Wicked Words* volume. This is the best in fun, sassy erotica from the UK and USA. **Another sizzling collection of wild fantasies from wicked women!**

VELVET GLOVE
Emma Holly
ISBN 0 352 33448 7

At the age of twenty-two, Audrey is an SM Goldilocks looking for the perfect master. Her first candidate – an icy cool banker – is too cruel. Her second choice – a childhood sweetheart – is far too tender. When she meets Patrick, the charismatic owner of a bar, he seems just right. But can Audrey trust the man behind the charm? Or will Patrick drag her deeper into submission than she will care to go? **Beautifully written erotica from Ms Holly, the Black Lace readers' favourite author.**

Coming in May

UNKNOWN TERRITORY
Rosamund Trench
ISBN 0 352 33794 X

Hazel loves sex. It is her hobby and her passion. Every fortnight she
meets up with the well-bred and impeccably mannered Alistair. Then
there is Nick, the young IT lad at work, who has taken to following Hazel
around like a lost puppy. Her greatest preoccupation, however, concerns
the mysterious Number Six – the suited executive she met one day in the
boardroom. When it transpires that Number Six is a colleague of
Alistair's, things are destined to get complicated. Especially as Hazel is
moving towards the 'unknown territory' her mother warned her about.
An unusual sexual exploration of the appeal of powerful men in suits!

A GENTLEMAN'S WAGER
Madelynne Ellis
ISBN 0352 33800 8

When Bella Rushdale finds herself fiercely attracted to landowner
Lucerne Marlinscar, she doesn't expect that the rival for his affections
will be another man. Handsome and decadent, Marquis Pennerley has
desired Lucerne for years and now, at the remote Lauwine Hall, he
intends to claim him. This leads to a passionate struggle for dominance –
at the risk of scandal – between a high-spirited lady and a debauched
aristocrat. Who will Lucerne choose? **A wonderfully decadent piece of
historical erotica with a twist.**

VIRTUOSO
Katrina Vincenzi-Thyne
ISBN O 352 32907 6

Mika and Serena, young ambitious members of classical music's jet-set,
inhabit a world of secluded passion and privilege. However, since Mika's
tragic injury, which halted his meteoric rise to fame as a solo violinist, he
has retired embittered. Serena is determined to change things. A
dedicated voluptuary, her sensuality cannot be ignored as she rekindles
Mika's zest for life. Together they share a dark secret. **A beautifully
written story of opulence and exotic, passionate indulgence.**

Coming in June

DRIVEN BY DESIRE
Savannah Smythe
ISBN 0352 33799 O

When Rachel's husband abandons both her and his taxi-cab business
and flees the country, she is left to pick up the pieces. However, this is a
blessing in disguise as Rachel, along with her friend Sharma, transforms
his business into an exclusive chauffeur service for discerning gentlemen
– with all the perks that offers. What Rachel doesn't know is that two of
her regular clients are jewel thieves with exotic tastes in sexual
experimentation. As Rachel is lured into an underworld lifestyle of
champagne, diamonds and lustful indulgence, she finds a familiar face is
involved in some very shady activity! **Another cracking story of strong
women and sexy double dealing from Savannah Smythe.**

FIGHTING OVER YOU
Laura Hamilton
ISBN O 352 33795 8

Yasmin and U seem like the perfect couple. She's a scriptwriter and he's
a magazine editor who has a knack for tapping into the latest trends.
One evening, however, U confesses to Yasmin that he's 'having a thing'
with a nineteen-year-old violinist – the precocious niece of Yasmin and
U's old boss, the formidable Pandora Fairchild. Amelia, the violinist, turns
out to be a catalyst for a whole series of erotic experiments that even
Yasmin finds intriguing. In a haze of absinthe, lust and wild abandon, all
parties find answers to questions about their sexuality they were once
too afraid to ask. **Contemporary erotica at its best from the author of the
bestselling *Fire and Ice*.**

THE LION LOVER
Mercedes Kelly
ISBN O 352 33162 3

Settling into life in 1930s Kenya, Mathilde Valentine finds herself sent to
a harem where the Sultan, his sadistic brother and adolescent son all
make sexual demands on her. Meanwhile, Olensky – the rugged game
hunter and 'lion lover' – plots her escape, but will she want to be
rescued? **A wonderful exploration of 'White Mischief' goings on in 1930s
Africa.**

Black Lace Booklist

Information is correct at time of printing. To avoid disappointment check availability before ordering. Go to www.blacklace-books.co.uk. All books are priced £6.99 unless another price is given.

BLACK LACE BOOKS WITH A CONTEMPORARY SETTING

☐ THE TOP OF HER GAME Emma Holly	ISBN 0 352 33337 5	£5.99
☐ IN THE FLESH Emma Holly	ISBN 0 352 33498 3	£5.99
☐ A PRIVATE VIEW Crystalle Valentino	ISBN 0 352 33308 1	£5.99
☐ SHAMELESS Stella Black	ISBN 0 352 33485 1	£5.99
☐ INTENSE BLUE Lyn Wood	ISBN 0 352 33496 7	£5.99
☐ THE NAKED TRUTH Natasha Rostova	ISBN 0 352 33497 5	£5.99
☐ ANIMAL PASSIONS Martine Marquand	ISBN 0 352 33499 1	£5.99
☐ A SPORTING CHANCE Susie Raymond	ISBN 0 352 33501 7	£5.99
☐ TAKING LIBERTIES Susie Raymond	ISBN 0 352 33357 X	£5.99
☐ A SCANDALOUS AFFAIR Holly Graham	ISBN 0 352 33523 8	£5.99
☐ THE NAKED FLAME Crystalle Valentino	ISBN 0 352 33528 9	£5.99
☐ ON THE EDGE Laura Hamilton	ISBN 0 352 33534 3	£5.99
☐ LURED BY LUST Tania Picarda	ISBN 0 352 33533 5	£5.99
☐ THE HOTTEST PLACE Tabitha Flyte	ISBN 0 352 33536 X	£5.99
☐ THE NINETY DAYS OF GENEVIEVE Lucinda Carrington	ISBN 0 352 33070 8	£5.99
☐ EARTHY DELIGHTS Tesni Morgan	ISBN 0 352 33548 3	£5.99
☐ MAN HUNT Cathleen Ross	ISBN 0 352 33583 1	
☐ MÉNAGE Emma Holly	ISBN 0 352 33231 X	
☐ DREAMING SPIRES Juliet Hastings	ISBN 0 352 33584 X	
☐ THE TRANSFORMATION Natasha Rostova	ISBN 0 352 33311 1	
☐ STELLA DOES HOLLYWOOD Stella Black	ISBN 0 352 33588 2	
☐ SIN.NET Helena Ravenscroft	ISBN 0 352 33598 X	
☐ HOTBED Portia Da Costa	ISBN 0 352 33614 5	
☐ TWO WEEKS IN TANGIER Annabel Lee	ISBN 0 352 33599 8	
☐ HIGHLAND FLING Jane Justine	ISBN 0 352 33616 1	
☐ PLAYING HARD Tina Troy	ISBN 0 352 33617 X	
☐ SYMPHONY X Jasmine Stone	ISBN 0 352 33629 3	

☐ THE HOUSE IN NEW ORLEANS Fleur Reynolds ISBN 0 352 32951 3
☐ NOBLE VICES Monica Belle ISBN 0 352 33738 9
☐ HEAT OF THE MOMENT Tesni Morgan ISBN 0 352 33742 7
☐ STORMY HAVEN Savannah Smythe ISBN 0 352 33757 5
☐ STICKY FINGERS Alison Tyler ISBN 0 352 33756 7
☐ THE WICKED STEPDAUGHTER Wendy Harris ISBN 0 352 33777 X
☐ DRAWN TOGETHER Robyn Russell ISBN 0 352 33269 7

BLACK LACE BOOKS WITH AN HISTORICAL SETTING

☐ PRIMAL SKIN Leona Benkt Rhys ISBN 0 352 33500 9 £5.99
☐ DEVIL'S FIRE Melissa MacNeal ISBN 0 352 33527 0 £5.99
☐ WILD KINGDOM Deanna Ashford ISBN 0 352 33549 1 £5.99
☐ DARKER THAN LOVE Kristina Lloyd ISBN 0 352 33279 4
☐ STAND AND DELIVER Helena Ravenscroft ISBN 0 352 33340 5 £5.99
☐ THE CAPTIVATION Natasha Rostova ISBN 0 352 33234 4
☐ CIRCO EROTICA Mercedes Kelley ISBN 0 352 33257 3
☐ MINX Megan Blythe ISBN 0 352 33638 2
☐ PLEASURE'S DAUGHTER Sedalia Johnson ISBN 0 352 33237 9
☐ JULIET RISING Cleo Cordell ISBN 0 352 32938 6
☐ DEMON'S DARE Melissa MacNeal ISBN 0 352 33683 8
☐ ELENA'S CONQUEST Lisette Allen ISBN 0 352 32950 5
☐ DIVINE TORMENT Janine Ashbless ISBN 0 352 33719 2
☐ THE CAPTIVE FLESH Cleo Cordell ISBN 0 352 32872 X
☐ SATAN'S ANGEL Melissa MacNeal ISBN 0 352 33726 5
☐ THE INTIMATE EYE Georgia Angelis ISBN 0 352 33004 X
☐ HANDMAIDEN OF PALMYRA Fleur Reynolds ISBN 0 352 32951 3
☐ OPAL DARKNESS Cleo Cordell ISBN 0 352 33033 3
☐ SILKEN CHAINS Jodi Nicol ISBN 0 352 33143 7

BLACK LACE ANTHOLOGIES

☐ CRUEL ENCHANTMENT Erotic Fairy Stories ISBN 0 352 33483 5 £5.99
 Janine Ashbless
☐ MORE WICKED WORDS Various ISBN 0 352 33487 8 £5.99
☐ WICKED WORDS 4 Various ISBN 0 352 33603 X
☐ WICKED WORDS 5 Various ISBN 0 352 33642 0
☐ WICKED WORDS 6 Various ISBN 0 352 33590 0

☐ WICKED WORDS 7 Various   ISBN 0 352 33743 5
☐ THE BEST OF BLACK LACE 2 Various   ISBN 0 352 33718 4
☐ A MULTITUDE OF SINS Kit Mason   ISBN 0 352 33737 0

BLACK LACE NON-FICTION

☐ THE BLACK LACE BOOK OF WOMEN'S SEXUAL   ISBN 0 352 33346 4   £5.99
    FANTASIES Ed. Kerri Sharp

To find out the latest information about Black Lace titles, check out the website: www.blacklace-books.co.uk or send for a booklist with complete synopses by writing to:

    Black Lace Booklist, Virgin Books Ltd
    Thames Wharf Studios
    Rainville Road
    London W6 9HA

Please include an SAE of decent size. Please note only British stamps are valid.

Our privacy policy
We will not disclose information you supply us to any other parties. We will not disclose any information which identifies you personally to any person without your express consent.

From time to time we may send out information about Black Lace books and special offers. Please tick here if you do <u>not</u> wish to receive Black Lace information.   ☐

Please send me the books I have ticked above.

Name ....

Address ....

....

....

....

Post Code ....

Send to: Cash Sales, Black Lace Books, Thames Wharf Studios, Rainville Road, London W6 9HA.

US customers: for prices and details of how to order books for delivery by mail, call 1-800-343-4499.

Please enclose a cheque or postal order, made payable to Virgin Books Ltd, to the value of the books you have ordered plus postage and packing costs as follows:

UK and BFPO – £1.00 for the first book, 50p for each subsequent book.

Overseas (including Republic of Ireland) – £2.00 for the first book, £1.00 for each subsequent book.

If you would prefer to pay by VISA, ACCESS/MASTERCARD, DINERS CLUB, AMEX or SWITCH, please write your card number and expiry date here:

....

Signature ....

Please allow up to 28 days for delivery.